REIGN
OF THE
WATCHERS

To Jean,
Remember the
Wonderful Promise !

12-25-14

REIGN
OF THE
WATCHERS

⊰⊱ BOOK 1 ⊰⊱
THE ANTEDILUVIAN
CHRONICLES

M. L. LERVOLD

TATE PUBLISHING
AND ENTERPRISES, LLC

Published by Tate Publishing & Enterprises, LLC
127 E. Trade Center Terrace | Mustang, Oklahoma 73064 USA
1.888.361.9473 | www.tatepublishing.com

Tate Publishing is committed to excellence in the publishing industry. The company reflects the philosophy established by the founders, based on Psalm 68:11,
"The Lord gave the word and great was the company of those who published it."

Book design copyright © 2012 by Tate Publishing, LLC. All rights reserved.
Cover design by Rtor Maghuyop
Interior design by Mary Jean Archival

Published in the United States of America

ISBN: 978-1-62147-791-4
1. Fiction / Christian / Historical
2. Fiction / Christian / Romance
12.11.16

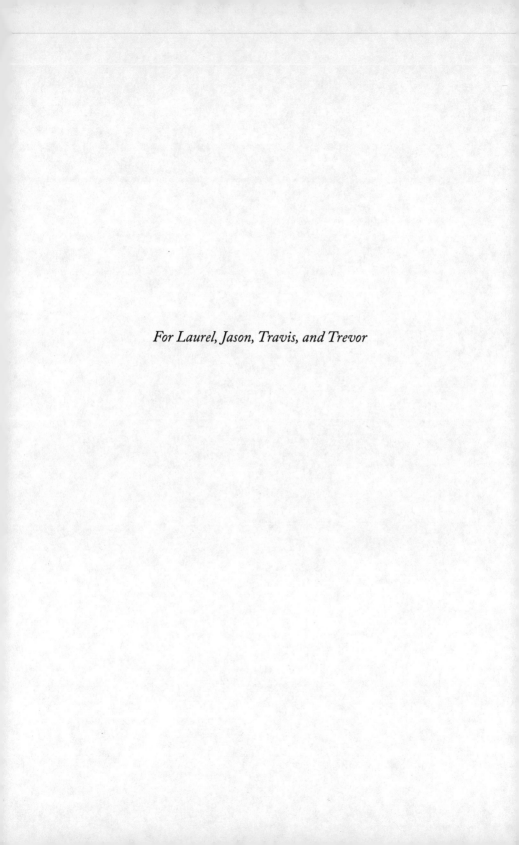

For Laurel, Jason, Travis, and Trevor

AUTHOR'S NOTE AND ACKNOWLEDGMENTS

Nearly forty years ago I sat in Dogmatics Professor Roland H. Hoenecke's History of Israel class at Dr. Martin Luther College (now just Martin Luther College) in New Ulm, Minnesota. We spent many months on the book of Genesis. He was a wonderful teacher and Hebrew scholar, and we students were always disappointed to hear the ending class bell ring. I owe the idea of this book to him, where one day in class we covered Genesis 6: 1-4. He explained the traditional Lutheran interpretation and then said, "But, some scholars believe…" Among the reasons for this alternate interpretation was that the "sons of God" Hebrew word used in the passages was only used elsewhere in the Old Testament as meaning angels and not ever used to mean godly men.

I've written this novel with the belief that the Holy Scripture is the inerrant and inspired Word of God, that Scripture interprets Scripture, and that Scripture does not contradict itself. And I have the solid belief that just because something in Scripture is difficult to wrap my mind around doesn't mean it isn't so.

I want to thank my family for the many readings and re-readings of my manuscript: my mom and dad, Barbara and Norman Lervold; my aunt Jackie Knierim; my sister-in-law, Cheryl; my niece, Hollie (I thoroughly appreciated a teenager's perspective and review); from Tate Publishing, Rachael Sweeden, Raimie McDaniel, and my excellent editors, Ashley Luckett and Meghan Gregg; for the beautiful layout and design, Kenna Davis, Rtor Maghuyop and Mary Jean Archival; and last but not least my cousin Steve Beck, for his numerous re-readings, wonderful suggestions and especially his insight that "a lie can hold many truths, but the truth cannot hold a single lie."

I want to thank my oldest son, Jason Dick, Ph.D., for the insights he's given me about the cosmic microwave background, the "first light of Creation." Interestingly, Dr. Martin Luther, back in the 1500s, wrote concerning the passage, "Let there be light," on the first day of Creation and the celestial lights created on the fourth day:

> But here a famous question is raised: "Of what sort, then, was that light by which the unformed mass of heaven and earth was illuminated? Although neither sun nor stars had been created, the text makes it clear that this light was true and physical."
> …Therefore I am of the opinion that this was true light and that its motion carried it in a circle, just as sunlight moves in a circle. Nevertheless, it was not such a clear and brilliant light as it was later on when it was increased, adorned, and perfected by the light of the sun. Similarly, the Holy Scriptures also bear witness that on the Last Day God will make more brilliant and glorious the present daylight of the sun, as though it were a weak light in comparison with the future glory (Isaiah 30:26). As, therefore, the present daylight is, so to speak, a crude and coarse mass of light if it is compared with

the future light, so that first light was crude when compared with the present light.

—*Martin Luther, Lectures on Genesis
Chapters 1-5, p. 19-20.*

Unbelievers throughout the years have ridiculed the Bible's account of Creation for having light created prior to the sun and stars, and believers throughout the centuries have held to the truth of it because God's Word said it was so, as shown by Martin Luther in the above quotations. But now today, after the discovery of the CMB (Cosmic Microwave Background) in 1964 by American radio astronomers Arno Penzias and Robert Wilson, even atheist scientists agree that there is indeed radiation (short photons of light) left over from an early stage in the development of the universe before the existence of stars. This discovery is considered a landmark test of the Big Bang model of the universe. Of course, Bible-believing Jews and Christians believe in the Big Bang as in "God said, 'Let there be,' and bang, there it was."

My book, based on the controversial passages of Genesis 6: 1-4, may raise some hackles on certain theologians who hold to the view that the "sons of God" in the text were merely godly men or "Sethites." I say to them, "They weren't so godly, then." I hold to the view that the Hebrew word in the text has the same meaning as when the identical Hebrew word is used in the texts Job 1:6; Job 2:1; and Job 38:7, none of which can be construed in any way as meaning human males at all.

I have also based my story upon the Book of Enoch (Ethiopian Enoch, translated by R.H. Charles, 1917.) Although, not considered part of the Old Testament canon of Scripture by the majority of the Christian Church at large, it always was considered part of the OT canon of the Ethiopian Church, as well as the Ethiopian Jewish community. This book was also found among the Dead Sea scrolls (an Aramaic translation) and was well known by the Jews at the time of Jesus and by the early Christian Church, quoted by Jude and referenced by Peter.

Furthermore, Enoch's several visions of heaven and the "Son of Man" at the throne of God is striking. It explains the Pharisees' total umbrage at Jesus's claim to be that "Son of Man," and their rightful understanding that Jesus was claiming to be the Messiah and equal with God by that phrase, one that is used explicitly and repeatedly in the Book of Enoch, but never so clearly in any of the rest of the Torah and Tenach.

Another issue that arises from the sons-of-God-are-angels interpretation is the question of who were these angels? Already fallen ones who rebelled earlier along with Satan? Or ones who were not in that first rebellion but succumbed to temptation afterward? I had been taught that after that first rebellion, those angels who did not rebel were "confirmed in righteousness" and put in a state where they could no longer sin. But nobody ever showed me the Scripture on that, and I rather doubt that it could be found. My story in this book works on the premise that the angels involved with lusting after human women were guardian angels (Watchers) who succumbed to temptation by Satan and left their appointed stations to do so. Jesus says that angels do not marry nor are given in marriage, but that does not mean they cannot disobey or that none ever had. I believe they have, to this day, free will. I believe that it is a testament to the fortitude of the holy angels to continue to watch over our affairs day after day, year after year, and still choose to remain sinless. Although, it is much easier on them now, since man's years have been shortened (to a tenth of what it was) since the time before the Flood. The temptation to exchange eternity for a few short years with a beautiful woman now is just not worth it, especially considering the consequences:

> And the angels who did not keep their proper domain, but left their own abode, He has reserved in everlasting chains under darkness for the judgment of the great day; as Sodom and Gomorrah, and the cities around them in a similar manner to these, having given themselves over to sexual immorality and

gone after strange flesh, are set forth as an example, suffering the vengeance of eternal fire.

Jude 1:6-7

And

For if God did not spare the angels who sinned, but cast them down to hell and delivered them into chains of darkness, to be reserved for judgment;

2 Peter 2:4

It is entirely possible also that Goliath and his brothers were not part of a "race" of giants, but rather their father, Anak, was a Watcher (probably already fallen but maybe not) who succumbed to temptation, and his sons, Goliath (slain by David), and his brothers (slain by David's mighty men) were Nephilim. That would explain the relatively small number and uniqueness of these giants. Besides the Scripture concerning these giants in I and II Samuel and I Chronicles, other references to giants in and near the land of Canaan occur is these passages: Numbers 13:33; Deuteronomy 2:11; Deuteronomy 2:20; Deuteronomy 3:11, 13; Joshua 12:4; Joshua 13:12; Joshua 17:15. Further, it appears that the word "Anakim" may be exchanged for the term "son(s) of Anak."

It also would have been some really unwise decision-making by Anak, who undoubtedly suffered the same consequences as the likewise offending antediluvian Watchers. And small wonder that the sin of the Canaanites wasn't complete and their fate marked for annihilation by God through the conquering Israelites, until their sin began to approach the levels that were rampant before the Flood. Besides the widespread idolatry and child sacrifice practiced by these people, the emergence of giants could very well have been an additional factor.

And still another argument that arises from dissenting theologians is the belief that angels fathering children with human women makes the incarnation of Christ not a unique and singular miraculous occurrence. The children (Nephelim or Giants) produced by these unions would still have fathers, albeit by "strange flesh" and forbidden unions, but their souls would not have existed prior to their conceptions—hence, no incarnations here.

Besides, in this day and age, where scientists (without angelic intervention) are producing sheep, pigs, and mice (and more) that have human genes in their DNA, who are we to say it is an impossible thing for sinning angels to produce children with human women, or even animals for that matter? If one thinks about it, where did all that ancient mythology originate from anyway? Mythology about gods, giants, god-men, and fantastic creatures are as old and pervasive throughout the world's cultures and peoples as are the Flood and Creation stories. Additionally, today's geneticists might want to think twice about what they're doing to God's Creation, considering what happened to the sinning sons of God. Just because it can be done, it doesn't necessarily follow that it should be done or that there won't be undesirable consequences.

I picture in my mind the sight I saw on a recent television program showing the beautiful pink faces of the sheep that were engineered with human genes. I felt sorry for them. My aunt Jackie says she'll really be concerned, though, when a mouse turns to her and says, "Get rid of the cat!"

I lastly would like to extend my special thanks to the Ancient Alien Astronaut theorists. They've done a fine job speaking to the evidence of ancient civilizations that were far more sophisticated than the traditional historians like to own up to. But I heartily disagree with their extraterrestrial visitors being alien astronauts. Curiously, their yet unsolved mystery about why their ancient astronauts suddenly disappeared from earth's general operations can be solved handily in, "the offenders are all locked up right now," thankfully!

—M. L. Lervold

"Now it came to pass, when men began to multiply on the face of the earth, and daughters were born to them, that the sons of God saw the daughters of men, that they were beautiful; and they took wives for themselves of all whom they chose. And the LORD said, 'My Spirit shall not abide with man forever, for he is indeed flesh; yet his days shall be one hundred and twenty years.' There were giants on the earth in those days, and also afterward, when the sons of God came in to the daughters of men and they bore children to them. Those were the mighty men who were of old, men of renown."

—Genesis 6:1–3

"And from them I heard everything, and from them I understood as I saw, but not for this generation, but for a remote one which is for to come."

—Enoch

"Everything one needs to know to be saved can be found in the first three chapters of Genesis."

—Unknown

BOOK 1

YEAR 718 A.C.
(AFTER CREATION)

To Freedom

The mist was so thick and saturated that drops of water formed on the great trees' leaves then descended with a gentle patter onto the thatched roof of the refuge. The mesmerizing, rhythmic sound was soothing to the young girl's soul. She'd never heard such peace before, or maybe it was the warmth of her sleeping mother's breath on her neck that warmed and calmed her fears and healed her wounds.

Wrapped in the arms of her mother, and in the arms of a newborn sensation of hope, Lelah drifted into the deep sleep of one who had finally reached a safe harbor after having known only violent storms. Her mother was safe; she was safe.

Her heart thudded in her chest. She was afraid it rocked so hard and loud that it would betray her hiding spot. She was crouched behind the back of the fountain, out of sight, she hoped, from the snarling, raging giant that stormed the courtyard. She could even feel the massive stones of the wall she was wedged against jolt and shift with each impact of her father's fist or foot. The sounds were the worst.

They always were—the screams, the noise of breaking, tearing flesh. "Amah! Amah!" the voiceless words repeated in her mind... "Amah!"

"Amah!" The shrill scream pierced the darkness.

Melenah awoke with a start next to her thrashing, sweaty, terror-filled daughter.

"Baby, baby, it's all right. I'm here. We're safe. He's not here. He's not here. We're safe," she said. She cradled the shaking Lelah in her arms and rocked her back and forth.

As she calmed and soothed her precious daughter, Melenah caught the aroma of something delicious wafting through the cracked window, mingling with the fresh smells of the dewy morning mist. The rustle of the giant ferns heralded the approach of the bearer of that good and welcome repast.

"Good morning, sojourners! A meal to give you strength and put some meat on your bones!" the kindly old woman said. She bustled through the doorway, carrying a tray of what looked like porridge in two steaming bowls. Slabs of cheese, fresh-baked bread, and a jug of water were piled high and looked like they might topple to the floor with the slightest of tipping. But all remained intact as she deftly settled the feast onto the small wooden table nestled in the corner of the cozy little cottage.

"You're so kind to us, Elloe. I don't know how to ever repay you for all you've done for us."

"Hush, child. Is it any wonder you're not used to kindness? Let's get you to the table. Lelah, get on the other side of your mother, and let's both get her to some good home cooking."

Although only twelve years old, Lelah was a head taller than her mother and was commonly taken for being older. After a sniffle and wiping the remnants of the sleep-terror tears from her cheeks with the back of her hand, she helped Elloe ease her mother up from the bed mat and guided her to a stool at the table.

Lelah settled down on the stool next to her mother, their eyes and all attention now on the meal before them. As they reached for the food, the likes of which they hadn't seen for many days, Elloe spoke.

"First," she said, "before you eat."

They halted their reach, and Elloe continued, "We call on the Name and give thanks."

A stab of paralyzing fear struck both mother and daughter. What name? Whose name? They'd thought they were safe, away from his power and reach. Samjaza? Was this all a trick?

Taking their frozen countenance as reverence, Elloe proceeded with, "We give thanks to the Name above all names for this bounty before us. May it strengthen these His children for the journey ahead. So shall it be."

As Elloe slipped out of the cottage, Melenah and Lelah maintained their frozen position until Melenah whispered, "It can't be Samjaza. She didn't draw the circle. She didn't say the chant." It was as much to reassure herself as it was to ease Lelah.

Finally moving, she slipped the medallion that hung around her neck out from its hiding place in her blouse. As both looked at it, the fear ebbed. The Name was in the center of one side, bounded by a circle of tiny crude images that looked like the sun, moon, stars, trees, fish, different animals, and two people. On the other side, there were curious undecipherable marks that looked like tiny letters spiraling from the outer side down to the center. At the very center were two words they could read: "The Seed."

Fingering the medallion, Melenah marveled at how the one side with the Name changed to a map in just the right light. This map, along with the possession of the thing itself, had been their ticket to freedom and their connection to the people who risked so much to enable their exodus.

"Elloe must mean the Name here. This is what's gotten us this far." She remembered the day her cousin Kaliyah had given it to her, saying an old man at the edge of the city had slipped two of them in her hand and whispered, "Freedom."

"Now, Lelah, let's eat!" Melenah stated with enthusiasm. They both were silent as they helped themselves to some of the best food they could remember eating. Or maybe food just tasted better when eaten in freedom.

Their final destination was still not attained. They were safe across the river, safe into territory that was not ruled by Samjaza or any other of his fellow Watchers, but there were still spies and eyes that could betray them even on this side. Precautions still must be made until they reached the mountain.

After they'd finished the meal, the young girl assisted her mother with washing, using the basins of fresh water set out for them the night before. To Lelah, it was primitive using a type of chamber pot and fresh water basins and cloths for their toiletries. Melenah had shown her daughter what was used for what when they'd been in hiding before the escape. She'd known these things from her childhood. With grateful hearts, they changed into the clean undergarments and soft robes that Elloe had provided. While dressing, they engaged in mother-daughter small talk, the normalcy of which was refreshing in itself.

"When do you think Kaliyah and Markkah will come too?"

"Well, honey, I know that they will come as soon as they possibly can. Kaliyah is smart and resourceful. I know you miss Markkah so much, and I also know in my heart that we will all be together again," she softly said, comforting her daughter.

Elloe knocked on the door to announce her arrival. "Now, are you ladies decent?"

"Here you go, precious ones. Your transport is ready, and there is a long day ahead of us," Enosh said. "I trust you've had a good breakfast and you're all set for travel."

From the cottage to the small clearing, they'd trodden a path through lush vegetation that included giant ferns and massive trees, the tops of which still couldn't be seen through the lifting morning mist, and before them was the very welcome transport, decidedly different from the ones used to travel thus far. The first had been the worst: a refuse scow that had been filled with rotten, dead, and moldy things. They'd been buried among the offal for nearly an entire day and half a night, at times gagging and retching as quietly as they could, keeping their sounds lower than the road and bustle noise of the city and traffic. Fortunately, their noses grew numb from the stench and the filter clothes that were over their bodies seemed to keep the most egregious of the content from getting in their eyes or in direct contact with their skin.

In this transport, the cargo that hid them was clean and sweet smelling: crates of fresh fruit and vegetables. There was a space lined in hay, covered with a soft cloth, between the outer crates. Enosh claimed Melenah from the supporting arms of Elloe and Lelah and gently lifted her into the space. Melenah was able to crawl herself to the fore of the space and settle into a nestled sitting position. Lelah followed, finding a spot next to her mother. It was roomy enough and comfortable. The relatively generous compartment even allowed them to move around a bit, which would be a welcome relief during their journey. The roof of the space was covered by boards that supported yet another row of crates. This time, there were small spaces between the lower rows of crates that not only let in fresh air but even allowed them to peer through to the outside to give them a glimpse of their surroundings. Comparatively, this felt like luxurious accommodations.

"Dear ones, here are provisions for along the way," said Elloe as she hoisted a large covered basket into the transport for Lelah to pull into their cubicle.

"Now, ladies," Enosh said, "I'm going to close you in with one row of crates. If you need to make a stop along the way, knock three times on one of the crates at the front. As soon as it's safe, I'll stop and let you out."

Elloe added, as Enosh began to enclose the rear, "May the Name be with you and keep you on your way, and may He bring you true peace. So shall it be."

This time, Elloe's calling on the Name did not evoke that paralyzing stab of fear. However, a strange other fear, of something unknown and very great, resonated in their beings. Melenah and Lelah looked at each other, recognizing their congruence of feeling.

Their compartment darkened, but not so much as to darken completely. The bit of light from between the crates cast soft images of the interior. Their voices were a bit muffled, but they could still hear the conversation of the kindly couple as they prepared to be apart for a few days.

"Now, Enosh, be careful. Don't stop unless it's completely safe. The wash near the cliffs is the best place. Don't get out of the wagon if there's a herd of raptogals around. You know they're small, but nasty—"

"Yes, dearest, I'll be quite careful. I've done this many times. I know what I'm doing."

"I've put extra robes, an extra pair of leggings, and sandals in your bag, in case you get wet."

"Thank you, Elloe. I don't know what I'd do without you."

"Enosh, now after you deliver the girls, don't hang around or gab with the men at Ralcho's. Remember there are unfriendly ears around."

"Yes, dearest, I'll behave and be careful."

In the compartment, the mother-daughter team chuckled softly at the overheard banter of a couple that had spent their whole lives together, and marveled at the patience of the man listening to the same advice that he'd probably heard for uncountable years. This simple conversation had been one totally unique for Lelah and one that jogged Melenah's memory of a time before her enslavement. Like the scent of the cargo, the exchange between Elloe and Enosh was consoling.

The ride was uneventful with little traffic on the road, so there had been no excitement or concerns along the way. Throughout the morning's ride they caught glimpses of a traveler or two, but not much could be seen through the narrow cracks of their hiding place. The most interesting occurrence was their rest stop along the way.

Enosh pulled the transport to a stop, got out, and opened the back of the transport. They had arrived at a secluded spot by a stream underneath majestic red cliffs. After helping her mother out, they led Melenah to a place by the stream. Enosh then gave the ladies the privacy to attend to their necessities. They were both happy to spend some time in that spot. Lelah, refreshed, stood breathing in the crisp air and taking in all the fragrances of the meadow. Her entire being surged with the sensation of freedom. She wanted to run and laugh, but didn't want to be heard by any travelers who might come down the nearby road. Instead, she laid herself prone with her face to the ground, deeply breathing in the sweet bouquet of rich green grass and moist fresh earth.

"What are you doing?" queried her mother.

Turning her head, laughing, she said, "I didn't know freedom smelled so wonderful!"

Her mother chuckled. "Indeed it does. Both our noses have certainly smelled far worse!"

Lelah rolled over and then sat up, running her hands through the grass. She wanted to take it all in. This was the first time in her life that she had been in such a place, and she felt like she never wanted to leave it. Suddenly, both heard a rustling in the woods close by. Startled, Lelah leapt to her feet and hastened to her mother's side. Just a few paces away bushes parted and out ambled a young essimudusu, or three-horned beast, chomping on a mouthful of leaves. He just stood, chewed, and gazed at the curious creatures in front of him.

Fascinated by the sight, Lelah thought it a curious thing to see this beast in the wild, since she'd only ever seen them in the city being used by the Watchen class to pull their transports or be ridden by them. That privileged class relished in the display of their power and position above all the other people. The poor and slaves were only allowed to use donkeys and oxen. That ruling class carried an open disdain of others, and it was clearly etched on their faces during any of their forays into the streets of the city, and especially at any of the required gatherings.

"Now what have we found here?" a voice whispered behind her.

Lelah jumped as she was startled out of her reverie. She turned to Enosh, who had his eyes on the beast and a smile that cracked his face.

"I think we had better get back into the transport now," he whispered while helping Melenah from her sitting spot. "This young fellow's mother might be close by."

Without making any swift movements, they made their way back to the transport and the women were settled back into their compartment. As their journey continued, thoughts of where they had come from turned to whispered speculation of where they were headed and what kind of life they might have. They had to control their conversation volume, observing precaution, but their spirits soared with every step closer to their new home. The basket from generous Elloe contained lots of choice food and more clean clothes. The treatment and respect they'd received had been so overwhelming and ever so welcome.

ABOMINATION

As twilight came, Enosh and their transport reached the outskirts of a small town that sat next to a languid river. The road they traveled had mostly been through dense forests, but now they entered a vast clearing, although it hadn't been seen by Melenah and Lelah until they were finally unloaded, along with the crates, in front of a large, barnlike shed attached to a house.

They were greeted by a middle-aged man with rusty red hair. It was rather difficult to tell anyone's age. So he must have been maybe two to three hundred years old, by Melenah's guess, not nearly as old as Enosh or Elloe.

"Brother Jaireck, here are your charges, Melenah and Lelah."

"Welcome, ladies! Let's hurry, get you out of sight. My wife has readied a room for you. Follow me."

One on each side, Enosh and Lelah helped Melenah hobble after Jaireck. He led them into the barn-shed through piles of hay, crates, and various tools to the back wall. The back wall boards looked like a solid wall, until their new host pushed on a board and part of the wall swung open to reveal a small room equipped with one narrow bed, one smaller cot, toiletries in the corner, and a table with two stools. There was a basin with fresh water on the table and a meal already laid out.

Behind them, they heard steps and a cheery voice. "I've brought extra blankets. It gets a bit chillier at night here than in the lowlands."

They turned to see a thin, pinch-faced woman with deep chestnut hair bound tightly in a knot at the back of her head. She had the look of one who had never had a hair out of place; the blankets she held were as precisely folded and her dress was wrinkle-free and flawless.

"Melenah and Lelah, this is my wife, Kahjeera."

"Welcome," said Kahjeera. She smiled and held out her hand to Melenah. It was only then that she realized that Melenah was being held up by Enosh and Lelah. She glanced down at the odd angle Melenah's legs made underneath the folds of her robes. The smile remained but seemed pasted on rather than thoroughly convincing.

She turned her attention to Lelah. "Why, dear, you are quite a bit older than we were told. We need to put another bed in here for you because you'll never fit on the cot. Jaireck, bring in the bed from the top room. This child will need one longer than her mother's.

"So, child, are you sixteen or seventeen years?"

"No, ma'am. Just twelve, last springtime."

"Oh, my—"

Enosh interjected, "My dear Kahjeera, how wonderful of you to provide this shelter for our sojourners. They've had a very long journey, and much of it under terrible circumstances. We appreciate all the efforts you've gone through, for these and all the others you've helped to freedom."

"Well, thank you, Enosh. Let's let the ladies refresh themselves and eat. You'll come in to eat with us in the house before you go."

Speaking again to Melenah, she said, "I'm sorry to seem rude, but we can't take the chance of anyone seeing you or that our routine is different." They said their good nights and left.

As the women sat down at the table, Melenah said, "I think we should give thanks first. I'm not sure who the Name is, so I hope He isn't upset that we thank Him anyway."

"We give thanks to the Name, who has gotten us this far and is leading us to freedom. And thank you for this food." And then she remembered to say, "So shall it be," just like Elloe. She hoped the words were right.

While they were enjoying their evening meal, Jaireck returned with the bed. He squeezed the larger bed into the space next to the other. There was no room on either side, with the beds wedged tightly between the walls. Wishing them a pleasant night, he left again, taking the small cot.

That night when Melenah lay in bed, she reached her hand to her daughter's head, caressing her long, dark hair. "Good night, sweetheart. I love you."

It wasn't but a few moments and Melenah was in a deep sleep. Lelah was too excited about their travels, and thoughts whirled through her mind, so sleep wasn't happening with her just yet. As she lay there, trying to imagine what life was ahead of them, she heard voices through the wall. Her bed was right up against the wall that adjoined the main house. It sounded like Kahjeera and Jaireck. She put her ear to the wall to try to make out the words.

"I just don't feel right about this," she heard Kahjeera say. "Didn't you get a good look at that girl?"

"Now, dear, they need help, just like the others."

"Mark my words, she's one of those half-breeds. She's an abomination. I have no problem at all helping people escape slavery, especially those who have been stolen from our lands, but to allow those, those—"

"Kahjeera, she's just a girl, and she seems like a well-behaved, good one at that—"

Jaireck was interrupted with, "Good girl, my foot! She's got bad blood, and she'll be nothing but a poison in our society. Pollution! We don't need that here. And what do you think that mother of hers is going to do? With her condition, she'll be nothing but a burden to everyone wherever she goes. Not to mention the nerve of that woman anyway, bringing that wicked thing with her! She ought to be ashamed of what she has consorted with! I don't care how nice you think she is. She is unclean! What in the world are we doing helping garbage like this?"

"They need help just like the others, and they want freedom too."

"Freedom to ruin us? I can't believe that the old man sent them. He, of all people, should know better, or—"

"I've had enough. I don't want to hear any more of this. You will stop…"

The arguing voices faded as they moved into a farther room and were heard no more. Slowly, Lelah moved her head from the wall, lay with eyes closed, her heart in her chest like lead and her stomach sickened. The words cut her so deeply she felt like she was crushed to the bed. No words other than *abomination*, *wicked*, and *garbage* entered her mind. She turned on her side and curled her knees to her chest. She tasted salty, silent tears as she wiped them from her face and shuddered with a chill not caused by any temperature change. The deep, cold shame permeated her being, and she drifted off into a fitful sleep punctured with visions of evil things, of which she was one.

The lifting morning mist and the warmth of the sun shining over their freedom had been so sweet, until this morning. Lelah awoke with her heart still leaden. She lay still with her eyes closed, wishing she hadn't awoken and wishing she were something other than what she was.

"Sweetheart, wake up. We've another wonderful day ahead! Closer to the mountain!"

Silence. Lelah couldn't tell her mother what she'd heard. Besides not having the words to describe, she didn't have the heart. She could never hurt her mother.

"Darling girl, get up!"

She gathered all the strength she could and opened her eyes to see her mother's smile and shining eyes. It crushed her and even angered her to think of anyone hurting her mother. That bit of anger energized her enough to get up and go through the motions of everything being fine. But the elation she'd felt these four days into freedom had evaporated.

They cleaned up, did their toiletries, dressed, and waited for directions for their next move. They heard footsteps approaching through the barn.

"Ladies, are you ready? We need to get on the road quickly!"

"We're all set," Melenah said with anticipation in her voice.

Jaireck, looking a bit anxious and weary for early morning, opened the wall door and greeted the women. Helping Lelah hold up her mother, Jaireck led them out to the entrance of the barn, where another cart had been backed into the opening. This transport, instead of vegetables and fruit, carried bolts of cloth and fabrics of all colors and textures. Like the carts before, there was a compartment in the midst of the cargo.

Lelah was greatly relieved to see that Kahjeera was nowhere to be seen. She noticed that Jaireck avoided looking at her, and the deep sense of shame and hurt intensified. She wanted to hide herself. She quickly helped her mother into their travel space and was happy that Jaireck moved just as quickly with sealing them in and out of sight. The basket that Elloe had given them was in the compartment, and there were still provisions enough in it for breakfast and for the rest of the day. It was obvious that Kahjeera hadn't prepared anything for them, but Melenah seemed not to notice as she dug into the basket for something to eat. Lelah let her assume that Kahjeera had known that they had enough food already.

"Honey, you're awfully quiet this morning."

"I'm just not feeling too well."

"Have something to eat. It might make you feel better."

"I'm not hungry. My stomach hurts."

"It's probably all the excitement. Just lay back and get some rest then, sweetheart, and you'll feel better soon."

"Thank you, Amah."

For most of the trip, Lelah lay next to her mother while her mother talked quietly of what she would like to do when they got to the mountain. As she talked, she stroked her daughter's hair.

The rocking of the transport and her mother's touch were soothing, but when her mother called her things like "beautiful daughter," the words pierced her like a knife. She knew she was an abomination. Maybe she could sleep and not wake up.

THE CITY

Kaliyah was biding her time. It had not been too difficult to get her cousins out of the city. They hadn't been missed because they'd been thought to be dead. Kaliyah had kept them hidden since the rampage that had taken the lives of twenty-three of the breeders, along with many of their children. In hiding, Melenah's broken bones had healed without the benefit of being set properly; hence, her once beautiful legs were twisted and nearly useless.

Kaliyah comforted herself now with the knowledge that she also had her daughter hidden away, so the only hurdle now was planning how she could arrange not to be missed. She needed enough time to get out of the city and through hostile countryside, at least three days.

It was a full moon tonight, and there would be two full moons to the Great Gather. People from all over Imin-Sár were already beginning to arrive. There had been nearly a full year of preparation for this event, with an entire outer city built to house the pilgrims and their livestock. This was definitely not just a local Gather event.

It had been fifteen long years of captivity. Kaliyah closed her eyes, blocking out the lights of the city, and pictured a gentle village in the country far away. Her mind's eye saw her mother and father, brothers, sisters, and her best friend and cousin. The images were hazy, all except Melenah's. She and Melenah had been the only ones from the village to survive the raid. The strong would have been conscripted into slavery, but instead of surrendering, they'd fought and died.

She was thankful for her father's guidance so long ago. She was her daughter's age then and grateful that her father had spoken to her of deep things. One thing she'd kept in her mind was what he told her about the Watchers. They were indeed "gods" of a different dimension and very powerful, but he'd said that they didn't know everything, they couldn't know one's thoughts, and they couldn't be in two places at one time. And he'd told her about those elite devotees of the Watchers, the all-human Watchen, who had been personally tutored by the Watchers in all manner of magic arts, weaponry, and the secret laws of nature. Her father had said that their magic was not as powerful, nor as accurate, as they'd led the people to believe. They could invade one's dreams, and their spells could be effective, but not all the time.

She'd tested this out too. While waiting upon a group of Watchen, she'd smiled and cleaned up after them, all the while deliberately thinking terrible thoughts about them. And they hadn't known the difference. She'd risked her life betting that her father had been right. He was, and it had given her courage.

Kaliyah hadn't started out life in the city as a servant. This had only begun after the rampage. When she and her cousin were taken captive, they'd been groomed and set aside to be breeders, along with countless other young women. First had been the Watchen girls, who had been more than willing to be consorts.

But when they didn't produce male offspring for the eldest son of the Watcher, girls were collected throughout the territory.

Samjaza, Lord of the Watchers, fathered twelve sons and daughters with his human wife, Herathah. Their eldest son was Enkara, who had fathered both Markkah and Lelah, along with sixty-two other girls. Samjaza's other sons had borne sons, but not Enkara. The giant, bad-tempered and mean to begin with, blamed the women. The rampage that had taken so many lives was the result of Enkara's focused rage against those who had failed him. The survivors of that attack were relegated to slave status and the remaining daughters taken away from their mothers to be trained in sorcery.

They'd been gathered to the courtyard for the selection. All daughters twelve years old were to be taken into apprenticeship under Herathah. All the mothers had seen what happened when girls before had been trained. Sweet natures became cruel and perverse, and the evil glow in their eyes reflected that of their grandmother's. They became possessed with power and devoid of love. Enkara, who'd always been the escort of the girls to present to his mother, was overcome with fury at, yet again, only presenting daughters. The slaughter began with his bare hands.

It grieved Kaliyah to think of that carnage, but she was grateful for the chaos that it had created, enabling her to get her loved ones into hiding. Melenah and Lelah had been near the front of the group of mothers and daughters, while Kaliyah and Markkah had been at the back. Panic ensued with the sound of the raging roar that issued from Enkara's mouth, made even more fearsome by his display of double rows of teeth that were not an uncommon thing among the children of the "gods." They'd begun to scatter for cover with the first swipe of the giant's mighty arm. Melenah had managed to shove Lelah into the space behind the fountain but was not quick enough to avert the blow that sent her flying against a stone bench. Lelah had heard the cracks of the bones as her mother's legs took the brunt of the impact.

Kaliyah, near the rear, shoved Markkah sprawling back through the entrance to the inside of their compound. As bodies were flying and Enkara was tearing one woman limb from limb, she'd spotted Melenah, crumpled and unconscious, at the foot of a bench. She ran to her and tried to pull her to safety. She spotted Lelah and called to her to come from her hiding spot to help. Kaliyah had to drag the petrified girl from the spot where she'd been wedged. Kaliyah slapped her in the face. Finally, shaken from her stupor, Lelah helped Kaliyah drag her mother into their compound, unnoticed by the murder-occupied monster.

At the time they hadn't had a plan for escape. It had been safer just to hide them and have them presumed to be among parts of the other dismembered bodies than to have Melenah's injuries known. Imperfection was not tolerated, and she would have been killed anyway. Kaliyah decided that she couldn't hide too. None of them could survive that way.

The hiding place was down. There was a vast system of connecting rooms that went deep beneath the compound where they lived. The sandstone was not strong enough to support huge caverns beneath the massive stone complex, but the smaller rooms, connected by walking tunnels, bore no threat to the stability of the foundation. And the sandstone had made it easier to carve out than if it had been granite. The multilayered honeycomb design of the rooms and tunnels also had numerous boreholes from the surface to the rooms that provided for air exchange. These rooms were storehouses for mainly food provisions and some general storage. Fortunately, the tunnels were too small for the giants to traverse, and this fact alone leant a feeling of security to the women. And thankfully, Kaliyah's subsequent slave status had sent her to the kitchens, which had given her more frequent and justifiable access to the honeycomb.

As she sat looking out her window, waiting for the time to slip down to see her daughter, she marveled at how the hiding could have turned out disastrous if she'd been sent away from the compound. But it hadn't happened. She felt like something or someone was looking out for them, but she didn't know who or what. She certainly knew who it wasn't. It wasn't Herathah and her magic, and it wasn't Samjaza, who was a self-serving god.

The thought of real escape from the city hadn't been discussed with Melenah. They both dearly wished it but had not even dared to hope it, at least not until Kaliyah met the old man. She fingered the medallion that hung from the chain around her neck and remembered the meeting. She'd been sent to a specialty spice market to pick up the cardamom that had been missing from the latest shipment of spices to the compound.

For some unknown reason, she had taken a different route back. That was a wonder too. Of all the routes to take, she'd decided to go down the road past the refuse complex. The odor alone should have sent her in another direction. But she walked that way anyway. It was outside the entrance that she'd seen the old man with the kindly eyes. At first when he spoke, she thought that he might be a beggar. Instead of his hand out to receive something, he had the two medallions in his hand, giving them to her and saying, "Freedom."

She'd asked, "How?"

He'd said no more words, just nodded his head toward the entryway where garbage was hauled. She knew that was the way out. The refuse was taken via large transports far out of the city every week. From the city, the smoke from the refuse burning could be seen far in the distance, but the smoke rarely reached the nostrils of the city residents.

The plan for escape had begun at that moment. For five long months she'd managed to care for her loved ones deep inside the honeycomb, bringing food and necessities to their little room behind crates of supplies and old furniture. They were hidden in a place not frequented by those who carted food in and out of the storehouses.

Her tasks in the kitchens had been the most humiliating. The regular slaves who'd once waited upon her and her daughter relished in her lowered status. They didn't hesitate to assign the foulest jobs to her. Besides transporting food in and out of the honeycomb, she cleaned up their messes, cleaned their latrines, disposed of the garbage, and listened to their verbal abuses. They occasionally physically lashed out at her if they thought that she wasn't humble enough for them. Actually, the errand for the cardamom had been a unique one with her being sent. Others higher up than her had been occupied with preparations of a great special meal to be given in honor of a visit of the grandmother. Had that been just circumstance too?

Her last chore of the day approached. It was the time of night to go into the honeycomb to retrieve the flour for the next day's baking. It had been a job despised because it was to be done in the dead of night, to get the flour to the kitchens before the bakers arrived. Kaliyah had taken care to make enough time to see her loved ones each time she'd made the trip. At the bottom of the cart she'd pushed, she was sure to take along whatever they needed. Now, over this last week, it'd been only her daughter hidden in the far reaches of the honeycomb. She ached for Markkah and her isolation, but both knew that it was just for a short time more. Kaliyah entered the underground system with great hope in her heart.

In the dead of night, the honeycomb was pitch black until she turned the knob at the right just inside the entrance. This connected two copper wires together that completed a circuit of energy generated by the large clay pot underneath the knob. The wires that made the circuit to and from the clay pot ran along the ceiling, and at intervals of about every ten arm lengths, they connected with a hollowed-out amber gourd, which emitted a soft glowing light. At the end of that first corridor and room, there were another two clay pots with knobs above. She turned the farther one on to light the next tunnel and room and then turned to switch the other knob off, extinguishing the lights of the former. Even at brightest daytime, these lights were needed to traverse the honeycomb. This had been one of the innovations that had come by instruction from the Watchers.

As she trundled the cart lower and lower, she picked up her pace. She knew the maze like the back of her hand now. At first she'd had to make little divots in the sandstone with a tiny knife she carried, marking the turns to the hideout. She rounded the final corner and entered a room lined with old crates. She tapped a few times on one of the crates.

"Amah!" an excited but lowered voice exclaimed from behind the crates. Both began to move the crates at the far end of the room. Kaliyah deftly rolled the cart into the space and just as deftly stacked the crates back up behind her. Only then did she embrace her daughter.

"Beautiful girl! We'll be free before we know it, honey! I'm so sorry you have to be left alone for so long. And I know you miss Lelah terribly too."

"Amah, don't apologize! You know there wasn't room enough for me to go with them. Besides, I only want to go when you go."

"You're a brave girl, Markkah. I'm so very proud of you. Many girls your age would complain and cry about their circumstances. You are very special."

Mother and daughter hugged for a long moment.

"Okay, sweetie, I've got a couple of things for you," Kaliyah whispered as she released her daughter. "Here are a few tasty treats from the kitchen, a nice fresh blanket, and some fresh clothes." And pulling a box out of the sack too, she said, "And here's a little puzzle for you so you're not so bored."

"Thank you, Amah!" Markkah chimed as she eagerly took the box from her mother. "A puzzle! I love puzzles!"

"Now, sweetie, I have to get going back up now. The time is getting nearer for our escape. Before you know it, we'll be with Melenah and Lelah again. Hold tight, and keep being patient."

"Yes, Amah."

They quickly and quietly moved the crates, got the cart out, indulged in one more quick hug, and then arranged the crates back to seal up the room. Kaliyah made her way back up through the tunnels and rooms to the place where she loaded the cart up with heavy bags full of flour. To compensate for the time spent with her daughter, she hurried as fast as she could. By the time she was out of the honeycomb and into the kitchen, she was quite out of breath. She hefted each large bag of flour to the large bin, unfastened the top, and poured the flour in. After all twelve bags were emptied, she looked like a ghost from the flour dust. Exhausted, finally her day was done.

THE MOUNTAIN

The cart slowed and came to a stop. Melenah gently shook Lelah's shoulder. "Honey, wake up. We're here."

Lelah really hadn't been asleep, but it had been easier to pretend sleep than to have to act like there was nothing wrong. She feigned awakening and then moved to help her mother to the rear of the transport as they heard the crates being taken out of the way.

Melenah took in the landscape. They were at the foot of a mountain. The setting sun was to her back, and the final rays reflected the top half of the mountain in front of her, making it look like it was topped in shimmering gold. The stunning sight caught her breath.

"Lelah, look at this!"

For the first time that day, Lelah looked up. Even through her depression, she saw the beauty of the mountain. But it increased her feeling of ugliness. She wanted to hide. She didn't belong there.

A little cottage was to the left of the cart. It looked like someone had started a fire in its fireplace. A fragrant smoke was slowly billowing out of the chimney. The giant trees behind the cottage were of a different sort than the trees of the lower jungle. They had huge trunks, and they tapered to a point at their tops. Instead of large leaves, theirs were long, gracefully drooping needles. In the waning light, they looked like majestic, dark sentinels standing guard. A tall man—for an all-human, that is—stood talking with Jaireck. They turned and headed to the rear of the transport.

"Melenah and Lelah, I'd like to introduce you to Metu, the man who'll lead you the rest of the way."

"It is very nice to meet you, sir," said Melenah.

With her head lowered, Lelah quietly spoke her greeting also.

"Well, ladies, let me show you to your cottage." To Jaireck he said, "Go ahead to the stables. Your cottage is the same as before."

Metu went to the other side of Melenah to assist Lelah with taking her mother to the shelter. As they walked down the path, Metu explained that the next day's travel would take them to a compound about halfway up the mountain, where they would be able to make their home for as long as they'd want or need. The news that they would be able to travel in the open was met with a cry of delight from Melenah.

"Real freedom! Lelah!"

Lelah forced a smile and an appropriate reply. Ordinarily, her mother would have noticed that there was something wrong with her daughter, but her excitement and delight overwhelmed her perceptions. But it did not go unnoticed by Metu.

He led them into the cottage, which was sparsely but comfortably appointed. There was a fire crackling in a stone fireplace and a meal on the table.

"I've left some extra wood in the box. You might want to put another log or two on the fire before you go to bed. It gets a bit colder up here in the high country than down in the lowlands."

"Thank you so much, Metu. My daughter and I appreciate your hospitality."

Metu had begun to think that Lelah might be a sullen child, not happy with her mother or their escape. He'd thought that perhaps she'd been one who would rather have stayed in the city. He'd seen that before in other young people. Cities these days, especially the great city, Eriduch, had many delights and action that attracted many of the young away from the agrarian country life.

Just as he'd begun to form that opinion of the girl, he caught a look at her and saw a tear track its way down her cheek. He also noticed the gentleness and care she showed while helping her mother. He sensed that maybe she was just deeply sad and not sullen. He decided to withhold judgment of the girl until he observed further.

As they settled down at the table, Metu asked if he could say a blessing.

"Oh, please do, Metu."

"We thank You, oh Name above all names, for protecting these Your children and bringing them to safety. Bless them, give them strength, gladden their hearts, and heal their wounds. Give them rest and refreshment this night. So shall it be.

"I shall now leave you ladies in peace. We'll leave at the break of dawn," Metu said as he left the cottage.

For the first time since the night before, Lelah felt like her heart wasn't quite so heavy. She also realized that she was famished. Both women set to the task of eating. Melenah was relieved to see that her daughter finally had an appetite. They chatted happily. This time Lelah's smile wasn't forced.

That night, again Melenah had no trouble falling asleep. But Lelah, having spent a good part of the day sleeping, had difficulties turning off her thoughts. She mulled over the happenings of the past days and tried to talk herself into thinking that maybe it'd be easier to have a life high up on the mountain. It would be easier to live and take care of her mother with not many people around. It could be almost like hiding. She wasn't sure what the conditions would be like, but she pictured a cottage not unlike the one they were in, and she hoped there weren't many people around. But even Metu's kindness didn't stop her from thinking that when he looked at her, he saw an abomination. He must have just been polite when he'd included her as "Your children" in his blessing. Still, the fact that he said it at all gave her a glimmer of hope, and she was grateful to him for that.

The next morning's mist had a chill to it that was new. Both Melenah and Lelah were thankful to find that the extra clothes provided for them were warm ones. They were ready and waiting when Metu arrived to escort them to their transport. The four harnessed oxen lowed as they finished their morning hay, and Metu lifted Melenah up into the front seat of the transport. Lelah pulled herself up into the seat next to her mother. Her robe had a hood that she pulled up, covering most of her face. In the chill, it didn't seem unusual. Metu checked that the cargo was secured and then climbed up into the seat on the other side of Melenah. He prodded the oxen, and they were on their way.

The climb took them in and out of treed lanes and clearings, with wide vistas of clearings, streams, lakes and farmlands being glimpsed between trees as they ascended. Looking down, they spotted some settlements they must have traveled through while still in concealment. The scenery was stunning in both directions. At least, that is what Melenah kept saying as they rode. Her enthusiasm was contagious. Lelah took in the sights with her mother and marveled at the panoramas. Lelah felt overwhelmed by the color green. She'd only been acquainted with the compound life in the city, with its colors of tan, gray, gold and brown of hewn stone and carved wood, so this was a whole other world to her. Despite herself and her feelings of dirtiness, Lelah breathed in the wild scents of strange blossoms and crisp clean air. She found herself forgetting for a few moments here and there how abnormal she was.

As the temperature rose, Melenah took off her outer robe. "Aren't you a little warm, honey?"

"Oh, I'm fine, Amah. I've just been a little colder than normal," she lied.

In early afternoon, a little village appeared as they rounded a bend in the road. It was more like a series of cottages tucked here and there at the edge of a great clearing. The top of the golden mountain loomed treeless before them. Metu pulled the oxen to a halt.

"Now, ladies, there are a few empty cottages, so you can take your pick. Our little compound houses refugees just like you. Some have stayed to make this their permanent home, and most have moved on to other places. The choice is yours, but you are welcome to stay here for as long as you wish."

Lelah whispered something in her mother's ear. Melenah turned to Metu and said, "Would you show us to one that's on the outskirts?"

"I know just the cottage for you, then. First let's introduce you to your neighbors, and then you can settle in."

"Metu! You're back!" cried a small child as he rushed out of the first cottage. He was followed by a young man and woman, who also ran up to the transport.

"Metu, who've we got here?" said the young man as he scooped up the child.

"Ramuel and Corah, I'd like you to meet Melenah and her daughter, Lelah."

"And I'm Kam!" squealed the child, wriggling in his father's arms, trying to get loose to climb into the transport. Metu reached for Kam, taking the squirming child into his arms to give him a big bear hug.

"And, ladies, this is my best little friend, Kam."

The gleeful child smiled and then acted bashful when Melenah held out her hand to the boy. He buried his face in Metu's shoulder and then peeked out with an impish grin to Melenah and Lelah. Then he buried his face again.

"Ramuel and Corah are one of our long-term resident families. They teach clothes making, if you are interested in learning. We teach a number of trades here so that refugees like yourselves can learn something other than what you've been doing in captivity. Or you may think of something else to do."

Corah interjected, "It helps to be productive, especially after feeling like you've been living on other's charity for a good while. You'll have time to check out what you're suited for and what you like best."

Metu handed Kam back to his father and then climbed out of the transport. He and Ramuel went to the rear and began to unload rolls of cloth and various other items. Loose again, the energetic little boy ran circles around the working men, cheerfully chattering to Metu, who answered him, showing great interest in the little boy's stories.

"There's a wonderful cottage right next to us that's available. It would be great if you would move into it," said Corah.

Melenah, after a quick look at her still-hooded daughter, said, "Metu says he knows the perfect cottage for us, but I don't know which one it is."

"Well, when he's ready to take you there, we can help you settle in."

"Thank you so much, Corah! You make us feel very welcome here."

Corah's eyes went to Lelah. Noticing the questioning look, she stated, "My daughter hasn't been feeling well for a couple of days now. I think she needs a little rest."

Understanding, Corah nodded.

Having unloaded the goods, the men came back to the front of the transport. Metu climbed back in.

"I'm taking these ladies to the cottage by the stream. I think it will most suit them," said Metu.

"I'd hoped that you would put them in next to us, but I guess you know best. I'll bring dinner up then when it's ready," chimed Corah.

By this time, their presence had become known to the other residents of the compound. They could see up the road where people who'd been in the fields and outside of their cottages had gathered near the road and were waiting for Metu to navigate their way.

Ramuel scooped up his enthusiastic son again as Metu prodded the oxen, and they lumbered up to the awaiting group. Again, Melenah and Lelah remained in their seats as introductions were made. Several beautiful young women were especially happy to see Metu. They gave cursory introductions and then turned their attentions the tall, handsome man who'd been their transporter. It was the first time that Lelah really looked at Metu. With his rakish dark curls and well-muscled arms, Metu had a presence about him that commanded attention, particulary the attention of women. She involuntarily sucked in her breath and her heart took a leap. However, it only served to make her retreat even deeper into her hooded robe. She could never be like those other girls—so happy, beautiful, and normal. She was acutely aware of her only part-humanness.

Melenah would need more time to be able to remember the names of all the people she met. There were farmers, shepherds, metalworkers, and carpenters among them. Most of the residents looked young to middle aged, and the children were plentiful. There were a few children around Lelah's age, but none nearly so tall as she.

Metu helped the men unload most of the rest of the transport's cargo. Different items went to different men and women, depending on their trades. Everyone had gotten some of the food staples. Lelah wondered if they'd all be as friendly and welcoming if they knew her mother was crippled and she was a half-breed.

Bidding the welcomers a good day, Metu prodded the oxen on to the cottage by the stream. It was the farthest cottage from the heart of the compound, out of the direct sight of any of the others. It had towering trees surrounding it and a babbling brook behind.

Metu jumped out of the transport and then reached up to help Melenah down as she scooted closer to the edge of the seat. Lelah got out on the other side and ran around to help with her mother.

"Well, you're feeling a little better, Lelah," said Metu.

Embarrassed, Lelah lowered her head and mumbled, "I am a bit better…now that we're here."

On either side of Melenah, the two helped her down the needle-strewn path and into the small stone cottage. Inside, it seemed more spacious than it appeared from the outside. It had one large main room and two smaller. There was a river-rock fireplace, and the entire place was furnished. After settling Melenah down on a chair, Metu went to the cupboards to inspect the contents.

"I'll be back," he said and exited the cottage. A few minutes later, he returned with a large crate filled with food items from the remainder of the cargo. He then loaded the oil, grain, and dried fruits into the cupboards.

"Lelah, come here. I want you to see where everything is, because you'll be taking care of your mother."

Still with a hood covering her head, she went into the kitchen corner and dutifully listened to Metu's directions. She was a puzzle to Metu. He still withheld judgment on her nature but had concluded that, at the least, she was attentive to her mother's needs. He suspected that her quietness and reclusive behavior might come from fear of people finding out she was the daughter of a giant, or Diǧir-na (god-man), as they preferred to be called.

He had been aware of her lineage since before their exodus from the city. He would keep an eye on her to be sure that it was a wise choice or not to extend freedom to ones so close to such evil. He hoped that his first impression, that she might be sullen and resentful of leaving their former abode, had been a false one.

He knew that there were many things the two didn't know as yet. Their worldview was entirely different and the things of old unknown to them. As he pondered these things, Corah knocked at the door. She had a steaming bowl of fragrant soup in her hands. Kam came quickly in after her, holding a cloth bag. He ran straight for Metu and leaped into his arms. Metu caught the bag that had gone flying in the process.

"Come in!" Melenah called.

"Here's your welcome meal!" she chimed.

And laughing, Metu added, "And it looks like Kam has brought flying biscuits too!"

"Thank you so much, Corah. We're famished!" said Melenah gratefully.

"Here, Amah, I'll help you to the table," Lelah said softly. She put her arm around her mother and lifted.

It was then that Corah realized Melenah's condition. She put the bowl down on the table and went to assist Lelah with Melenah.

"I'm sorry to see that you have difficulty walking, Melenah. But you know, that means you'll be able to learn clothes making easier than some of the other trades. I'd love to have you work with me."

"I don't know what to say, Corah. I'd be honored to work with you. I think I'd like that."

Lelah smiled. She thought she was going to like Corah very much.

Metu put the rescued biscuits on the table too.

"Metu, we'd be honored if you would say the blessing for us," said Melenah.

They reverently bowed their heads, and Metu invoked the Name, blessing the newcomers and their whole community.

Melenah thought to herself that she wanted to learn more about who the Name was and what these people were all about who'd risked so much to get slaves to freedom, even ones who really didn't belong to them.

For the first time since overhearing the devastating argument, Lelah was comforted. She let the hood fall to her shoulders. And Corah still genuinely smiled.

"Come on, Kam. Let's let these ladies enjoy their meal!" To Melenah and Lelah, he said, "I'm going up the mountain for a few days. I'll be back soon to check on you."

Mother and daughter now were alone in their new home. It was a delicious meal, and the elder was greatly relieved to see that the younger seemed to be feeling much better.

TRASH AND REFUSE

The muted light of the pre-dawn filtered into the small room where Kaliyah slept. She had gotten just a few hours' sleep before having to begin another day. As she blinked away the haziness of not quite enough rest, she counted it as one more day closer to freedom. She readied herself for the day and then went to report to her work.

Every morning she first went to the kitchens to clean up after the bakers. Only after she'd completed the cleaning there, she was allowed a small portion of some of the leftover bread or other food that was otherwise headed for pigs and other animals. Her next duty would be to clean the latrines, and then she would clean the courtyard of any animal droppings that might have soiled the paving stones. Some of the animals left rather large messes, depending upon who might have visited and by what transports they used. She would clean the kitchens after every meal preparation too. Her next-to-last duty of the day, which was usually late into the evening, was to open the doors of the trash room for the trash transporter and assist him with loading the refuse. And finally, the last task of the night took her into the honeycomb and her daughter.

This morning when she arrived in the kitchen, she was met by Nekoda, the chief steward of the compound. His repulsive face was matched by his attitude. Kaliyah had felt the brunt of his meanness and great tattooed arms more than once. She shuddered with foreboding.

"If it isn't the foreign piece of trash," he said with a cruel grin and to the delight of the other workers in the kitchen.

Kaliyah lowered her eyes and head and meekly said, "Yes, sir."

"I hear you're very good at shoveling dung. You're so good at it, I've got another job for you for a while."

A stab of fear shot through Kaliyah. Her present routine was critical for her ability to provide for her daughter. She couldn't be sent away, not right now.

Nekoda continued, "You are going to be on street-dung duty for the Gather."

She dared to speak. A few seconds of dead silence in the room followed her saying, "I'll need a day or two to train someone to do my job here first."

"What is wrong with the woman who did this job before you? Oh, I remember. She's dead." He emphasized the word *dead*, leading everyone to think that maybe he'd make short work of Kaliyah too, right there in the kitchen.

After another strained silence, he said, "You've got two days. Then you report to Abishag." Without striking her, he left the room.

Kaliyah began her kitchen duties, to the jeers of the delighted servants. Their mocking was inconsequential to her. While madly cleaning, she was also madly thinking about how to take care of Markkah. If she did not have her kitchen duties and was working out on the streets of the city, there would be no way she could continue to have access to the honeycomb.

Think fast, think fast! kept running through her mind. She had to get Markkah out of the honeycomb before she began her new duty. She willed herself to not panic but instead to plan. If Nekoda didn't present her with a trainee before the end of the day, she'd have time.

She thought if she could get Markkah up out of the honeycomb when she made the last trip of the night to get the flour, she could hide her in the trash room until tomorrow's trash pickup. But she'd have someone with her all day tomorrow to train for her job. She'd have to think of a diversion so they could get Markkah loaded into the trash transport without the other person knowing. For now, though, she was going to have to wait until trash pickup tonight to see what the trash collector, Ishmerai (known to everyone else as Maggot) thought would work. He was the one who had smuggled Melenah and Lelah out.

The day's work was frustratingly slow, but thankfully Nekoda didn't show up with her replacement yet. She kept hoping that her luck would hold out on that. Finally, the evening loomed, and she entered the trash room early, eager to meet Ishmerai. She reflected on that first realization that Ishmerai was connected to the old man and the medallions.

She had hidden her loved ones in the honeycomb after the rampage, with no idea how they were going to get out or even survive the hiding itself. Her subsequent slave status enabled her to care for them. The meeting with the old man who gave her the medallions had given her hope of the possibility of escape. She had had the medallions for nearly two moon cycles, with no idea about how they could help in that endeavor, when she was helping a trash transport driver load the transport. She'd bent over to pick up a basket, and the medallion, which she'd put on a chain around her neck, slipped out of her blouse. The man saw it. She remembered the fear she felt, thinking that it might not be good for him to see it. Instead, he had smiled and slipped an identical one out from his shirt and said, "Freedom." He was an ally of the old man and part of an underground network of people who helped others to escape slavery.

"My name is Ishmerai, but you really don't know that," he'd said, putting his finger to his lips.

When Melenah was healed enough, she and Lelah had been smuggled out with the trash, taken to the refuse transfer complex in town, then taken out of the city to the facility away in the distance, and then on from there.

Kaliyah heard the rattle of the wheels lumbering close to the gate. She ran to open it and was greatly cheered to see Ishmerai. Thankfully, the refuse business was of such a despised nature that rarely anyone but those of very low rank were around for the dealing with it. And right now, they were the lowest of the low. It worked in their favor. But they spoke in whispers anyway.

"Ishmerai, I need your help right away!"

"It's not safe to leave yet, Kaliyah."

"I know, not for me, my daughter."

Kaliyah explained the dilemma, her job change, and that she needed to get Markkah out of the honeycomb now.

Ishmerai pondered a few moments and said, "It won't work tomorrow, because someone else will be making the rounds. I won't take the refuse now. I'll make a few other stops first. Then I'll be back in about two hours. Have her here then. I'll keep her safe in hiding at the refuse compound until we can get you out too. It's good that you have the new job, because we can be in better contact. It'll be sometime during the Gather that conditions will be right to get you both out of the city."

"I knew you would have the solution!" Kaliyah said through tears of relief.

"Now get going. Get Markkah here as quickly as you can."

Kaliyah closed the gate as Ishmerai pulled away. Hurriedly, she made her way out of the trash room, into the kitchen to grab the flour cart, and then ran through the compound and to the entrance of the honeycomb. She gingerly turned the light knobs on and off as she descended down the tunnel. Leaving the cart at the flour room, she ran as fast as she could to the hiding place. Rounding the last bend, she began to unstack the crates before she gave the safe signal to her daughter. She heard a little gasp from inside.

"I'm sorry, honey. It's just me!"

"Amah, what's up? You're early."

"Markkah, we have to hurry. It's time for you to get out of here."

"Wonderful!"

"But, honey, it's a little bit different than we thought. I have to let you go ahead of me—"

"Amah! You know I'm not going without you."

"It's just for a short time. You'll just be in hiding in a different place. I promise we will escape together."

As Kaliyah explained why things were changing, she grabbed a couple of empty flour bags that had been used as bedding material. "Markkah, just like Melenah and Lelah did, you'll hide in these when I load the cart with the flour."

Markkah slipped her puzzle into her robe pocket. Her mother had her put on a couple layers of clothing because there was no way to pack or carry any kind of bag. They left the hiding place, replacing the crates back in order. Both ran as swiftly and as quietly as they could to the flour room.

Markkah helped her mother put the first several large bags in the cart. Then Kaliyah had Markkah climb into the cart. She put one bag over Markkah's head and slipped the other one up over her legs. It was uncomfortable, but Kaliyah stacked a few flour bags around her bagged daughter and a couple on top. She fussed with the arrangement to make the load look as normal as possible.

She whispered, "Can you breathe all right?"

"I'm fine, Amah. It doesn't feel good, but I'm okay."

"Let's do it, then," Kaliyah said as she pushed the heavy cart uphill and away from the flour room. It seemed to take forever to get out of the honeycomb. She hoped against hope that no one would notice that her schedule was not as usual. It was still late, and most of the people in the compound were in bed, but someone might be up and notice the difference.

She was almost to the kitchen when, to her horror, Nekoda rounded a corner and stopped in front of her. With him was a blood-streaked, bruised, and disheveled young woman he held roughly by the arm.

"I've got your trainee for you," he said with a cruel smirk. He shoved her roughly into the cart and added, "Maybe she scrubs better than she pleases me."

With that, he turned and left. The stunned girl leaned heavily on the cart. Kaliyah watched as Nekoda left the hall, and she muttered under her breath, "I can see the interviews are over."

As Kaliyah came up to her, she asked, "Are you all right?"

"I'm…I'm okay," she said shakily.

"What's your name?" asked Kaliyah.

"Hazael, but they don't call me that here. They call me Merah."

"Well, small wonder they don't want to call you 'God Sees' around here. But, I'll call you Hazael when no one is listening," said Kaliyah softly. "You're in no condition to work with me tonight. I want you to get some rest first, and we'll start in the morning.

"Let me put this cart in the kitchen first, and I'll be right back to show you to my quarters." Kaliyah helped her to a bench in a secluded alcove off of the hallway and then hastily wheeled the cart into the kitchen.

"Quick, Markkah," she whispered as she lifted flour bags off her daughter. She helped her daughter out of the sacks and led her out the other kitchen door and down a long hall to the refuse room.

"Amah, what did Nekoda do to that girl?" Markkah asked with concern.

"He hurt her badly, sweetheart, but she'll recover."

"I feel sorry for her."

"I do too, honey. But now I want you to hide in that corner. I'm sorry it smells so bad here. Take the empty sacks with you because you might need them. Be quiet as a mouse, and I'll be back as quickly as I can."

Kaliyah gave her daughter a quick hug and kiss and then helped to conceal her in her hiding place. She then ran out of the room, past the kitchen, and to Hazael, who was still sitting on the bench with her head leaning against the wall.

"Come, Hazael. I'll take you to my quarters," Kaliyah whispered gently as she helped the girl off the bench.

Unsteady on her feet, Hazael responded, "Thank you for your kindness."

The two made their way through rooms and hallways to the farthest part of the compound to the slave quarters. They passed the few slaves left still doing their last chores of the night. The privileged occupants, of which Kaliyah had once been, were in their quarters or, if chosen, would be in the upper reaches with Enkara. Kaliyah thought to herself that it was far better being the lowest slave in this place than a consort of the brutal giant.

Kaliyah showed Hazael where she could wash and then where to sleep. Since Kaliyah had such late-night duties, she had been put in a small space away from the larger slave quarters so she wouldn't disturb the sleeping servants when she came in, in the middle of the night.

"When I'm done with my duties tonight, I'll come back. Now you rest. We have a big day tomorrow, and it starts early."

"Thank you, Kaliyah," Hazael said with gratitude.

Without a further word, Kaliyah made haste to return to the refuse room. Entering, she was relieved to see that all was as she'd left it.

"Markkah, I'm back."

"Amah!"

"Sit quiet, honey, and listen to me. Ishmerai will be here soon. You will go with him, and he will hide you for some days until the time is right for me to join you. Then we will leave together."

"But, Amah! I don't—"

"Hush, child. We must do it this way. There is no other option. You know why. I told you before."

"But I'm afraid, Amah."

"I know. So am I. But trust Ishmerai. The old man trusts him, so I know we'll both be all right. It'll be a short time. I know it in my heart," she said soothingly.

"What old man?" Markkah asked.

"You know, the one who gave me this," she said as she drew the medallion out from her blouse.

They heard the rumbling of the refuse transport approaching. Kaliyah ran to the gate and opened it and as quickly ran back to Markkah and helped her out of her hiding spot. She took the medallion off from around her neck and slipped it over her daughter's head.

"Wear this for me. It's my promise. One day we'll be free, darling, and it'll be soon. Be brave. Be brave for me and Melenah and Lelah."

"Yes, Amah," she said through tears.

"Kaliyah, give me a hand so we can make this quick," said Ishmerai.

Upon Ishmerai's instructions, they took some of the crates and piles of garbage out of the transport. Markkah helped. Near the front, there was a discreet boxed compartment, the hiding spot. It was only large enough for two bodies at the most.

"I don't have the filter clothes with me, Kaliyah, but we can use those flour sacks. They'll at least help a bit. It won't be a long trip tonight."

And then, to Markkah the young man said, "I'm sorry, Markkah, to meet you like this."

He held out his hands to hold hers and continued, "I've promised your mother to take good care of you and keep you safe until you can both leave. But now we have to hurry."

Kaliyah gave Markkah a hug and kissed her on both teary cheeks. "I love you, and I'll be with you soon."

Ishmerai and Kaliyah helped Markkah into the hiding compartment.

"It'd be better for you to put the bags over you rather than put you in them for now. At least they'll shield you from anything leaking through the top. Keep facedown so you can breathe the air coming through the slats at the bottom. It may get a bit dusty, but at least it's fresh air," instructed Ishmerai.

"Honey, don't let the smell get to you. Just remind yourself that this nasty stuff is our ticket to freedom and our protection," added Kaliyah.

"I love you, Amah. I'll wait for you."

With tears running down her face, Kaliyah helped Ishmerai reload refuse and add the new refuse to the bed of the transport.

"The Name be with you, Kaliyah,"

"And with you, Ishmerai."

As she watched their deliverer pull the transport away from the gate and down the road, she was encouraged by the strength of the young man who bore her daughter away for safekeeping. She still did not know who the Name was, but she was confident she knew who the Name wasn't. And that was a good thing.

She pulled the gate shut and turned to her final duties of the day. She washed in the kitchen washroom and then turned her attentions to loading the flour into the vat. She finished just about the same time she usually finished this duty. In exhaustion and relief, she retired to her quarters to curl up next to the poor girl who would fill her shoes in this place.

Just before the break of dawn, Kaliyah shook Hazael awake. It took a few seconds before Hazael could remember where she was.

"You'd better call me Merah today, or we'll get in trouble."

"Okay, Merah, I'll remember."

Throughout the day, Kaliyah showed Hazael-Merah her routine and gave her pointers on how to avoid trouble. She felt sorry for the girl, with the knowledge that she had no hope for escape from her situation. She was almost tempted to tell her there was a way out, but she couldn't risk betrayal or even be assured that she had the authority to choose who should get out. She didn't know why that made a difference. She knew she'd been just a stranger walking down the street to the old man who gave her the medallions. But he'd impressed her with a feeling that he'd been waiting for her and had known about her and her loved ones. It didn't make any sense, and he certainly hadn't said so, but maybe it was an understanding that she'd read in his eyes. Somehow, he was the one who chose. At least that is what she felt, and she obeyed that instinct.

Hazael learned that the demeaning work would make it so she could do her work mostly undisturbed. The humiliating status made it so they were largely invisible to those in the household. No people, except the kitchen staff, acted like they saw them as they quietly and unobtrusively completed the duties. Kaliyah thought that Hazael's homely looks would also serve to keep her from the attentions of any who would do her more harm. Of course, no slave was immune to the cruelties of Nekoda, but it was a good thing he thought Hazael displeasing. Hopefully, the worst she could expect from him now would be his periodic beatings or unexpected blows. Kaliyah consoled her conscience with these thoughts.

During the last job of the night, when Kaliyah showed Hazael the honeycomb flour storage, she thought that she should run down to the hiding place to remove evidence of the hiding. But she could not think of an unsuspicious way of doing it. The best she could hope for was that it was so far tucked away in the honeycomb that it wouldn't be discovered for a long time. It was a risk, but she felt she had no choice.

❦   ❦

The first day alone in her new hiding place, Markkah took out her little wooden puzzle and occupied herself with still trying to discover its secret. She was grateful for something to do other than just sit and think. She'd been cooped up for so long, more than half a year, that she was growing impatient to be out in the open again.

Ishmerai had told her that he would not see her that night but would come in the morning. It had been his day to make the trip out of the city to the refuse site where sorting, burning, and reclaiming was done. It took a full sunrise to sunrise to make the round trip.

When she was tired of working the puzzle, she took off the medallion and puzzled over its secrets. She thought it had to be magic of some kind and a protective one at that, but she couldn't decipher the marks and figures on it. Then the thought hit her that if her mother didn't have it, she was unprotected and could be in danger. A feeling of dread and panic grew inside her, and the hours of the day faded into night with her apprehension growing. She'd known that Nekoda had badly hurt the woman who was taking her mother's place, so what would Amah's new master do to her?

Her earlier wish just to walk in the daylight turned to an urgent need to run in the open to help her mother. Could she sneak out and get back to the compound to give her mother the medallion? Would her mother still be there? But the knowledge that she didn't even know where she was in the city to get back there hit her hard. Ishmerai would know, and he would help. It took all her will and strength to resist the temptation to find a way out to the streets. She forced herself to wait and determined that she would go herself in the morning, if Ishmerai didn't come. She slept a fitful sleep holding on to the medallion.

In the pre-dawn hours of the next morning, Kaliyah prepared to meet with Nekoda for direction on her new assignment. Any reason to meet with Nekoda made her apprehensive, but it encouraged her to think that she wouldn't be dealing with him after this morning.

As Kaliyah and Merah entered the kitchen, they were met by Nekoda and a slimy, dirty man whose face made Nekoda's look handsome by comparison. The cruel smiles on each sent a shot of panic through both women's beings. They stood petrified, heads down, not looking Nekoda or the other man in the eyes.

"Merah! What are you doing standing there doing nothing? Get to work, you ugly pig." Nekoda sneered at Hazael. With great relief and enthusiasm, she hurriedly set about the duties she'd been shown to do the day before.

"And now, our little piece of trash, this is your new master," he said smoothly.

Kaliyah acknowledged the meeting with Abishag with a humble nod of her head.

Nekoda then coolly said, "You're not quite ready for your new job." She didn't see his smile, but she heard it in his voice. Her foreboding feeling was justified as she realized that her transition would not be without a final farewell from Nekoda.

"Strip," he commanded. The command gathered the attention of all the servants in the room. The only one who went about her business quietly was Hazael.

"I said strip!" he growled in a low, menacing tone when she hesitated.

She began undoing her garments and taking off her outer robe and blouse. She was left standing in just her undergarments. She was inwardly very thankful that she had impulsively given the medallion to Markkah. A feeling of relief surged through her even as she was being humiliated before the eyes of the two lechers and the gleeful eyes of the servants, who reveled in her debasement.

She gathered her discarded clothes and attempted to put them into her small bag. Before she could complete the task, Nekoda knocked her on the side of her head with his fist, nearly sending her to the floor. When she righted herself, he added a mean, hard pinch to her breast that took all her being not to scream in pain.

"You won't need any of that where you're going," he said, yanking the bag from her hand.

After what seemed like an eternity under leering eyes and to the snickers of the amused audience, she was told, "A trash rag for a trash hag," and then a filthy rag of a garment was thrown into her face.

She quickly put on the robe, which reeked of stale sweat and filth, and tied the belt. Nekoda shoved her over in front of her new master.

To the further amusement of the crowd, Abishag said to Kaliyah in sugared tones, "My dear, I'm not the least offended by the smell of trash."

Everyone there knew what the initiation into her new position would entail. Bruised, with her head pounding and dread in her heart, Kaliyah followed Abishag out of the kitchen.

In the early hours of the morning, an increasing feeling of urgency seized Ishmerai the closer he got to the city. He prodded the transport animals faster. Usually on this weekly trip, he was dragging by this time and looking forward to nothing but a few hours of daytime sleep until his nightly rounds began again. Thankfully, the refuse transport was empty, so the animals didn't balk so much when he prodded them faster.

He rounded the last corner and expertly steered the transport into the dock and stables area of the refuse facility. He unhooked the team, unharnessed them, and turned them loose faster than he'd ever done before. Observing the activity, a fellow slave, risen early to begin his daily tasks, threw a disgusted comment to Ishmerai.

"You, maggot, you're going to make the rest of us look bad working like that."

"Well, you do look bad, in more ways than one."

"You think you're so much better than all of us."

"It just so happens I am," he said with as much cockiness as he could muster.

Unlike the good-natured banter of men who respect each other and throw jibes as a form of affection, this exchange reflected truly hostile feelings. Ishmerai deliberately knocked into the fellow's shoulder when he hurried past him, heading for the far end of the compound to his quarters.

"Watch your back, Maggot," the man hissed back at Ishmerai when he regained his balance.

Weaving past mounds of trash of various descriptions and toward the rankest collection of the lot, Ishmerai made his way to Markkah's hiding place. He caught movement ahead and froze. Who would be near there? He caught sight of long, dark hair just disappearing behind a stack of broken crates. He rounded the other side of the same stack and found her crouched and attempting to hide.

"What in the world are you doing?" he urgently whispered.

"I...I was going to get out to look for my mother," she whispered back.

"I told you to stay put!" he said, taking her by the arm and leading her the short way back to her hiding place. They squeezed between two other piles of more or less permanent refuse and into the little room. The walls were constructed of various wooden boards salvaged from the site and completely surrounded by the refuse piled all the way to the ceiling. The inside was lit by light that found its way through cracks and holes in the boards and openings in the surrounding trash near the top. The ceiling wasn't flat but more like the inside of a cone.

"Now, what makes you think you have to find your mother?"

"I know my mother needs help! She's unprotected. She needs this," she whispered urgently, pulling the medallion off her neck. "Now you can take it to her...please!"

Taking the medallion into his hand, he asked, "What do you think this thing is?"

"Well, it's a protection amulet, isn't it? That's why Amah gave it to me, to keep me safe."

"No, Markkah, this is not magic. It is just a piece of metal that tells a story."

"But I'm afraid for my mother! You have to go find her."

"Markkah, sit down and calm down. Neither you nor I can go to your mother right now."

"But I have a terrible feeling that she's in trouble, Ishmerai!"

"There is something we can do," he said. He took her hands in his and did something she had not witnessed before.

Bowing his head, he spoke, "Creator of heaven and earth, in Your mercy, put out Your hand to be with Markkah's mother. Protect her from harm, and keep her safe until she can be with her daughter again. We ask this in the Name above all names. So shall it be."

The confused look on Markkah's face was the cue for Ishmerai to explain a bit.

"That was not a magic chant, Markkah. It was not a formula for producing a certain effect, nor was it a demand. It was a request."

There was so much that she didn't understand, but she was encouraged by his confidence and the strange chant he'd spoken.

"Will Amah be all right, then?"

"She's in the best hands she could be in. She is protected. Now, listen to me. You must stay put in here. I have to go to my quarters to sleep for a few hours. Then I go to work. I'll be back from my rounds before midnight, and I'll come see you then."

"Will you tell me the story then?"

"Story?"

"The story the medallion tells."

"Oh. Yes, I will. Tonight, we'll begin. And you stay put."

After traversing nearly half the city, Kaliyah found herself being led by Abishag into a building at the end of a block. It was mostly a factory area where there were large warehouses. The building looked lived in, but the residents were not at home. As soon as they were through the front door and hallway, Abishag slammed her against a wall. He liked to rough up a woman before assaulting her, and he liked a woman to fight and scream.

But something strange happened. As hard as she was flung against the wall, she didn't feel a severe impact; it was more like a bump. Then she looked at her assailant and was seized with fear at what she saw behind him. Abishag thought the fear was because of him and was thrilled with the reaction he was getting from his prey. It gave him a feeling of great power.

Kaliyah was riveted to the being behind him. Surely it was not Samjaza or any of the other beings she'd seen before. There was a great brilliance that shone from his face, and she was overwhelmed with a realization that this being was good. That was unique. Great fear seized her and also a feeling of great unworthiness. She fainted and fell to the floor.

She found her hand being taken by the being, and the perspective of the room changed. She was standing next to the being, looking down at her body while Abishag, enraged, began to kick her. For the force she could see being expended by Abishag, her body barely moved.

"He cannot hurt you," the being said.

Daring to speak, she asked, "Are you a Watcher?"

"Yes. Do not be afraid. I'm here to protect you."

"Why?" was all she could come up with.

"I was sent."

With amazement, she watched as Abishag grew more and more enraged, trying to hit and kick her body. With every blow that he tried to wield, he increased the force, but his blows registered no more than a tap to her. He wound up to throw the hardest punches he could muster, but he felt like his arm was prevented from making all but the softest contact. The harder he tried, the angrier he got, until he was exhausted. With that exhaustion came a fear and confusion. His prior plans of assault and violent pleasure dissipated, and the urgency to flee overtook him. He left the building, leaving her lying on the floor.

The next thing Kaliyah remembered was waking up on a cold, hard floor. She was alone. She gathered the filthy robe around her and stood, taking stock of herself. The only places that hurt were where Nekoda had punched her on the side of her head and where she'd been pinched. Had she dreamed the rest? If Abishag had beaten her up, she surely didn't find any effects from it. She'd been beaten before and knew full well how she should have felt.

As she stood, wondering what she should do, she heard the door open and what sounded like the entry of several people. She was greeted by four men and five women returning from their day at work. It was then that she noticed that it was already early evening.

"Well, here's our new worker," one said.

"Amazing! She's in good shape too!"

"Abishag must be slipping."

The oldest woman of the group came to Kaliyah and offered her hand in greeting. "I'm Hanan, and you are?"

"Kaliyah."

"Well, welcome to the east side street crew," she said warmly, adding, "It looks like you'll be ready to start work in the morning, then."

"Uh, I think so."

Hanan continued, "Usually when Abishag brings a woman slave in, she can't work for one or two days afterward." She whispered lower and closer to Kaliyah's ear, "That man is a real piece of work."

Introductions were made all around, and Kaliyah was made to feel welcome. Hanan, the older, calloused-handed woman, said that she was her new partner and seemed to be glad for it. She explained how they worked in pairs and that she'd not had a partner for several weeks. Her partner had been older, had collapsed under the workload, and had been taken away. She hadn't known to where.

Hanan showed Kaliyah around the place where they lived. There were a number of rooms with at least ten sleeping pads each, a communal kitchen and eating area, and one communal washroom. She was thankful the latrine was updated. One wall had a sitting trench that spanned it, with continually running water, and on the other wall was another higher trench with the same. Like most of the running water in the city, it came through aqueducts and pipes from the river.

This was better than the slave quarters at the compound. When Kaliyah remarked about it, Hanan explained that their labors were more valuable doing their duties out on the streets than to waste one worker who had to carry water and clean an antiquated latrine. As it was, turns were taken for the cleaning here, and the cooking and cleaning in the kitchen too. But those duties could easily be done when duty on the streets was done. It was the east side crew's week to cook and clean, so they were the first to return to the building that day. The other crews would be arriving soon.

Kaliyah helped Hanan with cooking chores and was thankful that here at least she seemed to have equal slave status with the others. She knew she was going to be doing the lowliest work in the city, but she welcomed it. And it was one step closer to freedom.

That night when she lay on her sleeping pad, she pondered the events of that day, and inexplicably, she felt very protected.

BITTER

Corah and Kam were regular visitors to the cottage. Out of consideration for Melenah's disability and the fact that it'd be easier to bring the work to Melenah, Corah came two days a week to give Melenah and Lelah clothes-making lessons. It did not take many days for both to catch onto the basics of sewing. It was the finer points of construction and design that would take some time to perfect, and that would entail lots of practice.

Both were quite taken with the process and enjoyed being creative. They worked with a number of bolts of cloth that had been in the transport with them when they first came. They would enthusiastically discuss ideas for designs. Being from Eriduch, they'd seen a variety of styles and thought that it might do to introduce similar items into the sparse selections they'd seen so far among the country folk.

On several occasions, Corah also helped Lelah learn to cook while Melenah entertained Kam, or rather Kam entertained Melenah with his antics.

After three weeks, provisions were running a bit low in their cottage. When Corah arrived for their lesson, Melenah asked her how they were to buy food and necessities.

"Well, ladies, you've made a number of garments that are good enough to be sold. I buy them from you, and then the items are transported to several towns where they are sold again."

It felt good to Melenah to be doing something to earn what they needed. Being a consort slave, nothing had been hers. She had had no real work to call her own, and even if she had, what she would have earned wouldn't have been hers. It was a unique and curious sensation, the realization that she felt wonderful building something for herself and her daughter. It gave her a feeling of self-worth that she hadn't felt in a very long time—if ever. She was glad that Lelah also seemed to gather confidence and enjoyment in the lessons and work.

They'd kept to themselves, not leaving from the close vicinity of the cottage. Melenah suspected that Metu had given direction saying they really preferred their privacy, and that was the major reason only their teacher and son had been there. This arrangement seemed to suit Lelah well, and since it was good for Lelah, it was good for her. *There will be opportunity and time for Lelah to feel more comfortable around people*, she said to herself.

"Lelah," said Corah, "how about you come with me this afternoon to spend your first earnings?"

Lelah hesitated.

"It's just here in our settlement, and there aren't that many of us. Every half-moon we hold a market and people trade, buy, or sell—or all three. You'll get to see what the others are learning, growing, or making too. I'd love for you to come."

Lelah saw the encouraging smile on her mother's face and decided to take the chance and go. After all, she could run home quickly if she had to.

With great apprehension and almost backing out, Lelah walked out of the cottage and followed Corah and Kam. It was a half-hour brisk walk to the center of the settlement that was not quite a village. But the center clearing was different from when she'd first seen it the day they'd come there. There were tables with all kinds of goods, and a lot more people than she'd thought lived in the area. Still, compared to the compound where she grew up and the city around it, this was really a small group of people. She consoled herself with this thought and sincerely hoped that the people who'd see her would treat her like Corah and her family treated her and her mother.

Corah had the newly made clothes on her arm, and Lelah had four small gold coins in her hand. This was a novel thing for her. She had never held money in her hand or had even ever bought anything in her life. It seemed her excitement about this might just outweigh her trepidation.

She had her outer robe on because of the chilly afternoon, but this time she did not have the hood of it concealing her face. As she approached the first table, she heard someone catch her breath, and the talking silenced. She looked at the things on the table instead of at the faces of those who looked at her. Corah rescued the moment by cheerily introducing her to the group of men and women.

She lifted her overly large, luminous eyes to meet the stares of the growing crowd. As she was being introduced, Corah also revealed which people lived there from those who were there from other places for the market. Lelah realized that the friendlier smiles and less-shocked stares were from those who lived in their settlement. She thought that they'd obviously been forewarned about her being only part-human.

She felt like a freak and wanted to turn, run home, and never come out of the cottage again. But Corah's demeanor was riveting; plus she had a good hold on her arm. The acceptance of Corah and a number of the others served to still her kneejerk reaction of flight.

With Corah's guidance, Lelah bought a basket and filled it with food items that would last for a while. She had three coins left, so she looked at other things for sale. While she perused the tables, she could hear low whisperings, and of course she thought that they whispered about her, of which she was probably right.

One man was a woodworker, and he had a wide variety of things for sale, small and large things—furniture, gadgets, toys, and things Lelah was not sure what they were used for.

"Can you make something that would help my mother walk?" she asked the man. He was almost startled that she spoke to him, but he recovered quickly.

"Your mother can't walk?" he asked, although he certainly would have known about it from the news in this small place.

"No, she can't. Her legs were hurt very badly, and they healed wrong. She can move them, but they don't hold her up."

After a few seconds' contemplation, he said, "Maybe I can make something for her. I'll have to come up to your place to see your mother and take measurements, though."

It was obvious that her mother had been right; their fellow residents had been told not to come by their place unless they'd been invited.

Lelah said, "First I'll ask my mother."

Corah was standing by during the conversation and added, "I think that is a wonderful idea!" And to the woodworker she said, "We'll get word back to you after Lelah talks to her mother. Thank you!"

As they continued to look at other wares, the people around drifted back to their usual behavior and conversations. The novelty of seeing a *Su-galam* (one stretched-tall) seemed to have worn off, at least outwardly. This was a relief to both Corah and Lelah. After a little while, Corah felt it was safe to let Lelah explore on her own. They were at opposite sides of the little market when Corah noticed the three girls, a bit older than Lelah, who happened to be at the same display table. She noted how Lelah was nearly a head taller than the older girls. She saw that they were smiling and thought to herself that it would be good that she have some friends around her own age, or at least her own size. Any of the other girls around twelve or thirteen would really be outsized by her. And she told herself, Lelah seemed mature for her age too. Seeing the smiles, her attention wandered away from the girls to the goods before her.

"Hi," said the girl closest to Lelah.

Startled, Lelah said, "Uh, hi."

"I'm Rannah, and this is Laniah and Orphra," she said.

"I'm Lelah."

Laniah said, "We hear you're learning clothes making with Corah."

"We're learning from her too, at her place," chimed in Orphra.

"So why aren't you taking the lessons with everybody else?" asked Laniah.

Even though she thought they were getting a little nosy, Lelah answered, "It's because of my mother. She can't walk."

"So you're a Su-galam?" asked Rannah.

"I suppose I am," said Lelah quietly.

"How old are you?"

"I'll be thirteen this spring."

"We can sure see why you're all called 'stretchers,'" said Rannah. The other two girls tittered with laughter.

"We'll call you 'Stretch,'" said Orphra.

"Yeah, you look like you were stretched out so much your eyes started popping out." Laniah laughed.

"Did your mom get crippled when she had you?" added Rannah.

After the comment about her mother, Lelah blocked out the rest of the things the girls were laughing about. She was dumbfounded. She'd thought they were being nice at first but then realized they were just making her the butt of their jokes. It was a blow to her stomach.

Lelah felt the prickle of heat creeping up her face, and her heart began to race as she turned away from the girls and made a direct line to the path back to her cottage. She wanted to run, but she didn't. She held her head high and with every step grew angrier with the snotty girls. She hated them and pictured herself slapping each one. The shame and hurt she'd recovered from earlier came back to haunt her too. By the time Corah noticed that she was marching back home and caught up with her, Lelah was thoroughly consumed with anger and hurt. She tried to hide it, but the color of her face betrayed her.

"Are you all right?" panted Corah, breathless from the run.

"I'm fine. I just think I've been away from Amah for too long," lied Lelah without turning to look at Corah. "I can find my way home."

With that, Corah took the cue to let Lelah go home by herself. She stopped walking and watched her walking determinedly home. She knew something must have been said to upset her, but Lelah wasn't sharing. She rightly suspected the three girls. Corah felt like kicking herself for not being right next to Lelah the whole time.

Just before turning the last bend in the path toward the cottage, Lelah stopped, turned, and headed into the forest to find a place to sit and stew. She found a downed tree that made a good seat. She didn't want to have her mother see her so angry and upset. The last thing she wanted was for her mother to be upset too, or to feel hurt.

Her tears were hot, angry tears, and the pit of her stomach felt like it held a rock. She felt resentful on top of it. Sure, freedom was great, but when she was in the compound back home, there were others like her and she had been treated like she belonged— that is, until the hiding. Her mother felt at home with all-humans because she was all-human. There had been a number of very nice people she'd met coming here, and she liked Corah very much, but she began to wonder if they secretly despised her for what she was.

And that was the whole issue. What was she really? What was a person if they weren't all-human? What was the other part, other than what she knew of Watchers? She consoled herself with knowing that the Watchers were otherworldly beings, spirits who could appear and disappear, take on different forms, and display great powers. They really were quite magnificent. *Were they not gods?* While wiping the tears from her face with the back of her hand, she felt a tickling on her feet. Looking down she spotted little brown beetles scurrying among the leaves. Then she thought with an involuntary smile, *It could be worse. They could have been rats or ugly bugs or something.*

She pictured, in her mind, her eyes even bigger and with pretty brown wings folded over her back. Chuckling aloud she said, "Now that would drive those little idiots to depair!" With that thought, her anger eased a bit, and indeed, as she considered these things, she consoled herself further and counted herself lucky to have the blood of the gods in her.

She walked a wide path around the cottage to reach the stream. Before she washed her face in an icy pool, she gazed at her reflection in the glassy water. Her eyes were rather large, but she didn't think they were unbecoming to her looks.

She said aloud, "I don't have to be ashamed of this face, you lousy girls. And you, too, Kahjeera," she threw in for good measure.

She washed her face and the last remnants of the tears before turning back and coming around to the front of their cottage and entering. She'd composed herself well enough to tell her mother about the woodworker who could make something that would help her walk on her own. Melenah was so excited about the prospect that her joy was a tonic. Her mother was also delighted with the items that she'd bought at the market. Those items were the fruits of their labors. Lelah felt herself comforted by that too.

Even as these things had eased Lelah's anger and hurt, a part of her heart hardened and a kernel of bitter hatred found its dwelling place.

Street Duty

Thankfully, Markkah's nose had grown immune to the stench that permeated her environment, and she barely noticed it anymore. The one bright spot of nearly every night was when Ishmerai came to visit for a short while and bring her provisions, necessities, and best of all, company. It was his encouragement and kindness that kept her from worrying about her mother.

She quickly grew to anticipate the sound of his approach and his little coded tap on the wall. She was well aware of his good looks, even though she thought he was trying to hide his well-chiseled features with a layer of grime and dirt. It seemed that the more she got to know him, the better those looks became, dirt and all. *Funny*, she thought, *I've known quite a few very pretty and handsome individuals whose looks became quite ugly when I came to know their natures.* That was another thing that had served to ease her mind and reassure her that she, her mother, and loved ones had put their trust in the right people.

Markkah was very mature for her age. She and Lelah had been born just two weeks apart. And like Lelah, she was already taller than her mother. They also looked quite like each other, being half sisters as well as second cousins. Their skin was fairer than most all-humans, and each had a somewhat elongated head similar to their father's, but not nearly as extreme as his. Both had long, silky, thick, raven-colored straight hair and luminous, larger than all-human, almond-shaped, slightly slanted eyes. Both had the eye color of their mothers, a deep rich russet brown. Most humans had a shade of brown for eye color and sometimes green. It was only with the Watchers, her grandfather included, who had the blazing blue eyes and dazzling white-blond hair; at least that was what she'd been told. From afar, the Watchers she'd seen all looked dazzlingly bright. She had never seen her grandfather up close and wouldn't now that she'd been saved from her grandmother's tutelage. It was not a sight that she'd miss, even with the curiosity of it all.

During the short visits with Ishmerai, it was not small talk that was engaged. He began instructing her in the deep things. She felt privileged to be spoken to not as a little child but as a person who could grasp things that mattered. She hung on his every word and learned many things that made her heart burn inside her.

He had started telling the story of the medallion, explaining a part of it each time. The side with the Name surrounded by the figures meant the Great Creator and all of creation. The two people pictured were the first, their greatest grandmother and grandfather.

"Even I'm from them?" she'd asked.

"Yes, even you, Markkah."

"My mother told me that her clan were musicians and from the grandfather named Cain, the marked one."

"He was their very first child."

And so the story had begun.

Ishmerai also spent his working hours thinking about his next visit with Markkah. He'd always been a doer and not one to teach the things that he strongly believed. That was why he'd been eager to turn his enslavement into working with the underground. In his first years of slavery, he'd been embittered, angry, and resentful, thinking that he'd been abandoned by the Name. It was the old man who had recruited him, and it was only then he realized that there was a reason he had been allowed to be in the place he was. The doer now had something very worthwhile doing.

He was thankful that Markkah was tucked away safely in the refuse compound. He chuckled to himself how well she was concealed from the other slaves who worked there. His former bitterness and anger had earlier alienated him from those fellows who so desperately needed to make their dismal lives a bit more tolerable by a certain camaraderie. He had only angered and depressed them more. But after he found the real purpose to his life, he changed his behavior toward the others and this time from one of a genuine nature to that of a feigned insufferable, obnoxious fool. This had been the last straw and one that had sent him away from the slave quarters to make his abode in the farthest reaches of the compound where the foulest of the refuse was stored and readied for transport. He was the shunned one, and no one knew his real name. They called him "kisim," or maggot. This isolation and rejection afforded him the privacy and space to conduct his underground activities. He marveled how his onetime alienation from his long-held beliefs had now contributed to the success of his missions.

He wasn't sure whether it was the teaching or just being with Markkah that held his attention the most. He was not unaware of her physical beauty, but it was the beauty of her thirsty spirit that impressed him. He had not been troubled by the fact that both Lelah and Markkah were daughters of one of the giants. The Su-galam were not so tall as their parents but still stood one or two heads taller than all-humans. Ishmerai had utter confidence in the choosing by the old man. Like his life, theirs and this too, had a reason. Just because he couldn't see what that reason was didn't mean it didn't exist.

Markkah was just a child, but he had to keep reminding himself of the fact. She stood nearly eye to eye with him, and he was not a short man. Still, he felt a bond growing between them that he knew would last a lifetime, no matter what form it might, or most likely might not, take in the future. He'd not become attached to any of the other slaves he'd smuggled. He'd never had the time to spend with any of them. This time spent with Markkah was truly special, and it made him acutely aware of what human communion he'd been lacking for so long.

Street duty was normally very labor intensive and one that kept many slaves working from sunup to sundown. But with the increased traffic from the travelers who'd come for the Great Gather, compounded by the increased traffic from the transports bringing supplies in preparation for the event, the cleanup work was greatly compounded.

The streets of Eriduch were paved with large flat stones, and a system of sewers effectively drained water from the streets. However, the masses of excrement from transport animals, particularly the larger ones used by the Watchen class and many of the travelers, was too great to wash into the sewers. Whereas the human refuse was washed into the sewers and down great pipes into the marshlands to the southwest of the city, the animal excrement was collected and shipped out to the refuse processing plant. There it was dried and processed into crop fertilizer.

Herathah, matriarch of the city, was a fanatic for cleanliness. She insisted that the streets be kept immaculate. Normally, it took over a thousand slaves to do this. Now the slave force had been almost tripled. Kaliyah and Hanan were assigned to the northeast corridor, the section closest to the center of the half-circle-shaped city. Their section was very near Herathah's palace, an unsettling thing for both women. They were also close to the foot of the massive ziggurat that bordered the entire east side of the city and had taken nearly thirty years to complete. This Great Gather was the dedication of the structure, named Mul-Eriduch, or Star of Eriduch.

The colossal structure had been built for the glory of Samjaza, Lord of the Watchers, and it was positioned precisely in the center of all Imin-Sár. Samjaza's fellow Watchers were eighteen in number, and they were, in turn, chiefs of ten lesser Watchers. Almost a hundred years before, they had sworn a pact to take themselves wives of the humans. Of the nearly two hundred Watchers, they fathered over three thousand children, all of whom were the giants, or Diğir-nas, as they were wont to be called. They varied somewhat in height, from eight to twelve cubits, but most were more than twice as tall as the tallest human males.

Each of the chief eighteen had claimed territory and built cities, but Samjaza, lord of them all, claimed the largest territory and built his city as the capitol of the whole world. Engineered by Samjaza himself, the project had entailed the labors of his sons, who in turn used thousands of conscripted human slaves and enormous animals. The stone quarry was west by northwest of Eriduch near the other great river, the Renenlil, that bordered Samjaza's territory. There the stones were mined and cut using the power of the river and diamonds on the edges of great water-driven saws.

The nearer river, the Alagan-ida, was from where the city's water supply came through the aqueducts and pipes. The waste marshlands to the south drained back into the river farther to the south. The refuse plant lay south of where the aqueducts came from the river, east by northeast of the city. The lands surrounding the city had once been lush tropical forests but had been cleared to make farmlands in recent years. The need for more and more crops and produce had increased exponentially with the increase in population and especially the increase in the giant population. The Digir-nas' appetites far eclipsed the normal demands of humans.

The water from the aqueducts entered the pipes east of Mul-Eriduch and ran beneath the center of the structure and from there into the city's water system. At strategic spots along each of the city's streets, there were water outlets that could be turned off and on by a valve. These were used to wash the streets once they'd had the bulk of any dung removed. There were slaves who did just that after others, like Kaliyah and Hanan had loaded their cart with what they'd collected.

It was backbreaking work, shoveling heavy piles of animal dung into the cart until it couldn't hold any more. Fortunately, the animals used for transports were all herbivores, so the odor wasn't nearly as bad as it could have been. However, since the Watchen from all over the world were prone to trying to outdo one another, they seemed to have brought with them their largest and most impressive livestock. Certainly, the droppings were quite impressive. And even though the visitors had quarters for themselves and their entourages outside the city, they felt the need to traverse within the city on a regular basis. However, the greatest amount of traffic was caused by the food transports as they brought in provisions to feed nearly a million people for seven days. At least these lowly transports were pulled by oxen.

It was easiest to work early in the morning and grew more difficult as the traffic increased during the middle of the day. It was helpful that the streets were very wide, and the animals that pulled the transports were naturals at avoiding obstacles in front of them. So wherever Kaliyah and Hanan were cleaning, the traffic just parted and moved around them. To the important passersby, the slaves were unseen and certainly unacknowledged. Both women both felt safety and not the intended insult in this.

Periodically, a larger dung transport would come by, and they would unload their cart's contents into it. These large transports traveled by the narrower alleyways that ran crossways to the six widest main streets that were laid out like the spokes of a half-wheel. Together, the layout of the city resembled a half of a great orb spider web. These streets converged into the main gathering area at the foot of the Mul-Eriduch on the east side and Herathah's palace on the west. The whole city was on a slight slope, the lower edges being the outer and the higher toward the center and Mul-Eriduch.

Despite the physical strain that her new job caused, Kaliyah enjoyed being out of the compound and out in the open air. She was grateful for Hanan, not only for her teamwork but also her gracious attitude just like her name. Kaliyah had never liked her own name, which bespoke of something dark. While toiling in the streets, she toyed with the idea of dropping the *K* on her name and going by "Aliyah" instead. *An "ascender" would fit me better*, she thought, especially when she was finally free. Her hopes for escape grew greater each day and fueled her energies for her work. Not a weakling to start with, she grew stronger than she'd ever been by the physical labor.

Except for the masses of excrement produced by the animals, Kaliyah loved to see the essimudusun, with their great bodies and enormous horns for eyebrows and nose top. She loved the shield that framed their faces and their gentle eyes. These beasts were the preferred transport animals of most of the travelers. When she was a child, there had been many of these animals near her village, and even then she'd loved them. They were gentle creatures, and their menacing horns were used for tearing up forest undergrowth to reach their preferred food, the tender shoots of certain plants. The farmers were happy to have an essimudusu nearby because it made clearing a forest for planting that much easier.

The occasional mahgid-gu, or great longneck beast, would grace their street and deposit droppings that would take the women several cartfuls to clean up after. You could almost tell what the owners thought of themselves by the beasts they used. Mostly mahgid-gu were used by the giants. The animals were very large but not the largest of their species, and their tails had to be paralyzed. When they were just small, the bases of their tails were pierced to sever the spinal cord, so the tails just dragged behind them. This enabled their use as pulling beasts with no damage to the trailing transports. When hitched to a transport, this immobile tail was harnessed to the underside of the vehicle. Kaliyah felt sorry for these beasts. Their eyes always looked so sad. These were the animals they had to be wary of, though, because they weren't so quick to realize what they might have in front of them or under their feet. Fortunately, it was easy to recognize their approach and get out of the way first.

On even lesser occasions, they saw a woolly amsi with its tusks trimmed off and riders atop. These were ridden by travelers from the north and great northeast, from the land of Nod. Kaliyah, being originally from close to the same region, recognized these animals also. They'd been used for transports by the people who would come to trade with their village.

Taking a little break between two spurts of traffic, with their street area cleaned by them and washed by the washing crew, Hanan and Kaliyah breathed a sigh of relief.

"We've got three more days before the Gather, so two more days of soiled streets," said Hanan.

"How's that?"

"I can see you haven't done this before."

"No, this is the first time for me."

"Well, you've been to Gathers before. Didn't you notice that there weren't any animals around?"

"I guess I hadn't thought about it, but now I think about it, I don't remember seeing any."

"Well, the day before the Gather, no animal transports are allowed on any of the streets of the city. We'll have to pitch in to make the streets shine, and we'll have to help load up the last of the dung for shipment out. Only foot traffic or small transports pulled by humans will be allowed during any of the seven Gather days after that."

"What are we supposed to be doing during that time?"

"We should be getting our orders soon, but usually it's cleaning the bathhouses or cleaning up after the continual feasts. Let's hope we get duty not so close to the center of it all."

Kaliyah wondered why Hanan wanted to be farther from the center of the city, but she didn't dare ask. She knew why she wanted to be farther away, thinking that it would make for a less-conspicuous escape during the height of the event. Twice during the past weeks, she's seen Ishmerai, who had been put on the large dung transport duty. They'd only acknowledged each other in public with a manner that was appropriate to the interaction of coworker slaves.

When she got close enough to him, he'd whispered, "Markkah is safe and sound." And the last time he said, "Stand by to be approached in the very early hours of the morning on the third day of the Gather."

It thrilled her to know that she and her daughter would soon be on their way to freedom, and she assumed that the escape would entail being ensconced in the foulest of refuse. She chuckled as she thought that she was thankful for her nose being so numb and her hands accustomed to the disgusting substance. On her way to freedom, she'd be as happy as a pig in a wallow, a phrase she'd remembered her father saying so many years ago. That indelicate thought struck her as even funnier.

"What's so funny?" Hanan asked.

"Oh, nothing really."

"Right," she said, shaking her head.

The women worked with vigor for the next two days, and when they returned to their quarters on the evening of the second, they and their coworkers were met by a messenger from Abishag who had a list with their new assignments.

BESTED

Melenah was greatly relieved and heartened by what seemed like Lelah's renewed vigor for life. She'd tried not to let her notice that she'd been concerned, fearing to exacerbate the problem. She had hoped that her positive and cheery attitude would be infective and then assumed that her method had worked. At any rate, she was thankful to see her daughter more willing to get out and stand taller among others. Lelah was growing up. She'd even gone back into the village by herself to invite the woodworker up to their cottage to do the measurements for the walking device.

Cain was the craftsman's name, and he was delighted to accompany Lelah back up to their cottage. Melenah graciously greeted him upon his arrival. He questioned her and measured her. Lelah helped her mother stand so he could see where she was able to hold some weight and how she could move. After the extensive interview, Lelah cheerily served a meal and they arrived at a price for his work: one gold piece. Again, the women were heartened that they were not receiving charity but were purchasing something with the fruits of their labors. Cain told them that he'd bring the apparatus to them in a week.

Exactly a week later, Cain arrived at the cottage, bearing the device he constructed. Actually, there were two pieces. He'd made two wooden poles, each with a carved cradle on the top part, wherein Melenah could slip her upper arms, and handles that she could grip with her hands. The edges were polished smooth and perfectly fitted. Melenah eagerly tried the poles out.

"They're beautiful, Cain!" she exclaimed as she took her first steps with them. Because she could put some weight on her crippled limbs, the poles were just what she needed. It took a bit of practice to arrive at the right coordination to make a few steps. She was absolutely beaming.

Lelah was pleased to see her mother so happy and thrilled that she would be able to get around so much better now.

"Thank you, Cain," she said sincerely.

"You're very welcome," he said, looking still at Melenah as she tried his creation.

After Cain left, Melenah walked as much as her strength would allow. She would have to practice a lot to both build her strength and coordination. She'd do it with great enthusiasm. Her daughter was warmed to see her mother's new sense of freedom and mobility, but she noted that because of her twisted legs, her mother was not nearly as tall as she used to be. Combined with Lelah's growth of nearly six inches since the rampage, she was almost a head and a half taller than her mother now. It made her want to protect her mother even more.

It was no longer necessary for Corah to give them sewing lessons, but the women kept busy making clothes. Corah would still stop by, sometimes bringing more cloth and sometimes just to visit. Corah was thrilled to see Melenah's newfound mobility.

"How wonderful it is to see you getting around!"

"I'm pretty thrilled myself. I can't wait to get good enough with these things to come visit you at your place!"

"You'll have to wait a bit on that and get good at walking outside first. Have you tried walking outside yet?"

"I plan on practicing out in the front first, with Lelah watching me."

"Good! I hope you'll let me make the first trip with you when you're ready."

"You can plan on it!"

Lelah made regular trips to take their creations into the village to sell to Corah. It would still be a few weeks until Melenah would be able to make her first trip. Lelah noticed with each trip that there were more people and more cottages being built each time. She also saw Metu with his transport, ferrying new residents to their new homes. Unlike the "catty trio" (as she was wont to call the three girls she despised), whom she'd seen more than once run up to Metu's arriving transport, Lelah did not approach him. It disgusted her the way the girls flirted with him and vied for his attentions. She snickered to herself as she witnessed how he did not succumb to their feminine wiles but would excuse himself from them and go about his business.

On this latest trip to the village, she spotted Metu once again surrounded by the giggling trio. She continued down the path toward Corah's home and was surprised to find Metu jogging up behind her and hailing her by name.

"Lelah, wait!"

She stopped and turned.

"Hi, Metu."

"I'm sorry to interrupt your trip, but I'd like a moment of your time."

"Sure," she said.

"I'm sorry I haven't been back to see you and your mother. I still mean to, but I've been quite occupied with transporting our new residents."

"I've noticed. But my mother and I are both wondering when you'll be bringing Kaliyah and Markkah."

"It won't be much longer now. Our new refugees have come from all over Imin-Sár, even from the farthest reaches of all the lands. The ones from Eriduch will be the last ones to come. It won't be safe to move them until the height of the Gather."

Lelah was relieved to hear that her sister and closest friend would be joining them soon. "Thank you so much for all of this, Metu."

"You don't need to thank me," he replied, adding, "And you and your mother are doing well?"

"We are doing very well," she said. Behind him, she saw the girls shooting glares at her. It encouraged her to smile sweetly.

"I hear your mother is getting around on poles that Cain carved."

"She is, and she's so happy about it. Soon she'll be able to walk to the village."

"I'm very glad to hear that. I wanted to tell you both that I'll be picking you up in three days to take you to the top of the mountain. Even with the walking poles, your mother will not be able to make the trip on foot like most of the others. Be ready on the morning of the third day. We will be on the mountain for several days, so pack provisions and necessities. Please give my regards to your mother."

It struck her that he wasn't asking; rather, he was ordering. But for the benefit of the still-glaring girls, Lelah held out her hand to Metu, who took her hand in both of his and bid her good-bye. Lelah turned and continued to Corah's with the clothing creations on her arm. She walked with her head held high and a spring in her step, pleased with herself that she'd bested the catty trio and excited to know that her sister would soon be beside her as well. *Life is good*, she thought.

Metu expertly but politely dodged the approaching girls, who seemed intent upon regaining his attentions, and he jumped into his empty transport. He steered it back down the road to rendezvous for another load of refugees. He thought about Lelah and was encouraged by her seeming normalcy and adjustment. He was still concerned about the wisdom of bringing a Su-galam into their society but vowed to keep an eye on her and her sister when she arrived. *At least*, he thought, *she is probably too young or it is not in her nature to be aggressively flirtatious like most of the other young women I regularly dodge.* Her demeanor made him feel comfortable talking with her, and he looked forward to the visits he would pay once the demands of his duties eased. There was much they needed to learn, and he felt personally responsible for ensuring this.

The Gather

The residents of the slave quarters stood as a group as Abishag's messenger began his announcement.

"Tomorrow, you are all to return to your regular street assignments and work to make the streets shine. The job is to be completed before noon. You are to be at your new stations just before noon. Not one of you is to be still working at the beginning of the Gather, or you will be dead."

He read off the list of assignments one by one with the men's first, then the women's.

"Hanan, you go to the northeast second bathhouse. Kaliyah, you go to the central first bathhouse..."

Kaliyah, along with the others, stood motionless at the orders. Her heart sank as she heard her assignment. She'd be right in the midst of the busiest section during the gather. How would Ishmerai know where to find her? She tried not to panic and hoped that during the last few hours of street duty she might see Ishmerai and let him know. And she realized that she was unsettled at being separated from Hanan. She'd grown close to her and had felt a sense of security at being her partner these last weeks.

That night on their pads, Kaliyah whispered to Hanan, "I'm going to miss you."

"Same here, Kaliyah."

Kaliyah was saddened that it would be more than just separated for a time. She didn't think she'd ever see Hanan again. She wished Hanan could escape to freedom too. She soon drifted off into a worried, fitful sleep.

Very early the next morning the slaves returned to their streets. This time there was no traffic. The city gates had been closed for the last of the preparations. They'd be opened for the ingress of all the attendees. City residents were finalizing their preparations within their houses and compounds. The official beginning of the Gather would commence exactly at noon, when the gates opened and processions would begin.

Working hard with Hanan and the two other cleaners scrubbing the paving stone slabs, Kaliyah marveled at how the color of the stones looked almost like gold. The rich stone shone, and she was surprised at the feeling of pride she felt when they finished and stepped back to review their work. The unsettling thing was that she'd not caught sight of Ishmerai. But then why should she? His duties would not have brought him anywhere near on this day. She could only hope that somehow he knew what he was doing and would find her. By the time they were done, there was just enough time for them to separate and head to their new posts, but not without her giving Hanan a warm hug first.

"Dearest, good-bye," Hanan whispered in her ear as they hugged each other.

Kaliyah almost thought that Hanan felt the finality of their separation. *How could she know? No, she couldn't*, she reassured herself. And even if she did, she felt in her bones that she wouldn't betray her.

Kaliyah arrived at her assigned bathhouse along with twenty other slaves. They reported to their master, who hurriedly gave them their immediate marching orders.

"We've got just a very short while until the procession begins. You are all to line up outside, against the wall. When the horn blows and the gates open, you are all to be on your knees and your heads bowed. Remain on your knees until everyone in the procession has passed by. Slaves will be the very last, and we will stay as a group at the bottom and outside the Gather area. When the ceremony is over and before the feast begins, I will lead you back here. Then I will give you your duty assignments. Now, out and line up."

They filed back out the door and lined up with their backs against the building's wall. Kaliyah could see up and down the great main street the same thing: slaves with their backs against walls. And gathered at almost every residence, compound, and side street were people in procession garb waiting to join the group to which each belonged. She remembered being in a different group during a Gather—as Enkara's slave consort and mother of a Su-galam, she had been in the fourth rank. Now she was at the very lowest. Funny how she'd barely noticed the slaves' position during earlier Gathers. But now the difference wasn't an insult, and she did not envy those above her.

The horns sounded and the music began. Since she was at the center of the city, it sounded far away. All the slaves knelt and bowed their heads. Kaliyah thought to herself that this was not going to be very comfortable at all. The stone she knelt on was clean and smooth, but it was still stone. But like the rest, she dare not move. Just to see the feet of the first group coming up the street seemed like an eternity. She did not need to look to know who the first group was.

The musicians led the processions, with six separate groups leading people up the six main streets of the city that culminated at the center Gather area. With horns and drums, the music was loud and rhythmic, suitable for the march. When they reached the large Gather area at the base of Mul-Eriduch, they stood in two lines that formed a large pathway to the stairs that led up the ziggurat. Then came the people in black robes, the lowest in rank of the all-humans, those who were poor freemen and laborers but loyal to the reigning Watchers. Their gathering place would be at the broad Gather area at the foot of Mul-Eriduch. They would fill the whole area, except for the pathway made by the musicians.

The next group was the well-to-do all-humans, the merchants and farmers, garbed in deep-blue robes. They filed between the musicians and ascended the steps to the lowest tier on the broadly terraced structure. The going was slow because of the crowds that converged at the entrance of the pathway between the musicians. Kaliyah's knees were beyond hurting now, and she wished that this Gather would have been a normal one that entailed just the residents of Samjaza's territory and not the whole Imin-Sár.

After the well-to-do came the Watchen in their red robes. There were not quite so many in this group as the former, but they made up for it in swagger, and they ascended to the second tier of the ziggurat. The next tier was filled with the slave consorts of the Diğir-nas in pale-blue robes. This had been Kaliyah's former group. The next higher tier was the Watchen consorts in their orange robes. Then came the children of the Diğir-nas, the Su-galam, with the older ones carrying the babies and little ones, all wearing white. Their number was staggering; they filled three tiers.

It had taken nearly three hours just to get this far, and Kaliyah could not feel her legs anymore. She hoped she would be able to move when it was finally time to stand. But the last procession was still to begin. The music changed; the tempo became more deliberate and marshal. Kaliyah tilted her head to get a glimpse of what was coming up the street. This she hadn't seen before.

Now came the giants, the god-men, in glistening silver robes. Instead of the usual just sons of Samjaza, these were all the

Watchers' sons and daughters. They filed up the six main streets, the women first and then the men. The last were the largest of the giants, all over two times larger than any all-human man, and they carried large stones. In groups of eight Diğir-nas apiece, four on each side, they carried one massive carved stone, resting on their shoulders, supported by their hands. Six of these stones were carried up each of the six streets. The sight was astonishing.

They were the last of the procession, and when the final one passed the slaves, the slaves were allowed to stand and face Mul-Eriduch. This was a difficult thing to do for Kaliyah and everyone else who'd been on his knees for several hours. She was glad that following her new master wouldn't be but a few steps from where they'd been. They were on the outer edges of the central area and couldn't get closer if they tried. She'd noticed that Enkara had been one of the stone carriers in the first group up their street. The eldest son of Samjaza did have his rank. The stone he helped carry, along with seven of his brothers, was unique among the rest of the stones. It had a curious top to it with a large, carved-out stone ring that stood on its edge in the center of the stone.

She and everyone else there watched in awe as the giants climbed the steps to their positions at the top two tiers of the structure. The last ones, the stone carriers, climbed all the way to the very top. The flat area on top already had numerous massive stone pillars standing erect in a large circle in the center. The giants holding the stones filed around the perimeter of those erect pillars and stood still.

The music stopped, and all was quiet. It was as if everyone stood watching with bated breath. Then movement could be seen. Coming to the edge at the pinnacle was a woman clothed in glittering gold. She was flanked by eighteen other wives of the chief Watchers, clad likewise. Behind them were the 180 wives of the lesser Watchers. It was as if by magic—and probably was—her voice could be heard to the farthest reaches of the gathered multitude.

"Tomorrow will be a new day. The dawn will bring a new era. We are gathered here not just to dedicate Mul-Eriduch to the service of our gods but to dedicate a new race. A mankind of god-men."

A deafening cheer rose from the whole host and continued for several minutes.

Herathah's voice rang again. "When an opponent declares, 'I will not come over to your side,' I calmly say, 'Your child belongs to us already. What are you? You will pass on. Your descendants, however, now stand in the new camp.' In a short time, they will know nothing else but this new community."[1]

Another great noise arose from the masses.

"Let the capstones be set, as the new race is mankind's capstone!"

With that last declaration, the giants held their stones high and set them atop the pillars, to the thundering roar of the people. Enkara's stone was set at the center easternmost edge of the circle of pillars. Kaliyah found herself caught up and mesmerized by the energy, the sound, and the magnificence of the event. She had to shake herself to get a grip on reality and not be sucked in to the collective mind and emotions of the crowd. It was the reminder of the bloodshed at the hands of these god-men that rescued her from being absorbed by the mass seduction.

"Let the feast begin!" sounded Herathah.

Tables that had lined the inner edges of each tier were uncovered, as well as the tables that had lined parts of the streets and outer edges of the gathering area below. Piled high was food of every description, and the slaves assigned to serving spread out to commence their duties. Kaliyah's group was ushered back to the bathhouse, with each grabbing a few food items along the way. It had been their only food since the early morning, and they needed sustenance before their duties would cease in the wee hours of the morning.

Once inside, their new master hurriedly directed each to a particular station. Kaliyah was assigned to the women's latrine on the west side of the baths. The assignments were nearly carried out when people began pouring in. The work was continual, as was the traffic in and out of the bathhouse. The workers slaved through the evening and well into the night. The baths became occupied by revelers until after midnight, when finally they lay down on pads for what was left of the night. Preparations for the event had included copious supplies of sleeping pads for the sojourners to bed down. Even those on the tiers of Mul-Eriduch had been supplied with these necessities. Kaliyah was thankful she had not been assigned to facilities on the ziggurat itself. All kept to their general areas so as to be ready and in place before the dawn, when the gods would come.

The slaves of the bathhouse also would get a few hours' sleep in a side room used to store supplies. Kaliyah was so exhausted she didn't even remember laying her head down that night. And she didn't dream. It took several shakes by a fellow slave the next morning to wake her up. Actually, it was at least an hour before dawn. The slave master had rousted everyone and was giving the days orders.

They were again to follow him to where they'd been the previous afternoon. The sleepers in the bathhouse had all awakened and returned to their places in the Gather area to await the advent of the gods. Kaliyah could see in the dim pre-dawn light that all were stirring and resuming their positions. Most had slept very close to their stations, and the mood was electric with anticipation.

The crowd hushed as the sound of voices from high atop Mul-Eriduch reached the ears of the people. The chant and the drums had begun. Herathah and the eighteen chief wives used long sticks with horsehairs at the end, dipped in the blood of a gisgal-usumlugal (mighty dragon-king,) to paint the circle within the stone pillar circle. The Watchen on their tier in their red robes swayed with the chant as the voices rose in intensity and fervor. With bated breath, the peoples looked to the orange-red sky and an immense craft that had appeared and hovered over Mul-Eriduch. The craft spanned nearly the entire ziggurat, its whirling, intersecting wheels within wheels creating only the sound of whispered wind.

Just as the sun rose, casting its blinding light directly through the stone circle atop the center capstone Enkara had laid, a collective gasp from the people accompanied a great beam that shot from the center of the hovering craft. It appeared that shining forms traversed the beams to the surface of the center of Mul-Eriduch. More beams from various parts underneath the craft shone down on the separate tiers and even down to the Gather area below. Beings traversed the beams and stood, towering over the peoples that surrounded. As one, all fell to their knees and bowed their heads in worship.

"The dwelling of the gods is with men!" boomed a great voice from the top of Mul-Eriduch. Samjaza, Lord of the Watchers, had spoken, his voice reverberating into the very bones of all who heard.

"Arise, mankind! Lift your eyes to the glory of the gods! You shall be as gods. Your children, the new race, the new community, are the very crown of this new immortal creation."

As one, the peoples arose, as did their voices, in a roaring cheer with their fists lifted high. Kaliyah lifted her fist with the rest, lest she appear different from others. She was careful not to give anyone pause about her loyalties. There were two Watchers close by. Their shimmering ethereal bodies towered over the surrounding people. The two, like the rest of the Watchers positioned throughout the crowds, seemed to be scrutinizing the peoples around them. Kaliyah lowered her eyes and tried to appear unnoticeable. She and the others knew what they were looking for.

The shorter of the two, with long, single-braided, platinum-blond hair and ice-blue eyes, rested his eyes upon a beautiful young peasant woman. He cut through the glut of worshipers and reached out his hand to her. She was overcome with awe and blushed a deep pink as she shakily held her hand up to his. The other, though he shone like the blond, was ruddier skinned, and his brilliant, long red hair cascaded down his back. His great orb eyes scanned in the direction of Kaliyah and her fellow slaves. She didn't meet his gaze but felt it burning into her. Just then, one of the other slaves, a young, ambitious beauty intent upon improving her status in life, jostled her aside and stood in front of her, proudly slipping off her outer robe. Her clothing underneath accentuated her assets, and the attention of the Watcher was refocused. Kaliyah breathed a silent gasp of relief as the Watcher reached his hand out for the young woman.

Although each of these Watchers had wives atop Mul-Eriduch, it was common for them to take consorts also. This was all for the sake of producing and growing the new race of god-men, at least that was the altruistic reason. In truth, they were just full of lust and were happy to have an acceptable excuse for it.

The voice of Samjaza again boomed from above. "Upon this day of dedication, I proclaim Mul-Eriduch to be my throne, the throne of power over the whole world, over all Imin-Sar. Those who oppose will soon be of no account. The only true race will be the race of god-men."

Deafening rhythmic cheers waved through the crowds once more. As he spoke again, the pulsating cheers hushed.

"I hereby decree that no longer will it be allowed for an all-human to marry or consort with another all-human. No all-human newborn will again be allowed to live. They shall be destroyed in the womb or at birth. Only the new race may flourish. The law of selection justifies this incessant struggle by allowing the survival of the fittest and the best. Mere humanity is a rebellion against natural law, a protest against nature. Those who cultivate the old

way only cultivate human failure.[2] To those few in the east who
think they have god on their side, where is their god? Is he here?
We are the gods who are here. We are the ones who have brought
the answer to the human problem."

While the multitude sounded its cheer, Kaliyah wondered
who they'd thought would do all the dirty work then. And she
wondered if there were any of the masses who thought the
things that she did, or were they all that stupid? Maybe many
just wanted to survive, just as she participated in the cheers so
that she wouldn't be thought a rebel. These, her thoughts, were
certainly not going to be shared with anyone around her. There
were obviously no others who'd share their own thoughts either,
if they had them.

"Let the feast of the new race begin!"

The great craft hovering above again shone beams to the
ziggurat and the ground where all the Watchers stood. The largest
central beam encompassed the entire top level of Mul-Eriduch.
The Watchers, the wives, and the newly collected consorts were
transported up the beams into the craft. The multitude hushed
at the sight and stared in awe as it then rose higher into the sky
and shot away in the blink of an eye. A roar and cheer rose from
the crowd, and the tables laden with food again were uncovered.
The slaves rushed to their serving stations, and the celebration
again commenced. Kaliyah and her fellow slaves, all except the
one ambitious beauty, were ushered back to their bathhouse to
resume their duties. The revelry continued throughout the day.
The giants, the Digir-na, took their fathers' example and spread
throughout the multitude taking women and the female Digir-na
taking men. Kaliyah was again thankful that her duties isolated
her from the basest of the celebration, and she counted herself
very blessed to be scrubbing and cleaning offal in the latrines.
And she was thankful that her daughter was safely tucked away,
far from all of this.

As the day turned into night, Kaliyah's anticipation eclipsed her exhaustion. In a few mere hours, she would be delivered from this evil city. It would be the morning of the third day. She didn't let herself worry about how Ishmerai would find her. Somehow she'd been delivered from Abishag's assault weeks earlier, and she counted that example as evidence that she would be found.

With that thought of Abishag, she was stunned to look up from scrubbing to see the man walk into the women's latrine and directly toward her. She froze in horror.

"You," he barked gruffly, "come with me."

She dropped her cleaning rags as he roughly grabbed her by the upper arm and pulled her up. He immediately turned, pulling her out of the room, past the latrine slave master, who merely nodded as they passed, and out the door. She dare not ask questions and dare not resist. He pulled her through the crowded main street and then turned down a smaller street, stepping around revelers there. Halfway down the block they came to a halt at the door to a building. Abishag fumbled with the lock and finally opened the door. Through the dark interior he dragged her until they reached a small room. He spun her around to face him and pinched her face in his left hand.

"I'll be back to finish where I left off," was all he said, and then he pushed her into the room and slammed the door. She heard the door bolt lock, and she found herself alone in an unfurnished cell that had only one narrow window to the outside high up on the wall. A dim light from the street behind filtered through the opening, which regrettably was far too small to crawl through.

Kaliyah was mortified. How could she escape this? She couldn't even think but just sat on the cold, hard floor and wept.

PRIESTS

B oth Melenah and Lelah were enthusiastic about the prospect of ascending the mountain with Metu—the mother, for a chance to get out of their little cottage for a change, and the daughter, for the chance to stick it to the catty trio once again. More often than not, Lelah dwelled on her hatred of those girls and any others who might be unappreciative of her person. She kept these things entirely to herself and worked hard to conceal even from her mother these thoughts of discontent, revenge, and anger. Lelah was a good actress.

They eagerly had packed clothing and provisions for their trip. They'd been told they'd be sleeping in tents and had packed accordingly. As they watched for Metu, both could see many people filing up the road past their dwelling. Most were walking; some had oxen-pulled transports. The pilgrims emitted a cheerful racket, and some were singing. Little children ran and played, circling their parents with squeals of glee and the occasional skinned knee and resultant whimper. This procession was far different from the ones they'd been party to in Eriduch. There was no pomp and circumstance to this one at all. Melenah thought this a breath of fresh air, and Lelah thought it was a bit dull; although, as always, she concurred openly with only her mother's estimation.

Finally, Metu came into sight. He steered his transport out of the procession and turned down their path. He pulled the oxen to a halt and leaped out. *Indeed, he is a fine-looking man*, thought Lelah. All the more fun it would be for her to know that the catty trio would be thoroughly bent out of shape about this arrangement. She smiled sweetly as they both helped her mother into the seat of the transport. Then Lelah climbed up. It was not an accident that she climbed in so that she would be sitting in the middle next to Metu. He swiftly loaded their packs into the back of the transport and then settled himself into the driver's seat.

As they traveled with the pilgrims, it was obvious that many people had come from far away, although *many* was a relative description. There were far more people than populated their little refugee village but not nearly so many as would attend even a small local Gather in Eriduch.

The pilgrims continued at a leisurely pace up the mountain. The climb was not steep, just steady, through conifers and intermittent meadows and across the occasional brook. Lelah was mesmerized by the movement of the transport and the glimpses of the lush valleys below that could be seen between stands of trees. It was late afternoon when the trees separated to reveal a vast meadow at the top of the mountain, and just to the north of the very top there stood a small stone cabin. The pilgrims who'd already reached the area were in various stages of putting up their tents and arranging their accommodations. Family groups clustered together. Melenah and Lelah both wondered if they'd be a group of two all to themselves. They had no relatives in this place. Their unspoken question was answered by Metu, who had been silent until now.

"You'll be camping with my family group," he said simply.

His family group was nearest the small stone structure, and Melenah and Lelah simultaneously recognized Enosh and Elloe as Metu slowed the transport to a stop.

"You're here!" Elloe cheered with her arms wide open.

Enosh's wrinkled face spread into a broad smile as he came to help Melenah out of the transport. Metu, leaping out of the transport, took Melenah's walking poles from Lelah and then gave his hand to assist her in climbing down.

"It is wonderful to see you!" Melenah said as she received hugs from both Enosh and Elloe. Metu and Lelah rounded the transport to the side of the greeters, and both received warm embraces from the old couple too.

Metu handed the walking poles to Melenah. She slipped her arms into the cradles and beamed with pride as she showed the kindly couple how she could now walk by herself.

Other members of Metu's family gathered around the newcomers, and both Melenah and Lelah felt truly warmed by the reception. It was as if they were members of the loving, close family, something Melenah hadn't felt in a very long time and Lelah ever. They were roundly introduced to more of the clan, including more grandparents. Mother and daughter were overwhelmed and could not begin to remember all their names. Metu collared three young nephews and enlisted them into pitching Melenah and Lelah's tent. Like a number of the younger of the group, they'd been openly gaping at Lelah. It was something that now she had become accustomed to. The young men eagerly erected the structure, stealing glances at Lelah all the while.

As the evening approached, all those gathered began to assemble around a stone altar at the very top of the mountain. Melenah and Lelah followed the rest of Metu's clan to the area directly in front of the altar that was piled high with kindling. Lelah was wondering where Metu was when she saw him following an older man to the altar, one they'd not seen before. He carried a ram—its legs bound and tied—over his shoulders.

All hushed as Metu laid the ram onto the kindling and then turned to speak.

"These are the words of the blessing of Enoch, wherewith he blesses the elect and righteous, who will be living in the day of tribulation, when all the wicked and godless are to be removed."

Lelah and Melenah were amazed at the man who stepped forward to speak. His countenance seemed to glow with an inner light, or was it the reflection of the setting sun, and they stood in awe along with the rest of the people.

The older man spoke, saying,

> Enoch a righteous man, whose eyes were opened by God, saw the vision of the Holy One in the heavens, which the angels showed me, and from them I heard everything, and from them I understood as I saw, but not for this generation but for a remote one which is to come. Concerning the elect, I said and took up my parable concerning them:
>
> "The Holy Great One will come forth from his dwelling, and the eternal God will tread upon the earth, even on Mount Sinai, and appear from his camp and appear in the strength of His might from the heaven of heavens.
>
> "And all shall be smitten with fear, and the Watchers shall quake, and great fear and trembling shall seize them unto the ends of the earth.
>
> "And the high mountains shall be shaken, and the high hills shall be made low and shall melt like wax before the flame.
>
> "And the earth shall be wholly rent in sunder, and all that is upon the earth shall perish, and there shall be a judgment upon all.
>
> "But with the righteous He will make peace and will protect the elect, and mercy shall be upon them. And they shall all belong to God, and they shall be prospered, and they shall all be blessed. And He will help them all, and

light shall appear unto them, and He will make peace with them.

"And behold! He cometh with ten thousands of His holy ones to execute judgment upon all and to destroy all the ungodly and to convict all flesh of all the works of their ungodliness, which they have ungodly committed, and of all the hard things that ungodly sinners have spoken against Him."[3]

With one solemn voice, the people bowed their heads and said, "So shall it be."

Enoch then turned to Metu and said, "My son, Methuselah, let us make our offering."

Enoch turned, held a knife high above his head, and then plunged it into the heart of the ram. Its struggles were brief as he then swiftly slit the animal's throat and collected the blood in a bowl. He took the full bowl and, dipping his hand into it, sprinkled the blood all over the top of the altar. Methuselah then held the flame to light the kindling. The flame grew and began to consume the wood and the ram. As the smoke was rising into the brilliant orange-red evening sky, all faced the altar, including Methuselah and Enoch, and bowed their heads.

Enoch, raising his arms to heaven, said these words: "Lord God, King of all Creation, Name above all names, accept this, our offering. According to Your eternal, infallible Word and Promise, may this sacrifice be pleasing to You as we look to You alone awaiting the fulfillment of Your Promise and our redemption. Protect the elect, those whom You have called. Deliver us from sin, and grant us Your peace."

"So shall it be," the congregation said with one voice.

"As we await Your promised Seed, redeem us, and deliver us from evil and evildoers."

"So shall it be."

Methuselah began singing a song and all the others, except Melenah and Lelah, joined in. It was a simple melody, and the words were of praise. It was decidedly different from the music to which they'd been accustomed. The words seemed to be the important thing, not the beat. It gave altogether a different effect too. The loud, rhythmic beats of the music they were used to always produced a feeling of absorption into a mind-numbing movement, but this plain song engendered a lifting of the heart. Melenah was captured by the beauty of it. Lelah was likewise intrigued, but she was more confused about the whole of what she'd witnessed, although she did want the safe deliverance of her sister and Kaliyah too. She hoped they had at least got that right. Then she looked around at the singers and spotted the catty trio off to the left. And she scanned the crowd for another face. She saw that one too. Kahjeera.

What a bunch of nonsense, she thought. *Some nice words for sure, but how many of these people are just like them, acting all righteous but are actually mean and ugly?* As she dwelled on these thoughts, she suddenly realized that the sacrifice was over; the crowd began to dismiss. Lelah accompanied Metu's clan back to their area. All over the mountaintop, food was spread out on blankets on the ground, and the evening meal began. Melenah unpacked their food and added it to the bounty provided by the others. Each group had a campfire around which they all sat that evening. Looking at other groups nearby, Lelah could make out faces. She was glad when Metu sat down next to her and her mother. If the catty trio looked over, and even Kahjeera, they'd see whom she was sitting with. With a smile, she joined in the conversation. *So Metu is short for Methuselah. It means "man of the dart." Interesting*, she thought. *This is a good gathering after all.*

KINGS

There were no more tears to shed. Kaliyah just felt weak and defeated as she sat on the cold, stone floor hugging her knees. There was no way out of this one. She thought about Markkah and the heartbreak she would have and then had to think of something else because she couldn't bear it anymore.

Suddenly, she heard steps approaching from the hall. Her heart began thudding wildly in her chest. She stood. Could she fight the man and escape? There was nothing she could use in the room for a weapon, and she began to shake when the lock on the door began to rattle and the latch sounded its release.

She backed against the wall near the hinged side of the door. Maybe if she rushed him, she could get by him and run. The door opened, but the man didn't step in.

"My child, it's time to leave now," whispered a kindly voice.

She was too stunned to say anything. It was not Abishag.

"Come now. Put this on," said the man in the red robe of a Watchen as he stepped into the room. He held out another red robe to her.

It was then that she recognized the wrinkled face of the very old man who'd given her the medallions several moon-times ago. Relief coursed through her body, and she regained her ability to move. She gratefully slipped on the robe and watched as he relocked the room when they left. She followed him silently down the hallway and down out to the street. They both had their hoods pulled over their heads, concealing their faces in the dim light of the street. No one they passed seemed to pay attention, or if they did, they respectfully nodded as they walked by. They stepped around groups of revelers and made their way north and east around the outer edge of the lower central Gather area toward the north end of the ziggurat.

Kaliyah burned with questions but didn't dare speak until they were well away from any of the crowd and out through the north gate of Eriduch. The trees lining the path they traveled concealed their escape from any eyes that might have spied their movement away from Eriduch. Past vacant farmlands and houses, they made their way toward the river directly east of the city. At the edge of the farmlands and beginning of an untamed jungle, Kaliyah finally spoke.

"Where is my daughter?"

"She's waiting for you, along with some others."

"I thought Ishmerai would come to get me, and how did you ever know where to find me?"

"Ishmerai is meeting us, and to your other question, I have my connections."

"And, sir, what should I call you?"

"Kaliyah, my child, you may call me 'Old Man,'" he said.

She saw in the moonlight a twinkle in the old man's eye. She could tell they were now approaching what looked like a small transport just at the edge of the jungle. Excited, she knew she would soon have her beloved daughter in her arms. She fairly ran to the transport as Markkah leaped out of it.

"Hush, you two!" was Ishmerai's urgent whisper as the reunion threatened to alert the whole area if there was anyone there to alert.

Weeping tears of joy, the mother and daughter embraced for many moments, prompting Ishmerai to gently intervene.

"Come now, ladies. There will be time enough to enjoy each other's company along the way," he said softly. "Now do climb into the transport."

The old man climbed first into the cargo area and held out his hand to assist the ladies. It was only then that Kaliyah noticed that two other people were already settled within. One was an unknown middle-aged man, and to her great surprise, the other she knew.

"Hanan! I can't believe my eyes!"

"Kaliyah! Our parting was not forever after all! Here, let me introduce you to my son, Bahman."

They shook hands. Bahman looked like he'd been used to many years of hard labor. As he shook Kaliyah's hand, he apologized.

"I'm sorry for my rough hands. I've been in the quarries for a long time," he said as he held her hand in his.

Kaliyah noted that his hands were indeed more calloused than his mother's, but she was glad to see one so strong accompanying them on their flight. She had measured the old man as being intelligent and agile for one who was quite old, but she felt a lot safer with a large, brawny man on the team.

Ishmerai guided the small transport into the jungle along a narrow path. It was nearly pitch black, but the oxen seemed to know the trail, or if they didn't, there really wasn't any way to make a wrong turn or even wander off the trail. The jungle on either side was thick and impassable. The oxen ambled steadily toward the river.

"This is a lot different a route and travel than I expected," Kaliyah commented.

"And it'll get a lot different yet," replied Ishmerai.

The group quietly talked until the transport reached a small clearing, one that was sufficient for a turn-around. Ishmerai pulled the oxen to a halt.

"Well, this is it."

"Is what?" questioned the women.

"This is where I leave you."

"Ishmerai!" spoke Markkah. "Aren't you coming with us?"

"No, Markkah," said Ishmerai as he turned around. "There's more work for me to do here."

After the old man and Bahman helped the women out of the transport, Markkah ran around to the side to address Ishmerai.

"You have to come!" she pleaded earnestly. "You want to be free too!"

"Dearest Markkah, I am already free."

Kaliyah sensed the bond that seemed to be between the two and felt sad to think that they probably wouldn't see each other again. These were not good times, and she knew the increased danger there'd be in the city, especially after the latest decrees of Samjaza. There would undoubtedly be more of those wishing to escape also.

Markkah reached her hand up to Ishmerai and tearily spoke. "Ishmerai, you've been my teacher and protector. May the Name be with you and keep you safe."

"May the Name be with you and keep you safe," he returned as he held her hand in his.

And both said together, "So shall it be."

"Come," said the old man. "We've got little time to be across the river. We must reach the other side before dawn."

It occurred to Kaliyah that if she hadn't been taken by Abishag from her latrine job early that night, she wouldn't have been able to get out of the city so soon and they wouldn't have had time to reach the river and cross it before dawn. She pondered about the things that had been so terrible and had ultimately turned out to be the best thing after all.

Ishmerai turned the transport around and left by the same path they'd come. He would have to deliver the "borrowed" transport to the farm just outside the city where he'd appropriated it earlier. He'd have just enough time to slip into the refuse facility to begin another day's work, behaving like he'd had a good night's sleep. He was thankful he was still young and strong enough to pull it off. But with a heavy heart, he thought that he was really going to miss Markkah.

It had been a shorter route straight east to the river than if they'd made the trip by the road to the refuse plant; however, it was rougher territory. It was providential that the jungle on the west side of the river between the farmlands and the river had been cleared of wild animals. The giants and Watchen had effectively hunted out the predatory animals in the area. The increased need for farmland necessitated the taming of the surrounding jungles.

The old man led the way down a narrow trail. They could hear but not see the river ahead. All but the old man wondered how they were going to cross the huge river. No one dared ask.

They followed the old man as he made his way down a steep bank to the water's edge. They pushed aside vegetation and ended up under a large tree whose branches reached out and drooped way out over the water. The moonlight barely filtered through the leaves to reveal a log raft that was tethered to the trunk, the answer to how they'd cross the river before them.

The old man clambered over onto the raft, and he held out his hand to the women, helping each to balance them as they stepped on.

"It's best to sit down," he said, "and, Bahman, grab the poles and hand them to me."

Bahman located the two long poles lying by the tree trunk and deftly handed them to the old man.

"Now, untie the rope and get on."

The strong man did as he was told, and soon, with the women huddled in the middle and the men standing, each with a pole in hand, they pushed the raft out from under the tree and onto the river. In the moonlight, they could barely make out the farther bank of the Alagan-ida. It was an enormous river, wide and mighty. There was a ferry much farther north that was used by the trade route. The fertilizer from the refuse plant was regularly ferried over to the east side by the ferry, and produce and foodstuffs were ferried back. That had been the route over which Melenah and Lelah had been smuggled. Here there was no ferry.

"This raft is going to take us far to the south before we get to the other side," Bahman said with a hint of concern in his voice.

"Indeed it will," replied the old man.

With a matter-of-fact, controlled tone, Bahman added, "Won't that put us deep into the Idim-kur?"

"Most certainly."

The exchange between the men brought stabs of fear to the older two of the listening women. Markkah was not concerned, because she seemed unaware of the implied dangers of the Wild-lands.

Then the old man softly added, "Don't be afraid. Greater is He who is with us than he that is in the world."

"I wasn't thinking about any 'he.' I was thinking about the 'whats,'" said the still-rattled Bahman.

"It's the same difference," the old man calmly added.

Kaliyah noticed that the old man had a smile on his face. He was enjoying this. Exactly who were they with, anyhow? The men pushed the poles for what seemed an eternity. The long poles were landing on the river bottom deeper and deeper. The men were fairly leaning over, grasping the tops of the poles as they pushed. After a long while of pushing, the poles couldn't touch the river bottom anymore. They drew the poles up, sat down, and the raft drifted with the current for a while.

After some silence, the old man spoke again, "All is going according to the plan. We're well guarded, and we will all arrive safely. The route is just a bit different than the one others have taken before you."

Kaliyah, looking out over the dark waters with the moon at her back, gave out a startled gasp.

"What is it, Amah?"

"Oh, nothing," she replied, not wanting to worry Markkah about the shining pairs of eyes of differing sizes that she'd noticed on the surface of the water.

Hanan saw the eyes too and said nothing. She put her hand over Kaliyah's and gave her a reassuring squeeze.

"All right, Bahman, it's time to check for the bottom again."

The men arose and once more lowered their poles into the river. This time they found bottom and pushed to propel the raft closer to the destined shore. Kaliyah kept her eyes on the eyes in the water. She was relieved to see that none had appeared closer. All seemed to be keeping a distance, and she hoped it would stay that way. Was the Watcher who'd rescued her from Abishag on duty here? She sincerely hoped that he was, even though she couldn't see him. Then she looked up into the night sky and saw the shape of a mahgu-usum silhouetted by the moon. The great bird-dragon made graceful arcs as it glided in the night sky. Her attention was torn from the eyes on the water to the great beast with the elongated snout and back of head soaring high up in the air. The other two women turned their eyes to the sky following Kaliyah's gaze. They noticed that the beast changed its direction, interested in something upon the river. As it spiraled down and closer, Hanan reached for Markkah's hand also.

"Oh, Lord of Spirits, King of all Creation, the Name above all names, protect us from danger," said Hanan softly as she bowed her head.

"So shall it be," said the old man and Markkah in unison.

Kaliyah's eyes had not left the approaching mahgu-usum. She saw then how it abruptly changed its direction and returned to its earlier soaring heights. She breathed a sigh of relief and was assured that indeed there was a Watcher on duty. This was magic of which she had never before known.

She marveled at her daughter also, who had not shown any concern or fear. She concluded that it was not an ignorance of the dangers that produced this. She would have many questions of her daughter in the near future. She sensed a distinct change in her, but she couldn't discern exactly what that was.

A thickening mist began to arise on the surface of the river, and the nearing shore soon vanished from their sight. They knew the shore was getting closer by the men's poles that grew longer as the river bottom shallowed and the current ebbed. Suddenly the branches of a large tree appeared through the mist.

"Aim for that tree," said the old man, and they pushed harder against the bottom. Bahman's muscles could be seen working mightily under the sleeves of his robe. Kaliyah was again solaced by the strength of the man.

The old man spoke again, another order, "Ready yourselves, everyone. As soon as we meet the shore, immediately climb the tree."

No one entertained any thought to question or to do otherwise. The urgency of the command compelled obedience. Questions could be asked later. As soon as the raft bumped against the bank, the men dropped their poles and assisted the women in climbing up the tree. Markkah and Kaliyah were pushed up first and told to keep climbing, then Hanan and Bahman. After the old man lashed the raft's rope to a large branch, Bahman reached his hand down and hoisted the old man up last.

They climbed the tree whose trunk had a diameter the height of two full-grown men higher and higher until they found a spot between the spread of three branches that could accommodate all of them. Hanan, Bahman, and the old man unlashed their satchels that had been strapped to their waists. Out came bread and dried fruits. Thirstily, they drank from the giant leaves' puddled waters that had condensed from the mist. Hungrily, they feasted, and wearily, they laid down to rest. As the dawn broke, they all dropped off into a welcome and dreamless sleep. Their snores mingled with the sounds of the awakening jungle whose mist brightened with the rising sun.

Kaliyah was awoken by Bahman's voice. It took her a few seconds to orient herself to where she was. Her initial confusion dissipated as she sat up and rubbed her face. She was in the tree, and Markkah was still sleeping peacefully by her side. It seemed to be late in the afternoon. They'd slept nearly all day. She listened to the noises of the jungle, bursting with life and sounds. Then she paid attention to what Bahman was saying.

"Uh, Old Man, are you awake?" he asked quietly again. Looking way down at the base of the tree, he continued, "Here's the 'whats' I was concerned about."

As Kaliyah stood up and moved to the edge of their resting place to stand next to Bahman, Markkah and Hanan began to stir from their sleep. She followed Bahman's gaze, and to her mortification, she saw the animals. Circling the tree and stopping at intervals to cock their heads up in their direction were umbin-sutum. The vicious talon-lizards were making low-pitched chucking, clicking noises, communicating with each other. As Kaliyah looked around, she saw more of the beasts moving on the ground. She counted at least twenty of them. She'd never seen one before but knew what they were from the descriptions she'd heard. The hair on the back of her neck stood up, and a chill went down her spine.

"Unless we've got a whole lot of poison darts on us, I don't think we're going to be traveling anywhere anytime soon," stated Bahman with a note of disappointment and not a little bit of fear.

Markkah and Hanan joined the two at the edge and looked down.

"Well, son," spoke Hanan as she slapped him on the back, "this is really going to get interesting."

"Good grief, Mother, is that all you can say?"

With a loud snort, the old man abruptly awoke. He sat up, stretched, and began to brush the tree dander off his long white beard. Bahman couldn't wait for him to finish his lengthy awakening process.

"Old Man, do you know what's down there on the ground?" Bahman exclaimed, perturbation thick in his voice.

"Well, of course," Old Man replied unconcernedly. "Why do you think I had you all climb this tree so fast?"

"Son, stop being so disrespectful!" demanded Hanan.

"It's all right, Hanan. He'll learn in time."

Kaliyah felt faint and began to teeter on the edge. Bahman caught her from falling, guided her back to the middle of the notch, and helped her to sit down.

"Before we go on, we need to eat again. It'll be a while before our next meal, and we will all need our strength," said the old man.

Out came more food from the satchels, and they relished the food like it might be their last meal. When they'd finished, all looked to the old man expectantly. No one wanted to be the first to ask him what the plan was. It was Markkah who broke the silence.

"I need to take care of necessities."

"That may be a little tricky right now," said her mother, "but if it makes you feel any better, I do too."

"Well then, I think it's about time we make our move," stated the old man.

The hearers' universal unspoken question was, "What move?" as they listened to the continuing noises below.

The old man stood and faced east into the depths of the jungle. He put his fingers to his lips and whistled a long, loud, shrill whistle. He repeated it twice more, in slightly different directions. After the third time, a faraway, resounding roar was heard that sent echoes throughout the jungle. The noises of the jungle silenced. The birds stopped their singing, the monkeys' their chatter, and the umbin-sutum their chucking-clicking sounds. Bahman stepped to the edge again and looked down. He saw that the talon-lizards' attention was no longer on them. All the ones he saw had their heads pointing in the direction of the sound they'd just heard. He knew what a gisgal-usumlugal, or mighty dragon king, sounded like and wondered whether this was really a good idea…or not.

BEASTS

The gatherers on the mountain spent two days after the sacrifice involved with a number of activities. Besides being a family reunion time, the first of the two days were spent with Metu and Enoch holding court. Various public matters, concerns, and disputes were brought before the men for adjudication. Some of the people sat and listened to the testimonies and speeches of those who needed their issues resolved or problems solved. Those who weren't involved or listening attended to visiting, supervising the playing children, or preparing meals for those in their groups.

Cain, the woodworker of the village, paid visits to Melenah and was satisfied to see her happy with his creation. They even went for several short walks, enjoying one another's conversation. Melenah learned that he'd lost his wife and children when the giants raided his village in the southwest. He'd been a woodworker then, but his slavery had relegated him to working in the fields for forty long years. He'd been free for nearly ten years now and loved living in the refuge village, teaching and plying his trade.

Melenah shared with him memories of her childhood before her enslavement. Her years as Enkara's consort were a sore spot, one that she didn't want to recount. The only bright spot of those years was Lelah, and she enjoyed sharing of stories of her growing up.

With her mother's attentions not focusing on her, Lelah sought ways to occupy her time. She did not want to join in with any children her age because she'd feel awkward being so much taller than any of them. She certainly didn't want to associate with any of the older girls who were also shorter than her. She knew how that'd turn out. She decided to sit with the audience and participants of the legal sessions being run by Metu and Enoch because she thought maybe she'd learn more about how they thought. Plus, it would occupy her time without her having to join a group and have that group accept her. She understood some things they covered, and other things were beyond her. A thought that kept occurring in her mind was the question of how all these people who thought of themselves as "righteous" and "elect" could have so many disputes and problems? Wouldn't someone who was "righteous" do everything the "right" way in the first place?

She sat and listened for most of the morning until her least-favorite trio decided to join the group and sit down on the ground directly in front of her. She thought that just their positioning was an intended insult to her. Ignoring her, they began to whisper between each other, making comments about Metu.

"He just looked over here right at me," whispered one.

"No, he was looking at me," whispered another.

"Don't you just love his hair?"

"I really like what he's wearing."

"He's got some really great muscles, doesn't he?"

Lelah couldn't listen to any more of this and felt like smacking each one on the back of the head. She decided then that maybe this would be a good time for her to find something else to do. And besides being annoyed by the girls, she decided that she surely didn't want Metu to think that he was the reason she was sitting there in the first place. She got up and left.

Since it was approaching the midday mealtime, she ambled back to their camp and pitched in to help with the preparations. She felt the most comfortable with the older women and grandmothers of Metu's clan. She did notice, however, that there seemed to be a number of young men, teenagers, who were keeping track of her movements. They'd been listening at the legal session and then ended up not far from where Lelah was helping with the meal. It unnerved her , and she ignored them the best that she could.

She sat with her mother and Cain when they ate. She mainly listened to their conversation and rarely joined in. Basically, she smiled and talked little. She was glad to see her mother so animated and felt that this outing was really a good idea for her. For herself, she wasn't so sure. But for the rest of the afternoon and evening, she stayed mainly with the women of Metu's clan and enjoyed listening to their conversations and helping where she could.

The next day there was no "open court" for an audience, but Metu and Enoch held private sessions for people who wanted to discuss private issues alone with them. As Lelah stayed with the women of the clan again, she noted that the two men held these private sessions within Enoch's little cottage nearby. People periodically moved in and out of the building, and at some times during the day there was even a line of people waiting outside the cottage. In the early afternoon, she noticed Kahjeera, along with her husband and a group with them, waiting their turn. She'd felt like there were eyes burning into her back, so she turned around and caught them scowling at her. A pang of hurt mixed with anger and fear shot through her, and she abruptly turned away. Lelah felt an overwhelming need to flee, to get away. With heart pounding and her face feeling a prickly flush, she turned toward her tent. But there were more people blocking the way and she couldn't bring herself to squeeze through them. With great effort she suppressed the urge to run and tried to behave as naturally as possible, forcing smiles and nods to the few who greeted her as she walked. Weaving between tents and campsites, she spotted a massive tree with branches reaching to the ground. Glancing back, she could tell she was out of the eyeshot of Kahjeera's group and then deftly parted two branches and slipped between them.

The branches of the tree made a completely secluded room. Lelah spotted a stone slab next to the trunk. Sitting down on it, her breaths were nearly as rapid as her heartbeat. She tried to calm herself down, willing the panic to go away, cupping her hands over her face. Wild thoughts ran through her mind. *What if* Kahjeera *persuades Enoch and Methuselah they've made a big mistake? Will everyone turn against me and my mother? What will we do and where will we go? Could we go back to Eriduch? I know I could, but my mother surely could not. And what will happen to Markkah and Kaliyah when they get here?*

Tears streamed down her face as her body wracked, but she managed to keep silent. The last thing she wanted was to have anyone find her. Gradually, her breathing calmed as she steeled herself for whatever outcome may develop. She told herself that somehow her loved ones would get through this. Uncupping her hands, she wiped away her tears and then breathed in the pungent scent of the tree's needles. The fragrance seemed to calm her further as she inhaled deeply. *Surely Metu won't be pushed around by that witch,* she thought, *I don't think anyone could easily intimidate him.*

After what seemed an eternity, Lelah gained control of herself and decided that she should probably start back to her mother, or else she would begin to worry about Lelah's disappearance. She stood up and walked the five strides to the branches. But, just as she reached out to part them she heard voices close by, right on the other side. She knew full well who it was and she froze.

"You should have backed me up!" Kahjeera shouted accusingly at her husband.

Lelah heard no response from Jaireck, and her heart began pounding again.

"Didn't I tell you that abomination of a child would corrupt the whole lot of us? Do you see the way Enoch's family treats her like she is one of them? Mark my words—she has set her sights on marrying Methuselah."

Lelah couldn't believe her ears and she thought, *What?* She quickly put her hand over her mouth because she nearly spoke the word. Trembling from head to toe, she listened despite the fact that the last thing in the world she wanted to hear was more abuse from that woman.

Now Jaireck spoke. "She is still only a child…"

Interrupting, Kahjeera ranted, "I saw the way she sat there watching him during the hearings. I saw how they sat together at the meals. She's setting to defile the priestly line!"

Silence.

"I refuse to participate in any more of this slave-smuggling business. Not only are these 'slaves' including part-humans, but some of the pure-humans are descendents of Cain—and that abomination is both!"

"Woman, will you keep your voice down?"

"I most certainly will not!" she retorted. "They are all foolish! Enoch and Methuselah think they're so high and mighty, and they listen to the Old Man, who is getting so senile he thinks he can make the bad people good. The ungodly are ungodly, and they'll always be ungodly. They are a pollution to the righteous."

Silence.

"And to think that they are polluting Mount Moriah, Zion itself, with the presence of that woman and her offspring. What a sacrilege to have the ungodly desecrate holy ground!"

Silence.

"I felt like a fool in there trying to talk sense into those two men. They might have listened if you'd have backed me up. I'm ashamed of you."

Silence.

"Don't just stand there saying nothing! You treat me like I'm the only one who feels this way. You've heard what the others in our family and other families too have said about this disgrace— I'm not alone in this. Zibiah and Caleb didn't come to this Gather because they think the priests are not doing their job, and they don't even know about this latest travesty. Caleb would do a much better job leading our people and protecting us."

Finally he broke his silence and pleaded, "Woman, be quiet. I've listened to you and heard more than enough. We will not be involved in the smuggling business any more. And, I'll have a talk with Caleb when we get home. Now give it a rest. Please."

"Good."

"I can't imagine how anyone could think that bringing—"

"Woman! Shut your mouth!"

Lelah could hear the conversation getting farther away from the tree. Relief flushed through her because she had been terrified they'd never leave or that they would discover her. Even with their increasing distance, the fresh insults had put her into a condition where she was now not ready to leave the shelter of the tree room, not yet. When the relief and shock passed, a fury then raged like a beast in her chest, and she pictured herself mauling the witch to shreds. It was all she could do not to roar out loud. She sat down on the stone slab again with her face in her hands. After some time, she calmed herself with the fact that she and her mother had not been rejected by Enoch's clan. She thought, *If Enoch and Methuselah had been convinced by that witch, I would then say that there is nothing righteous about 'the righteous' at all.* But, at the same time she wondered, *How many of the so-called 'righteous' feel the same way as that woman?*

With the beast finally quelled to a leaden mass in her chest, and when it seemed there was no longer anyone near the tree, Lelah parted branches on the opposite side where she had heard the conversation. There was no one in sight, so she stepped out.

Breathing a sigh of relief, she turned to her right and after a few steps nearly walked into a very short woman who was rounding the tree.

"Pardon me!" Lelah was startled.

"That is all right, dear, I've been walked over before," the woman said with a smile. "You are the Su-galam child, are you not?"

"Yes, Ma'am, I am."

"I hear you are learning clothes-making."

"Yes, Ma'am, I am."

"Well, dearie, you are probably using some of the materials that I sell."

"Oh?"

"My name is Hulda. This is my first Gather here too."

"Really?"

"Indeed. I travel all over the Iman-Sar plying my trade."

Lelah was in no mood to hold a long conversation with the woman, and there was something about her that seemed creepy. She couldn't put a finger on what that was. Perhaps her smile? She said, "It is nice to meet you, but my mother is looking for me."

"Well, then, hurry on, dearie."

It was the *dearie* thing that Lelah didn't like, and she hastened to increase the distance between them, before the beast could raise its ugly head again.

After making it back to her own campsite, Lelah decided to take refuge in their tent for the rest of the afternoon. She was surprised that her mother hadn't even noticed her absence, until she realized how pre-occupied she was with Cain. Melenah just cheerily greeted her daughter and then stated that she was going for a little walk with him. Back in the tent, Lelah lay down on her sleeping pad and closed her eyes, trying to sleep with her chest a leaden mass. But, the noise and activity around the tent interfered with the attempt, so she sat back up and hugged her knees. The flap of her tent then opened.

"Lelah, are you in there?"

She recognized Corah's voice.

"Come in," she replied quietly.

Corah ducked through the opening and entered, saying, "I was wondering where you were!"

"Oh, I'm just taking a little rest."

"I'm not surprised. This gathering can wear anyone out," she said kindly.

"Yes, it can."

"May I visit with you a while?"

"Of course."

Corah sat down next to Lelah and said, "I've been so busy with my family group, I haven't had time until now to come see you. Kam has worn himself out so much he's taking a nap. It is nice to have a break."

"He is full of energy, for sure," Lelah said with a smile. She enjoyed the little boy's antics.

"And I was wondering whether you and your mother would like to join our family group for the evening meal tonight."

Lelah hesitated. She wasn't sure whether she wanted to venture anywhere else the rest of the day. At last she responded, "You'll have to ask my mother. She's taking a walk with Cain."

"Oh, we'll have to have Cain come too! I'll go out and look for them. And, Lelah, I'm glad to notice that you are getting on so well with Metu's family. They are happy to have you here."

The comment was solacing to the young girl, and she sincerely replied, "I'm glad to be here with them too. They've been very nice to me."

"Well, I'll be off to find your mother then. We'll see you soon!"

After Corah left, Lelah felt encouraged enough to leave her tent again and join the women of Metu's clan. They were sitting in a group, conversing, and welcomed her when she came to sit down with them. Being quiet, she did not enter into the conversation but listened to the women, enjoying their conversations about everyday life and family. It took her mind off Kahjeera and her ilk and made her feel a bit less like running back to Eriduch. It was only her mortal fear of her father and the love for her mother that made her want to belong to this group.

That evening, Melenah, Lelah, and Cain joined Corah and Ramuel's family. She was thankful that they were not nearby to Kahjeera's family group. Lelah enjoyed the final evening of the gathering the best. Little Kam was ecstatic to see her when they arrived, and she spent most of the time there playing with him. He had to sit next to her while they ate. She picked Kam up in her arms and gave the energetic youngster a last squeeze before they bid their good night.

To the nods and smiles of the others, the little child said, "You have pretty eyes."

She decided that it hadn't been such a bad trip for her after all.

Early the next morning, the entire group gathered in front of Enoch's cottage. Enoch, with Metu by his side, blessed the people and bid them safe travel back to their homes. Then all commenced to pack up their belongings and begin the journey home. Melenah and Lelah were the last to leave because they were with Metu, who had to attend to some last business with his father. While the men spoke outside, they joined Edna, Metu's mother, inside the humble dwelling. It was well after the midday meal when Metu was ready to begin the journey back down the mountain. The half-day trip would put them back to their cottage well after darkfall.

Finally, they headed home. Along the way, Melenah asked Metu, "Are Kaliyah and Markkah on their way here now?"

"Indeed, they are."

"Oh, I'm so glad!" exclaimed the usually quiet Lelah.

"Are you going down to get them?"

"I will. They'll be with you in two and a half days."

Figuring the timing, Melenah added, "But that would put them at Enosh and Elloe's tonight. But Enosh and Elloe aren't there yet."

"They're coming by a different route."

Knowing this, Lelah was glad that they wouldn't have to stay at Kahjeera's. And Metu wasn't volunteering any information about where they were instead. Both the women understood that secrecy was the greater part of the slave-smuggling business and didn't question further. Lelah retreated back into silence, dreaming about being with her beloved sister again.

In the orange light of dusk, with still a way to go to the refuge village and home, they were startled by a form that darted out from between the trees. A huge yellow-and-black blur lunged onto the neck of one of the oxen. The women screamed, the oxen bellowed, and the transport jolted to a halt, nearly throwing its occupants out. In a flash, Metu reached into his cloak, put a blower to his mouth, and shot a dart directly into the right eye of the beast. The next dart landed between two vertebrae. The animal, stunned by the punctures, released the ox, roared in pain, and staggered back into the forest.

Leaping out of the transport, Metu commanded, "Stay put!"

The mother and daughter clutched each other, shaking and crying, while Metu pursued the wounded animal. The ox was dead, killed almost instantly when the enormous fangs of the mahkur-tidnum snapped its neck. The other ox struggled to get out of its yoke.

To Melenah and Lelah, time crept like a snail before they heard Metu's approach. He was dragging the skin of the beast and had two giant bloody fangs tethered to his belt. He lifted the slippery hide into the back of the transport. His hands were covered with blood. The almost metallic odor of all the blood from both the ox and the beast sickened both women. With part of their clothing both women covered their noses.

"Are you ladies all right?"

"We're fine," Melenah answered, not too convincingly.

Metu attended to the oxen, unharnessing the deceased one and rearranging the remaining. He dragged the one off the path and to the side. He made swift work of skinning the ox and putting its hide next to the tiger's. The carcass was left. Humans did not eat animals, so the remains were left for the scavengers to feast upon. Darkness had enveloped them by the time they set out again.

"I didn't think we had those animals around here," broached Melenah.

"Usually we don't. The civilized lands are fairly well hunted, and the predators have been cleared out. In this part of the Iminsar, they stay south of the Pishon in the Idim-kur for the most part. This animal was old and perhaps sick and probably driven out of its territory. Its attack on the ox was out of desperation. The beast was starving. I'm just very thankful it didn't attack any of the earlier travelers. Praise be to the Name for watching over us all."

A viscious thought entered Lehah's mind. *Too bad that beast didn't attack Kahjeera or those disgusting girls!* Then the thought of little Kam passing by this way not too many hours earlier gave Lelah a chill. In the end, she was glad too that it had been just an ox that had suffered. As it was, she and her mother were both more than impressed by Metu's skill with the poison darts.

Lelah finally spoke, saying, "Now we know why you're called Methuselah, the man of the dart."

He chuckled at that and replied, "I had no choice but to try to live up to the name my father gave me. It would not have been a good thing to bear my name and be a poor shot."

It was cathartic to laugh a bit.

IN OUR IMAGE

The Old Man stood at the edge of the tree cradle, listening into the jungle where the fading echo of the roar was the only sound that lingered. The others felt like they were riveted in time, with wild thoughts in their heads about what would soon be upon them. Soon they felt the hint of a repeated rhythmic vibration in the tree itself that with each pulse seemed to course up their legs into their very beings. Then they could hear the crashing of trees and breaking of branches. The vibrations turned into the heard stomps of a beast of enormous size. The jungle was too dense to enable long sight, and they knew that when they'd finally see what was coming, it would be directly in front of them.

To the gasps of all but the Old Man, a gigantic head appeared, level with their perching spot. Its mouth opened, and another deafening roar boomed. The Old Man had covered his ears and held his breath. Bahman made quick to grab the women and begin to push them higher up into the tree. The women were in agreement with this move, but the roar came accompanied with a blast of disgusting breath that nearly made them lose their grips.

From several branches higher, the companions turned to see what would become of the Old Man. To their astonishment, they witnessed the old man speaking softly to the beast and rubbing its immense nose. The beast was by far the largest gisgal-usumlugal that Bahman had ever seen or even heard of. He was stunned.

"My wondrous Lugal, my old friend, it is always good to see you," he said lovingly. The animal turned the side of its head, the height of which was taller than the Old Man himself, to let the Old Man scratch him on his cheek. As he was being scratched, the beast uttered a low, guttural purr that rumbled and resonated to the bones of the ones who watched and questioned reality. Hanan and Markkah were the first to climb down.

"Markkah, no!" exclaimed Kaliyah.

"Mother!" exclaimed Bahman at the same time.

"My old friend, I'd like to introduce you to some new friends," the Old Man cooed without turning his head to see Hanan and Markkah's approach. The beast turned his head again, lifted his nostrils to sniff the air, and leaned its head in closer to the notch.

"It's all right, ladies. Come closer. You may touch him."

In awe, Hanan and Markkah felt the rough skin of the beast and couldn't find any words to express what they felt. Still with trepidation, Bahman helped Kaliyah back down to the tree cradle. Neither felt comfortable touching the animal. It was then that Bahman noticed that the animal wore a basket-weaved leather netting that attached over the upper torso of the creature. On the topside, it covered the shoulder area, lower neck, and upper back and was strapped and lashed on the underside of the upper chest.

"It's best we get started before nightfall."

"Uh, I still have to take care of necessities," said Markkah softly to Hanan.

"Old Man, is it safe to descend?" Hanan asked.

"Oh, yes, yes. We can all go down now and take a little time to take care of necessities. Just stay out from under Lugal's feet."

As they gathered their few things, Kaliyah whispered to Hanan that she needed something. Gladly, Hanan reached into her satchel and discreetly pulled out a clean undergarment. She quickly slipped it to the embarrassed Kaliyah. They all climbed down the tree. As they descended, Hanan asked whether it was safe for them to wash at the river's edge.

"It's safe enough now," replied the Old Man. "Just stay close by and hurry."

After they reached ground, the women went behind some vegetation to the river's edge, and the men found another spot on the water relatively close by. They took care of necessities and washed. When they were nearly done with their ablutions, a sudden crashing nearly knocked them over, and the women screamed in terror. They heard the sound of crunching flesh, and blood spattered their newly washed selves. The men yelled and rushed to the women. With eyes closed, the women huddled hysterically, thinking this would be the last of them.

Lugal had in his mouth a large umbin-sutum, evidently one that had been either more foolhardy or hungrier than his fellows. The mighty dragon king killed the beast with one crunch of his jaws and proceeded to relish his tasty find. No one had seen the umbin-sutum coming, and all, when recovered from the shock of it, were very grateful for their unlikely protector. While shaking his head in the process of shredding his dinner, a dismembered talon flew through the air directly at Bahman. In a reflex reaction, he reached out his hand and caught it.

Looking at his hand that held the bloody talon, which was as long as his forearm, Bahman was dumbfounded.

The Old Man clapped him on the back and said, "Now that's a trophy you'll have fun telling tales about!"

Recovering his composure, Bahman replied, "I'll have to tell tales because the truth won't be believed!" He fastened the talon in the front loop of his belt.

The rattled women hurriedly finished their cleanup and joined the men. They looked to the Old Man for directions.

"Now, we need to climb back up the tree to that second long branch," he said, pointing to a limb that looked to be about sixteen or seventeen cubits high.

All climbed, including the Old Man. They waited for Lugal to finish the last remains of his meal. Then the Old Man let out a low whistle, and the great beast turned and approached. Lugal ducked his great head under the branch where they perched and stopped at the Old Man's direction.

"Come closer, just a little bit more," he coaxed the beast. The Old Man reached out, grabbed hold of a leather strap, and pulled himself over onto Lugal's upper back.

"The women next," he ordered.

Markkah was the first. She maneuvered with ease over to the straps and climbed the netting to seat herself just behind the Old Man. Hanan followed. The great beast shifted, unbalancing Kaliyah as she tried to span the distance between branch and beast. Bahman grabbed hold of her, swift to keep her from falling, and she then shakily made the transfer from branch to beast.

"Thanks," she said to Bahman. "That would have hurt!"

"Anytime, dear lady." He smiled as he made the transfer himself.

They all ducked too, holding themselves close to the netting as Lugal moved away from the tree. Out from under the branch, they could arrange themselves a little more comfortably in their seats on the netting.

"Wedge your feet into a strap joint, and hold on," guided the Old Man. They sat closely in single file, with the Old Man just above Lugal's shoulder blades and on his lower neck. He stroked and patted Lugal. As the orange light of the evening enveloped the jungle, the Old Man whistled another low whistle and the mighty dragon king, with his charges aloft, lumbered off into the depths of the jungle.

Kaliyah whispered back to Bahman, "Would you please move that talon over to the side? It's hurting me."

"I'm sorry. Of course," he said gently as he moved the talon to the side of his belt.

Awe, exhilaration, a wondrousness—these were all feelings among those riding the gisgal-usumlugal. Markkah was the most entranced with the thrill of it all and hoped the trip would take a long time. She was glad that the animal was not running, although they covered ground quite well even at his ambling pace. The stars were brilliant above; the feel of the great beast's hide under her fingers was fascinating. She patted him through the netting and willed herself to remember the feel of it for the rest of her life.

She thought she knew who the Old Man was from what she had learned from Ishmerai, but she was too timid to ask. As the night wore on, she determined that she would ask him when they stopped to rest.

As the wee hours of the morning approached, the mist began to envelop the endless jungle. The time for traveling stopped, the stars being no longer seen for navigation. The Old Man let out a low whistle and patted Lugal on both sides of his neck. The beast understood the direction and came to a halt. The jungle was not quite so thick in this part, and the Old Man directed the beast over to a tall tree for their debarkment.

They climbed off Lugal and onto the tree and then down the tree to the ground to take care of necessities. The tree, being of the same sort as their previous sleeping quarters, was reclimbed. It was not because they were afraid of other animals, but rather it was safer to be out of the way of Lugal's tail or just out from under his feet. They took out the last of the provisions on hand and feasted.

"Before we leave tomorrow, or rather this afternoon, we'll take time to collect some more food. There's plenty around," stated the Old Man.

All during the meal, Markkah thought of how to ask the Old Man about himself. After putting several questions together and rejecting them, finally she just blurted, "You named Lugal, didn't you?"

"Why, yes, I did," answered the Old Man. "Do you not think it is fitting for him?"

"I think it's the perfect name for him."

"Indeed, well said. It was perfect," he said with a hint of sadness in his voice.

She slipped the medallion out from her blouse and off from around her neck. She held it out to him and pointed to the two people figures on the one side.

"You're him, aren't you? You're the greatest grandfather."

"I don't like to be called that, because there is nothing great about me."

Kaliyah, Bahman, and Hanan were holding close attention. Hanan had believed the stories about the Creator since she was a child and had thought that the Old Man was one of the grandfathers. She was amazed to learn that he was the first.

"Was Lugal with you in the garden then?" continued Markkah.

"Yes, he was. Both he and his mate. And I must confess, he was always my favorite. Of course, in those days, his favorite food was big melons. Even today, he eats one for a treat from time to time."

"So he's so big because he's as old as you."

"Exactly. He's kept growing, and I've just grown old."

"Where do you keep him?"

"I don't keep him anywhere. He's free, just like all of creation longs to be."

"Ishmerai told me about the Creation, but I would like to hear it from you."

The others agreed. They wanted to hear too.

For a number of reasons, the Old Man was hesitant to talk of it, but after a hesitation, he began.

"I was not there when the world was created, but the Lord of Spirits told me how it was done. And this is what He told me to teach my children and their children:

"In the beginning God created the heavens and the earth. The earth was without form, and void; and darkness was on the face of the deep. And the Spirit of God was hovering over the face of the waters.

"Then God said, 'Let there be light'; and there was light. And God saw the light, that it was good; and God divided the light from the darkness. God called the light day, and the darkness He called night. So the evening and the morning were the first day.

"Then God said, 'Let there be a firmament in the midst of the waters, and let it divide the waters from the waters.' Thus God made the firmament, and divided the waters which were under the firmament from the waters which were above the firmament; and it was so. And God called the firmament heaven. So the evening and the morning were the second day.

"Then God said, 'Let the waters under the heavens be gathered together into one place, and let the dry land appear'; and it was so. And God called the dry land earth, and the gathering together of the waters He called seas. And God saw that it was good.

"Then God said, 'Let the earth bring forth grass, the herb that yields seed, and the fruit tree that yields fruit according to its kind, whose seed is in itself, on the earth'; and it was so. And the earth brought forth grass, the herb that yields seed according to its kind, and the tree that yields fruit, whose seed is in itself according to its kind. And God saw that it was good. So the evening and the morning were the third day.

"Then God said, 'Let there be lights in the firmament of the heavens to divide the day from the night; and let them be for signs and seasons, and for days and years; and let them be for lights in the firmament of the heavens to give light on the earth'; and it was so. Then God made two great lights: the greater light to rule the day, and the lesser light to rule the night. He made the stars also. God set them in the firmament of the heavens to give light on the earth, and to rule over the day and over the night, and to divide the light from the darkness. And God saw that it was good. So the evening and the morning were the fourth day.

"Then God said, 'Let the waters abound with an abundance of living creatures, and let birds fly above the earth across the face of the firmament of the heavens.' So God created great sea creatures and every living thing that moves, with which the waters abounded, according to their kind, and every winged bird according to its kind. And God saw that it was good. And God blessed them, saying, 'Be fruitful and multiply, and fill the waters in the seas, and let birds multiply on the earth.' So the evening and the morning were the fifth day.

"Then God said, 'Let the earth bring forth the living creature according to its kind: cattle and creeping thing and beast of the earth, each according to its kind'; and it was so. And God made the beast of the earth according to its kind, cattle according to its kind, and everything that creeps on the earth according to its kind. And God saw that it was good.

"Then God said, 'Let Us make man in Our image, according to Our likeness; let them have dominion over the fish of the sea, over the birds of the air, and over the cattle, over all the earth and over every creeping thing that creeps on the earth.' So God created man in His own image; in the image of God He created him; male and female He created them.

"Then God blessed them, and said to them, 'Be fruitful and multiply; fill the earth and subdue it; have dominion over the fish of the sea, over the birds of the air, and over every living thing that moves on the earth.'

"And God said, 'See, I have given you every herb that yields seed which is on the face of all the earth, and every tree whose fruit yields seed; to you it shall be for food. Also, to every beast of the earth, to every bird of the air, and to everything that creeps on the earth, in which there is life, I have given every green herb for food' and it was so.

"Then God saw everything that He had made, and indeed it was very good. So the evening and the morning were the sixth day.

"Thus the heavens and the earth, and all the host of them, were finished. And on the seventh day God ended His work which He had done, and He rested on the seventh day from all His work which He had done. Then God blessed the seventh day and sanctified it, because in it He rested from all His work which God had created and made."[4]

Markkah was full of questions, and since she'd been brave enough to ask the Old Man thus far, she decided she'd push it further with, "What does it mean that God created the heavens and the earth and it was formless and void?"

"To create is to make something out of nothing. That first day, He brought into existence from out of nothing everything in the entire universe, both seen and unseen, but it was a formless, unorganized mass. And out of this created substance, everything was formed and structured during the six days in the order that He states."

"What was God's Spirit doing hovering over the face of the waters?"

"The hovering is best described as brooding, like a hen broods her eggs, keeping them warm in order to hatch her chicks. The Spirit brings life," replied the Old Man.

Markkah was not nearly done with her questions, so she next asked, "How could there be light created on the first day, but the sun, moon, and stars were not made until the fourth day?"

"Markkah, don't be rude," said Kaliyah. "It's not polite to question like this."

"On the contrary, Kaliyah. It is a very good thing to ask questions. How else will there be understanding?" reprimanded the Old Man softly. "Now, to answer your question, Markkah, there is a light that exists that does not come from any stars or the sun. It was the first light of Creation, and it still remains."

"How do you know?"

"Because He created it and didn't take it away."

"How do you know for sure?"

"Because He said so."

Markkah was on a roll, so the next question was, "When God said, 'Let Us make man in Our image,' does that mean there is more than one God?"

"Indeed, no. There is only one God, one Creator."

"Then why does He say 'Us' and 'Our'?"

"Even when I was in the garden, still a friend to Him, and I walked and talked with Him, I did not fully understand Him. He is so far above and beyond our comprehension. But I've suspected that it has something to do with His Spirit hovering and Him speaking."

"That doesn't make any sense."

"If God made total sense to us, then He wouldn't be greater than us, and He wouldn't be God."

"Now, that makes sense."

Kaliyah had heard the Creation story when she was a child, but it was quite a different one. She was too timid to ask about it. Bahman and Hanan knew the story too, but not in this detail. All had more questions. Markkah was doing a good job of asking, so they kept silent, listening attentively.

"Ishmerai says that you named the animals on the sixth day, the day both they and you were created. Is that right?" Markkah continued.

"Yes, that's correct. Old Lugal here was the first I named too. Maybe that's why he is my favorite. He's always had a way of making his presence known."

The beast, as if he knew they were talking about him, let out a roar and scratched at the saddle netting. Lugal circled a spot, mashed down some brush, and then lay down with a huff and a thump that sent an earth tremor through the jungle and rattled the tree and its occupants to the core. The Old Man looked lovingly at the beast, and memories seemed to swim in his eyes.

Markkah wasn't done with her questioning. "So your name is 'Man' from the beginning?"

He chuckled, "Indeed it is, but 'Old' Man now is more descriptive."

"What does it mean when God said He created you 'in Our image'?"

The Old Man paused and then softly said, "Truly amazing words. No words can I find that would do justice to the great things God intended for me or for all of us. I was created very differently from the animals. The Lord of Spirits did not just say, 'Let there be,' as with all other parts of Creation. There was a purpose and a plan for me, for us. And although we have flesh like the animals, have similarities of design, and have similar bodily needs for food and comfort, we alone were created in His image and possess a spirit, a soul. In the day I was created, I was perfect and holy and walked with Him without fear. It is not just for this life in the flesh alone that we were created."

Another pause. The Old Man's words were a lot to digest.

Markkah broke the silence again with, "Where is our greatest grandmother? Is she waiting for you at home?"

Another silence ensued, but this one was nearly as thick as the mist enveloping them. Markkah worried that she'd gone too far, when finally the Old Man spoke again.

"I think we've all heard enough for one night, or early morning as it is. I'll tell you the answer on the morrow. Now it's time for sleep."

They all adjusted their sleeping areas as best they could in the cradle of the tree. Kaliyah caught a glimpse in the dim light, a glistening of tears on the Old Man's face as he shifted around for a comfortable spot.

THE MISSING

The small woman twisted her unruly hair back into a knot as best she could in the wind that whipped the ferry and slowed its progress over to the west bank of the river. Hulda was eager for the reward she knew would be coming her way. Her regular travel to Eriduch to deliver fine cloth to market was sweetened with the possession of news that would profit her handsomely. Her one-ox cart was laden with fine silks and linens, and she ran over in her mind how she would juggle her trade with her intelligence delivery.

She reflected on Herathah, who was aware of the slaves somehow escaping her realm but had not been able to discover the culprits involved, nor the manner by which they were getting away. The existence of coconspirators, especially those within the walls of Eriduch, was a thorn in the ruler's side, who took it as a personal insult to herself and her husband that there were Watchers who thwarted them and guarded the so-called "righteous priests" in the east. Herathah knew that, ultimately, Enoch and

Methuselah were at the bottom of it, because she was aware of the refuge village they'd provided. A generous reward was offered for information that led to the capture of anyone involved in this smuggling. Knowing these things, Hulda had her ears and eyes on the lookout wherever she was at, making a habit, especially in the freelands, of ingratiating herself with the locals with the intent of cashing in if the opportunity arrived. *Payday is near*, she thought.

The ferry was not as crowded as usual. The traffic was light because of the Great Gather still in process in Eriduch. She traveled with a small group of other peddlers intent on the same prospect of sales. There would be several markets in action on the western outskirts where the bulk of the foreign gatherers had set up temporary housekeeping. Her ox transport would not be allowed into the city proper, so she would have to skirt the outside of the city on the north to get to the western outskirts to sell her cloth. She calculated that by the time she completed her sales, the Gather would be nearly over, and then she would be able to cash in on her information. As she traveled, she was spending in her head the money she'd make.

Abishag had been consumed through the remaining days of the Gather with trying to come up with a plausible, non-incriminating excuse for losing the borrowed slave, Kaliyah. He would undoubtedly be known to have been the last person to be seen with the woman. He was convinced that magic was connected with her and her disappearance somehow. When he'd discovered her gone, he'd run back to the street. He'd had the presence of mind at least to ask those nearby if they'd seen anyone pass by. One man said that he'd seen two Watchen in their red robes walk from the direction he'd come and that they'd turned down another street. He pointed to the way he'd seen them go. The man's observation intensified Abishag's suspicion that the magic of the Watchen was at play.

He could tell Nekoda that she was taken by some Watchen. Then there'd be an inquiry into why she was taken without giving compensation to her owner. He couldn't testify as to which Watchen were involved. He was the last one seen with her, so the slave thief or thieves could accuse him of anything. He didn't want their magic aimed at him...or maybe it already was.

And what if she were taken by a Watcher? She'd be coming back holding an entirely different position in society than when she left. She would have the power and authority to exact retribution. Any way he looked at it, he was in a vulnerable situation, and his fear eclipsed his anger. Not much time was left before he'd have to give an accounting.

THE PROMISE

Midafternoon found the Old Man's newly awakened entourage gathering fruits, berries, and other edibles from the jungle nearby their sleeping tree. For the hungry travelers, it was two berries or fruits in the mouth and one into the satchel with every picking. By the time they'd collected the provisions, they were quite full.

The gisgal-usumlugal stayed close by, his nostrils sniffing the air for scents of possible meals. The Old Man patted his haunch and said, "We'll be to the river tonight, where the tasty Uzka-Sutum will be plentiful."

The mightly Lugal let out one of his deafening roars, startling the food gatherers. One would have thought that the great beast understood what the Old Man said and knew that his favorite duck-billed lizard was soon to be on the menu.

The steed-mounting routine then began with the Old Man guiding Lugal to the sleeping tree and then all climbing to a place where they could cross over onto the net-saddle. And the ride commenced into the late afternoon and evening and finally into the night through the jungle, guided by the stars. Again, the travelers were immersed in the sensations of wonder and awe. It was not just the extraordinary means of transportation that stirred the hearts of the Old Man's companions, but it was their thoughts of what they'd learned so few hours before. All had more questions to ask of the Old Man when they'd stop again. And all were thankful that he'd promised to tell them more. The words they exchanged between themselves were sparse while they rode through the jungle. Lugal seemed to have picked up his pace too, most likely because of the meal awaiting him at their night's destination, the Pishon River.

Markkah was torn. She loved the ride and wanted it to go on forever, but then she wanted it to end so she could learn more from the Old Man. She again formed questions in her mind but kept rewording them so she wouldn't be rude. At least she tried to. She decided that instead of asking where the greatest grandmother was now, she'd ask about her creation. That might be a happier thing for the Old Man to talk about. That settled in her mind, she looked forward to the end of their night's journey.

They arrived at the Pishon River not long after midnight and well before the mists began to form. The Old Man said that it would be better to cross the river in the daytime, so he guided Lugal along the riverbank in search of another sleeping tree. It was not long before they located a suitable one. Lugal was more restless, owing to his meal prospects close by, so they dismounted quickly. They hurriedly attended to their necessities and readied their quarters for the rest of the night. Finally, the Old Man patted Lugal on his leg and told him to go find something good to eat. He was the last to climb the tree to join the others.

Fruits, roots, and berries were brought out for the meal. While they feasted, they heard crashing and noise from up the river that indicated that Lugal had found his dinner too. When all were sated, they sat back, expectantly looking at the Old Man to begin the story again. They were all glad for the shorter travel because that meant earlier answers to their questions. And again, it was Markkah who began the questioning.

"Greatest-Grandfather, you said last night that God made you differently from the animals and the rest of Creation. If He did not make you by saying, 'Let there be,' how then did He do it?"

The Old Man took a deep breath and answered, "This is how the Lord of Spirits told me He made me: He formed me out of the dust of the ground and breathed into my nostrils the breath of life, and that is how I became a living soul."

"Did He make our greatest grandmother at the same time too?"

"Actually, no, He didn't. That first day of my life, my first memory is that the Lord of Spirits took me and put me into a beautiful garden called Eden that He'd made for me to tend. When He set me there, He commanded me, saying, 'Of every tree of the garden you may freely eat, but of the tree of the knowledge of good and evil you shall not eat, for in the day that you eat of it you shall surely die.'"

"And you were alone? Where was our greatest grandmother?"

"I'm getting there. This is what happened. The Lord of Spirits said, 'It is not good that man should be alone. I will make a helper comparable to him.' Then He brought the animals and birds and creatures that He'd created to me to see what I would name them."

"And Lugal you named first."

"Indeed, he was at the front of the line, along with his mate."

"So you named all of them?"

"It was a long day's work, and I was wondering where this helper was that the Lord God said He'd make. I did not find one in all the creatures that were brought before me."

"Then what happened when you were done?"

"The Lord God caused me to go into a deep sleep, and when I woke up, I found this on my side," he said as he parted his cloak and shirt to show a faint scar and slight indentation right over his aged left breast.

To the slight gasps of the listeners, he continued, "I was missing a rib, from right over my heart."

He paused, drew a breath, and then continued. "I turned then and saw what the Lord of Spirits was bringing to me. I saw your greatest grandmother for the first time. The Lord God had built her out of my rib."

With misty eyes and a bit of a choked voice, he said, "And then I said, 'This is now bone of my bones and flesh of my flesh; she shall be called woman, because she was taken out of man. Therefore, a man shall leave his father and mother and be joined to his wife, and they shall become one flesh.'"

The listeners were silent as the Old Man composed himself with a couple more deep breaths and a wiping of a tear off his cheek. Then he said with a little chuckle, "She was the most beautiful woman in the world."

The ever-questioning Markkah once again asked, "Why do you think He built her out of your rib?"

Smiling, the Old Man said, "I'd wondered the same thing. But then I knew why. She was not made out of my foot bone so I would walk on her. She was not made out of my head so I would rule over her. She was made out of my rib because it was closest to my heart, just as she always was. She was made for me to love, and I did."

It was the past tense of his speaking that answered the question about whether she was waiting for him at home or not. They knew then she was no longer living.

Perceiving this, Markkah asked another question, but this one she thought would be on the lighter side.

"Lugal was your favorite animal, but what was our greatest grandmother's favorite one?"

The question caused an unexpected reaction from the Old Man. His demeanor, instead of one recalling pleasant memories, produced a darkened look, and they heard a controlled anger in his voice when he answered.

"Her favorite was a beautiful little creature," he said through clenched teeth.

His emphasis of the word *beautiful* suggested a derision for the creature, but he continued. "The animal was long and sleek, with brilliantly colored, shiny skin that sparkled like jewels, and it had many delicate little legs and feet that undulated and shimmered in rhythm as it walked. My Eve loved to play with the animal, and it would circle around her neck like a jeweled necklace or coil on her arm like a bracelet. Both the animal and its mate would be her almost constant companions while we tended the garden we'd been given."

As the Old Man spoke, they noticed his repeated reference to "the animal," of which he surely knew the name, for he'd named it. An unspoken question went through the minds of the listeners: *Could the Old Man have been jealous of the animal?*

He continued. "One morning when the mists lifted, my Eve discovered her pet missing. We both went looking for the animal. We caught glimpses of a sparkle and a shimmer and followed its movements toward the center of the garden, toward the commandment tree."

"The commandment tree?" Markkah interrupted.

"I called it that because it was this tree, the tree of the knowledge of good and evil, of which the Lord God commanded we shall not eat, for in the day that we eat of it we would die."

"Oh."

"I had told my Eve the command about this tree. We both knew of it and were disposed to have no other idea except to obey it. However, when we caught up to 'the animal,' it was coiled playfully around one of its branches."

He paused again. When he spoke again, there was regret and sadness mixed with the anger in his voice. "The 'animal' spoke. Now, I should have done something right there. I knew all the animals and what their capabilities were. Speaking rationally with us was not one of them, and it certainly was not a capability of that particular animal. But I ignored this and just listened. He had addressed my Eve as she reached up her hand in an attempt to coax him down from the branch. Instead, he moved just out of her reach and said, *'Has God really said, "You shall not eat of every tree of the garden"?'*

"Now, here again, I should have stopped it. Not only did I allow the animal to talk to my Eve, I remained silent as he said, *'Has God really said…'* I knew exactly what God really said, and I didn't attempt to clarify the truth of it. I was silent as I let my Eve answer her pet as she said, *"We may eat the fruit of the trees of the garden, but of the fruit of the tree which is in the middle of the garden, God has said, "You shall not eat it, nor shall you touch it, lest you die.""*

"Even when my Eve didn't get the command exactly straight, for God never told me not to touch the fruit, I didn't intervene. It had been my command only to my Eve to never even touch it, not the command of the Lord of Spirits.

"Then the animal replied to her, *'You will not surely die. For God knows that in the day you eat of it your eyes will be opened and you will be like God, knowing good and evil.'*

"The thought struck me that maybe God had been holding out on us, denying us something great. I saw that the fruit might be something desirable after all. Yet even as my Eve perceived the same thing, that the tree would make one wise, I held back and let her be the one to test it out first. When she took the fruit and ate it, I saw that it was good and she didn't die. She handed a fruit to me also, and I ate of it."

"What happened? Did you both become wise like God?"

"Well, our eyes were opened, and we both saw that we were naked. It shamed us to be so, and we sewed together fig leaves to cover ourselves."

"Didn't you know you were naked before that?" Markkah asked incredulously.

"No, nothing about ourselves shamed us before that. We hadn't felt ashamed or like we were lacking anything, but after eating the fruit, we did."

"So neither of you died then, of course. Does that mean that God lied to you?"

"Absolutely not. Indeed, though we did not drop dead on the spot, death began in not only us but all of Creation at that moment. We didn't understand that at the time, though. In fact, my previously clear intellect diminished immediately, and my thoughts were entirely corrupted from that point on. It had been corrupted so much that to this day, I can't even fully recall the blissful state I was in before this event occurred."

This time it was Kaliyah who asked, "What did you two do after this?"

"We heard the sound of the Lord God walking in the garden in the cool of the day that afternoon. We were afraid, and we hid ourselves in the trees and bushes. He called to me, and said, *'Man, where are you?'* Out of the hiding spot, I answered and said, *'I heard Your voice in the garden, and I was afraid because I was naked, and I hid myself.'* I could not even reply with the truth then. I had the sewn fig leaves on and had known I was naked before He'd walked in the garden and called my name that day.

"And He questioned me, saying, *'Who told you that you were naked? Have you eaten from the tree of which I commanded you that you should not eat?'*

"Then I replied, *'The woman whom You gave to be with me, she gave me of the tree, and I ate.'* I was unable to admit what I'd done. Instead, I laid the blame on the Lord God Himself, as if it were His fault because it was He who had given me the woman, who gave me the forbidden fruit. I accused my Creator and excused myself.

"Then the Lord God said to my Eve, *'What is this you have done?'*

"She answered, *'The serpent deceived me, and I ate.'*"

At the mention of the animal's name, Kaliyah let out a shriek and fainted. The attention of all was directed toward Kaliyah. Bahman cradled her in his arms and fanned her face with his hand. After some seconds, she revived.

"Kaliyah, are you all right?" said Hanan.

Kaliyah began to cry, and she choked out the words, "I was taught…from when I was young…that the serpent *was* the Creator."

Surprisingly, the Old Man sadly replied, "You would have been taught that. You are a descendant of Cain."

Markkah asked, "So God the Creator is not a serpent?"

"Most emphatically, no, He is not. The serpent was a creation of the Lord of Spirits, as was the spirit who talked through it. Indeed, everything that exists was created by God, including all creatures, seen and unseen, including the Watchers, the spirits, the sons of God, and those who claim to be gods."

Haltingly, Kaliyah asked, "What did the Lord God do then to the serpent and to you?"

"Well, He certainly could have just destroyed us all right then and there and started over with a better, more obedient batch of beings. But He did not. Instead He said to the serpent, who was still with us, *'Because you have done this, You are cursed more than all cattle and more than every beast of the field. On your belly you shall go, and you shall eat dust all the days of your life. And I will put enmity between you and the woman and between your seed and her seed; it shall crush your head, and you shall bruise its heel.'*

"Immediately, my Eve's little pet lost both its beauty and its legs. It became a most ugly, repulsive beast. And then He turned to my Eve and said, *'I will greatly multiply your sorrow and your conception. In pain you shall bring forth children. Your desire shall be for your husband, and he shall rule over you.'*

"Then to me He said, *'Because you have heeded the voice of your wife and have eaten from the tree of which I commanded you, saying, "You shall not eat of it": Cursed is the ground for your sake. In toil you shall eat of it all the days of your life. Both thorns and thistles it shall bring forth for you, and you shall eat the herb of the field. In the sweat of your face you shall eat bread, until you return to the ground, for out of it you were taken. For dust you are, and to dust you shall return.'*

"Then we saw the very first death."

Markkah let out a little gasp and the eyes of the others grew wider, and with bated breath all waited for the Old Man to continue.

"The Lord God slaughtered two sheep and fashioned their skins into tunics for our clothing."

The Old Man, looking into the faces of his audience, surmised correctly that they didn't comprehend the significance of what he was saying. "Don't look so relieved that it was merely the death of animals, now," he chided. "Death was non-existent in our perfect world before my great sin. The death of anyone or anything is a result of that sin. It is an enemy of all of Creation and it is the great price of sin. It is not natural even though we've become accustomed to it."

"Oh," said Markkah with wide eyes.

He continued. "The clothing that we had fashioned for ourselves out of fig leaves was not acceptable to the Lord of Spirits. It took His action alone and the shedding of blood to make us presentable enough to stand before Him. He did for us what we could not do for ourselves."

Markkah blurted out, "But people can make clothing out of skins." She gave a start when she felt a sharp poke of disapproval in her back as her mother discreetly attempted to discourage her apparently rude questioning.

Smiling, unperturbed by Markkah directness, the Old Man explained, "The point is this: we tried by ourselves to cover our sin, shame, and nakedness. It didn't work. To be acceptable to the Lord God, only the shedding of blood and His direct action alone was sufficient to cover us. Our sin could only be covered by this great price; bloodshed in our once perfect world. That is why to this day, when the priests of the Most High come before the Lord to make sacrifices for the sins of the people, they sacrifice an animal. This is done because we understand that we can't make ourselves presentable to Him by our own efforts, we cannot cover our sins on our own, but rather that it takes the Lord of Spirits alone to do so, as He first did for my Eve and me."

Observing nods of understanding, the Old Man went on. "And then the Lord God drove us out of the garden. A mighty spirit, a cherubim, was placed to guard the entrance so that no one could enter and eat of the tree of life and live forever."

Markkah said quietly, "How terrible to lose all that you had and were."

"Terrible doesn't even come close," replied the Old Man. "Everything, every decision, every thought after that has been flawed, tainted, and corrupted. Even my good intentions have not been good enough."

Kaliyah asked, "The curse you received, was there nothing but pain, misery, and death to look forward to?"

"Ah, now, listen. It was the curse given to the serpent that gave us something to look forward to. The curse on him is our hope. It is just one little sentence that the Lord God spoke, but it gave us then and gives us now a wondrous hope. The Lord of Spirits promised that the Seed of the woman would crush the enemy's head, a destroying deathblow. The serpent would merely hurt the Seed's heel, a wound, but not one that would destroy. There will be some day a man born of a woman who will utterly destroy the serpent and the evil and the death he brought to this world. In this promise, we believe and hope. Our Creator, the Lord God, loved my Eve and me so much that instead of destroying us, He forgave us, and He provided a way and a plan to bring us back to the state of being He intended. Through my rebellion, I lost wholly that image of God for myself, my Eve, and all of our future children on that terrible sinning day, but one day all who believe and hope in the promised Seed will regain that image."

Markkah took out her medallion again, held it up to the Old Man, and asked, "What then is this map that shows only in the moonlight?"

The Old Man smiled and said, "It is not a map to a physical place. It is the map for the heart and soul. It points the only way to redemption, to restoration, to freedom, through the Seed."

"So that's why Ishmerai said he was not a slave, that he was already free," said Markkah.

"Indeed."

"I want to be free too," Kaliyah softly said.

"Then realize that you cannot restore yourself to that image of God any more than my Eve and I could...and believe the Promise."

"I believe," they all said in unison.

And this time, the tears that were wept were ones of joy.

ACCOUNTABLE

Hulda watched from afar the finale of the Great Gather in Eriduch. The people who'd come in and out of the market during the past two days were all back in the city again for the closing events. The only ones outside the city were those guarding their market goods and those guarding the camps and animals of the travelers. Hulda's supplies were almost sold out, so she could have taken the chance to attend the ceremony in the city, but she really wasn't that interested with the religiosity of it all. Money and wealth were top on her priority list.

From where she sat, she had a view directly through the gate and up the center-north street that led to the foot of the ziggurat. She was much too far away to hear any of the speeches, but she could hear the roars of the people as they cheered their agreement with whatever it was that was being declared. And as the sun began to set, she could hear the deep, rhythmic chanting of the Watchen as they conjured in the airships of the Watchers. This time, instead of the single massive ship that spanned the entire ziggurat, there were about twenty smaller craft that appeared. One passed directly over her head as it flew toward the ziggurat. She could see the whirling intersecting wheels on the underside but heard only the faintest sound as a soft wind as it passed. As the rays of the setting sun gave an orange glow to the sky, it reflected on the ziggurat and the airships hovering above. Hulda admitted to herself that the Watchers could sure put on a good show.

When she had arrived, she heard the news about Samjaza's decree about allowing no more purely human children to be born throughout all the lands of the Watchers. This did not surprise her. Her grown children, some of whom were practicing Watchen and some merely Watcher supporters, were all enthusiastic about mere humans becoming a race of god-men. In fact, she had a number of Digir-na for grandchildren. Hulda wondered how long it would be before the peoples in the free lands would be affected by this. The territory of the free lands was getting smaller and smaller as the Watchers extended their rule. Those who traded with the Watchers' cities eventually became a part of their territory, either willingly or by force.

There was a great competition that had begun with the Watchers. Each of the twenty chief Watchers had established cities and monuments all over Imin-sar, all seemingly in an attempt to outdo one another. The lesser Watchers assisted their chiefs in these endeavors. Samjaza's ziggurat was the most massive one built between all of them yet. Over the years, Hulda had traveled to nearly all of the Watchers' cities, selling her cloth, and had found it most interesting to see what was new and spectacular with each one. Her favorite monument was in her own hometown, the city to the south, Ineb-Hedg, founded by Armaros, Samjaza's first lieutenant; it was a lion with the human-featured head of Armaros.

She reflected how years before when her husband was still alive and they were raising their family what he'd said about the Watchers, those other-dimensional spirits who could take on physical form for periods of time. And he would have known, because he was involved with the planning of a number of the monuments, including her favorite one. He'd said, "They're a bunch of blowhards. They like to make men think they're so much more superior, and granted, they do have some unique abilities and knowledge about secret laws, but they are no brain powerhouses. We engineers do all the major calculations and designs, and they get all the credit."

What the Watchers did have over and above mere all-humans were oversized, aggressive children who grew to be excellent at intimidation, slave-driving, and basic territorial expansion. The giants also were great and strong workers for the most difficult tasks of stone construction, whether by using their own brute strength alone or handling the massive animals conscripted for the tasks. She reflected that these Digir-na, the Watchers' sons and daughters, were even a bit more lacking in intellectual abilities than their fathers; definitely more brawn than brain. Maybe she was being too critical in her mind, but at least she thought that the race of god-men would improve as more human blood was thrown into the mix. She never spoke these rebellious thoughts to anyone, even her many children. She knew that her husband met an untimely death because he'd expressed his feelings one too many times to the wrong person. For herself, she was glad for her independence, enjoyed the travel and sights, and could look forward to a very comfortable retirement. And with cashing in on her recently acquired intelligence, she'd gain a retirement that would happen a bit sooner than originally figured.

As the sky darkened into night, the only sights left were the glowing beams and lights of the Watchers' aircrafts. The music and chanting grew to a pitch that vibrated even the outskirts of the city. To the resounding cheers of the masses, the airships soared with astounding speed in all directions and up and out of sight. She turned into her tent; it was time to sleep. She'd have a big day on the morrow. She estimated that the last of her goods

REIGN OF THE WATCHERS

would be sold well before midday, and then she would make her information trip into the city.

Midmorning on the day after the final Gather night seemed to be as good a time as any to Abishag to have that talk with Nekoda about the missing slave. To his great consternation, he'd just been informed that another of his slaves had come up missing. At least the slave, Hanan, was not a borrowed one. Still, he'd have to make an accounting to his superior for her absence also. He would deal with that problem after he had his talk with Nekoda.

As he walked through the courtyard gate into Enkara's compound, he was still trying to form in his mind exactly what he'd say. At least it was much better to talk with the hard-dealing man now than in a week's time, when he was supposed to return Kaliyah to her master. He went to the side entrance of the great house and down the hallway to Nekoda's office. He rapped on the door and immediately heard a gruff, probably hungover bark to enter.

"Well, Abishag, I'd have thought you'd be busy directing the rather extensive cleanup rather than paying me a visit," snarled the man.

This probably won't go very well, thought Abishag, but he had no choice but to forge ahead with, "I'm sorry, but I have some disturbing news."

"Well, spit it out."

"I've lost the slave Kaliyah, and I can't find her anywhere."

"Who was in charge of her? Bring him to me."

"Well, that's the bit of trouble. I took her from her assignment to have her do some other work for me."

"I'm sure you had some 'work' for her," Nekoda sneered.

"I was called away on another urgent matter, so I locked her in a room for safekeeping until I came back. When I returned, she was gone."

"Well, did you search for her?"

"Yes, I did."

"Did anyone else see anything?"

At this point, he hedged. It was a serious thing to accuse the Watchen, so he decided to lie. "No one saw anything. She just vanished into thin air."

"Only the Watchers can do that." Then Nekoda, rubbing the temples of his aching head, added, "You know Enkara will be pretty unhappy that you've lost the woman. Even if she was one of his throwaways, he doesn't like losing anything, unless he's the one who's doing the dispatching. In fact, he doesn't like it so much that I'm going to let you be the one to tell him."

Abishag's heart sank. *This is really not going well.*

"Sit there and wait until I have you summoned," he ordered. Then he rose and left his office.

Abishag fidgeted as sweat started to drip off his forehead. He even contemplated fleeing, but he knew that would only worsen his position. He had no choice but to go through with the encounter. Interminable minutes seemed to stretch by, and his dread worsened with each one. Finally, he heard steps coming down the hallway. A thin young slave boy came through the door.

"Sir, you are to follow me."

Silently, Abishag followed the boy up the grand staircase that led to Enkara's lavish quarters. They passed three giggling young women going the other way. Down the long, wide hallway, Abishag could see Nekoda standing at a huge pair of ornately carved wooden doors. This was his first time in the private quarters of a giant. He'd of course seen many Digir-na, and Enkara more than most, but that was on the streets. The sheer size of everything here made him feel like he was a miniature.

"Enkara is expecting you," Nekoda said as he opened the door and gestured for him to enter, alone. Clenching his teeth, Abishag put one foot in front of the other and entered the room. He didn't at first see Enkara. The vast room featured several seating and lounging areas. He spotted movement in the dining alcove and then realized where the giant was.

"So, who is this who brings me foul news so early in the morning?" rumbled a low, gravelly voice.

Nearly noon wasn't close to being "so early in the morning," but Abishag lacked the nerve to beg the difference. He did manage to answer, "Abishag, sir."

The enormous Digir-na was seated at a long dining table piled high with mounds of fruits, breads, cheeses, sauces, and pitchers of drink. Through a mouthful of food, some bits of which ejected from his mouth as he spoke, Enkara indistinctly ordered, "Gi ore here so I c'hear you."

Abishag thought he heard correctly and walked toward the eating area.

Enkara swallowed the mouthful and again ordered, "Sit down," as he pointed to a chair opposite him.

"Yes, sir," Abishag answered. Sitting down was more like climbing up. The dining chairs were all fashioned for giants, and the seat alone was level with his shoulders. Thankfully, the chair had steps on which to climb, which he did. Instead of sitting on the seat, he stood, putting him in a position to rest his elbows on the tabletop. He could see Enkara stuffing his face over the platters of food, with his double rows of teeth making him all the more intimidating.

"Now, who are you again?" asked the giant between bites.

"I'm Abishag, chief of the central and north sector city street cleaners."

Shoving another fistful of food into his mouth, he again spoke with his mouth full, "So wa' th' 'roblem?"

Nervously, Abishag began to explain, saying, "A moon before the Great Gather, I had to increase the street cleaning crews. I borrowed a number of slaves from all the houses for the needs of the event." He drew in a breath and continued. "The slave I borrowed from you is missing."

Enkara swallowed and glared at Abishag. With menace in his low, growling voice, he said, "So you can't bring me back what is mine?"

Abishag swallowed too, but it was just spit, and he answered, "No."

"What slave of mine is this whom you've 'misplaced'?"

"Her name is Kaliyah, sir." Enkara didn't seem to recognize the name, and Abishag didn't attempt to remind him of her former status with him.

"Have you made efforts to find her?"

"Yes, sir, and I could not."

"Where was she last seen?"

Sweating profusely, Abishag recounted the story he'd told Nekoda.

Booming at the top of his voice, Enkara called Nekoda's name, demanding his presence. Nekoda hastened to enter the room and made to stand at the entrance of the dining alcove. "Yes, sir," he said, with a respectful nod of his head.

"Who is this Kaliyah?" the giant growled.

"Sir, she was one of your slave consorts who was assigned to other duties earlier in the past year," he said as delicately as he could without pointing out the violent event that had led to that altered status.

A brilliant red coloring flushed the giant's face. Through clenched teeth, he turned to Abishag and said, "You will pay for my loss."

The giant, moving more swiftly than one would have thought for one of his size, stood up abruptly, sending his chair tumbling behind him. He reached his hand over the table and seized Abishag by the front of his shirt, lifting him off the chair, over the food-laden table, and held his face mere inches from his own.

"This will be reported to my mother and father," he growled into his face. And then he threw him.

Abishag went sailing out of the dining alcove, knocking over several pieces of furniture before he smashed against the stone wall on the opposite side of the great room.

To Nekoda, he said, "Take that piece of street trash out of here, and send someone in to clean up the mess."

"Yes, sir," he said with a bow.

"Check out anything else you can about this. I want you to make the report to my mother and take the trash with you when you do it too."

"Yes, sir," he said again. Nekoda made haste to retrieve Abishag, dragging the unconscious and bloody man out of the giant's quarters.

NEVER FORGET

It was late morning, and the mists had already lifted in the jungle. The tree sleepers awoke to another beautiful day. Only it seemed this day was more beautiful than most. The Old Man had awoken earlier than the others and had managed to put together a fresh breakfast for all. They were all eager to begin the day's journey. The Old Man put his fingers to his lips and whistled for Lugal. The beast was not far away and made his appearance in short order.

The river crossing was next. Hanan looked out over the wide river and spotted what she thought was a man with an ox transport.

"Old Man, I think I see someone on the other side of the river," she said with concern in her voice.

The Old Man looked in the direction she pointed and said, "Excellent! He's right on time!"

Knowing the Old Man expected the newcomer eased everyone's minds. They hastened to ready themselves for their journey, and like experts at riding a mighty dragon king, they easily mounted their steed. It was apparent that Lugal was not fond of fording rivers, but he did so anyway on his old friend's command.

"Hold tightly!" the Old Man ordered as the beast steadily walked deeper and deeper into the river channel. At one point they thought that Lugal was actually swimming, and they once or twice had their heads submerged. Thankfully, the river wasn't nearly as wide or as swift as the Alagan-ida had been. They made their way slowly but surely to the other side.

The man on the other side had bound strips of cloth on the heads of the two oxen, blindfolding them. He also had their yoke tied securely to a tree. All figured that the man knew what transport they'd be using and didn't want his animals to be spooked. They reached the shore just downstream of the man and his ox transport. The Old Man immediately directed Lugal to a suitable tree for dismounting.

The Old Man was the first to make it to the ground. The waiting man hurried to greet the Old Man with a handshake and then a strong embrace.

"Come here," he beckoned his charges. "Hanan, Bahman, Kaliyah, and Markkah, I'd like you to meet my great-great-great-great-great grandson, Methuselah, known as Metu for short."

"And, Metu, these are my latest absconded-with children!"

After the handshakes and greetings were made, the Old Man turned his attention to Lugal.

"Metu, Bahman, would you like to give me a hand with this?"

The Old Man coaxed Lugal into lying down on his side. When he did, the men helped the Old Man to unfasten the net saddle from the underside of the beast's chest and gingerly maneuver the saddle so they could slip it off.

Freed from the leather net-saddle, Lugal stood and gave himself a good shake and an ear-shattering roar. Metu ran to his hysterical oxen to try to calm them as best he could. The Old Man walked with the beast down to the riverbank. The others watched as the mighty beast lowered his nose to touch the Old Man's head.

They couldn't hear what the Old Man said to his old friend, but they saw him pat the animal one last time on his haunch as the beast entered the water for his return to the wilds of Idim-kur.

They gathered again by the transport, with Metu finally getting his oxen under control and unblindfolded.

"To Moriah we go!" exclaimed the Old Man as they climbed aboard the transport. The Old Man sat with Metu on the front, and the others situated themselves in the back. There was a sense of excitement in their conversation as they discussed plans for the future. Markkah and Kaliyah were looking forward to seeing Melenah and Lelah again and asked Metu many questions as to their well-being and activities. Metu described the place where they lived and about the refuge village and people. Both women were interested in their loved ones' newfound occupation and expressed interest in doing the same. Hanan told how many years before she had learned how to spin and weave woolen cloth and that she would love to pursue that occupation. Bahman related that he wasn't just a stoneworker but that he had tended sheep in his days before slavery and would enjoy doing so again. They were so absorbed in their conversation that before they knew it, the terrain had changed from jungle to forest as they climbed higher in elevation toward a mountain to the northwest.

Just before sundown, they arrived at the mountaintop home of Enoch and Edna. Introductions, greetings, tears, hugs, and cheers ensued. Edna had a meal all prepared for the hungry travelers. The sun had disappeared beneath the horizon by the time they sat at a rustic wooden table laden with fresh breads, cheeses, and a wonderfully aromatic soup.

While Edna lit the candles on the table, Enoch said, "Old Man, we would be honored if you would say the blessing for our meal."

Humbly and solemnly, the Old Man chided, "My children, never forget that you have *not* been honored by me. You have inherited only a corrupted nature, the curse, and death from me. It is because of my rebellion that Almighty God holds us all accountable for our sins. But we are all honored by the loving Lord God who has laid a plan and paved a way to restore what I broke, and it is He alone Who will repair that separation from Him that I caused. In the Name I will bless this meal."

They held hands around the table, bowing their heads, and the Old Man prayed, "Almighty God, Creator of all things, seen and unseen, King of the universe, Lord God of the promise, bless us Your children and the food You have provided. May it nourish and strengthen our bodies, as Your Word nourishes and strengthens our souls. Blessed be Your name forever."

And they all said, "So shall it be."

INFORMATION

Sitting in a chair, tapping her foot, Hulda waited to be summoned by the city's security chief. She had refused to talk with anyone but the superior, and her wait would be a lengthy one. The minutes ticked by like hours as both her nervousness and impatience grew. When she could sit no longer, she paced back and forth in the small, windowless, sterile room. And then she would sit and tap her foot again. She even toyed with the idea of leaving to go look for the man, but she restrained herself because the last thing she wanted to do was alienate him.

At long last, a young man entered and asked her to follow him. She stood, straightened her garment, and followed the man across a courtyard and into another building. Inside the security compound connected to Herathah's palace, she was led up a wide flight of stairs to a suite of offices, the farthest one being the security chief's.

Opening the massive door to the office, the young man announced Hulda's arrival. The room was furnished to accommodate giants, all-humans, and anything in between. The chief himself was all-human, but his wife was a daughter of Herathah and Samjaza, which made him brother-in-law to Enkara. For an all-human, the aptly named Enkum, meaning Guardian, was of better-than-average height. His demeanor and presence, was commanding, not to mention intimidating.

Hulda steeled herself, despite her diminutive stature, to bargain for what she could get from the information she had. She was ordered to approach the large marble desk and told to sit down on a chair in front of it. Sitting down, she felt even smaller, with her head just level with the desktop. She thought disgustedly that they'd put that chair there just for her benefit.

The chief shuffled a pile of leather parchments into another arrangement on the desk and then finally deigned to give her his attention, saying, "Now what is this very important information you have to offer me?"

"Sir, I have information about escaped slaves."

"We know we have escaped slaves and where they've been ending up."

"Yes, sir, I know, sir, but I don't think you know about these."

"Pray tell, then, who are the ones you wish to tell me about?" he asked.

"The slave's name is Melenah, and she was a consort of one of Samjaza's sons. Lelah, their daughter and one of Herathah's granddaughters, is with her."

"We have not been missing any consorts or their children."

"As I live and breathe, you are, and they are living under the protection of Enoch."

"I expect that you wish a reward for your information?"

Gathering all her nerve, she answered, "Yes, I do."

"I will have you wait then while I verify your information." He then called for the young man who had been standing at the door during their conversation, and addressing him, he said, "Take this woman to the lounge and get her some refreshment and send me three runners."

Again, the waiting resumed, although this time it was in a better environment. She wondered how long it would be this time, but at least she was encouraged that the chief had taken her seriously and was checking into what she claimed.

It took a bit of doing to revive Abishag. Nekoda set two women slaves to the task of cleaning the man up and attending to his wounds. Providentially, he had escaped with mere broken ribs, a few lacerations, and a severely mangled nose. His already unbecoming looks would definitely not be made better for this. While the women attended to the man, Nekoda set off to do some investigation about the missing Kaliyah and any other business involving Abishag that might shed some light on the event.

Consequently, he was not at Enkara's compound when the runner from chief Enkum arrived to inquire if a consort by the name of Melenah had been missing. Instead of Nekoda, the runner was directed to Enkara's harem master. He was informed by the master that there had been a consort named Melenah who had been killed, along with her daughter, during Enkara's rampage well over a half year before.

"Did you identify the bodies?"

"We did the best we could. There were quite a number who were killed that day, and they were all mangled and in pieces. As I recall, their particular bodies were identified by another consort named Kaliyah. That woman lost her own daughter also."

That was all the information the runner needed to know. He then made haste to return to the security offices, leaving the harem master wondering what the questioning was all about.

JOY

A sacrifice of thanksgiving was offered in the early morning hours of the day of rest. Enoch officiated, with Methuselah assisting. The small group sang songs of praise, and their voices echoed through the woods. And then Enoch arose and opened a scroll.

He said, "These are the words of the vision I was given by the Lord of Spirits. I have written them down for all generations to come. It concerns the seed of the woman, the promised One."

And he began to read,

> And there I saw one who had a head of days, and his head was white like wool, and with him was another being whose countenance had the appearance of a man, and his face was full of graciousness, like one of the holy angels.
>
> And I asked the angel who went with me and showed me all the hidden things, concerning that Son of Man, who He was and whence He was and why He went with the Head of Days?

And he answered and said to me: "This is the Son of Man who has righteousness, with whom dwells righteousness, and who reveals all the treasures of that which is hidden, because the Lord of Spirits has chosen Him and whose lot has the pre-eminence before the Lord of Spirits in uprightness forever. And this Son of Man whom you have seen shall draw up the kings and the mighty from their seats and the strong from their thrones and shall loosen the reins of the strong and break the teeth of the sinners."[5]

Again, Enoch picked up another scroll and said, "Concerning again the promised seed of the woman, another vision was given to me."

"And in that place I saw the fountain of righteousness which was inexhaustible: and around it were many fountains of wisdom: And all the thirsty drank of them and were filled with wisdom, and their dwellings were with the righteous and holy and elect.

And at that hour that Son of Man was named in the presence of the Lord of Spirits and His Name before the Head of Days.

Yea, before the sun and the signs were created, before the stars of the heaven were made, His Name was named before the Lord of Spirits.

He shall be a staff to the righteous whereon to steady themselves and not fall, and He shall be the light of the Gentiles and the hope of those who are troubled of heart.

All who dwell on earth shall fall down and worship before Him and will praise and bless and celebrate with song the Lord of Spirits.

And for this reason had He been chosen and hidden before Him, before the creation of the world and for evermore.

And the wisdom of the Lord of Spirits has revealed Him to the holy and righteous, for He has preserved the lot of the righteous because they have hated and despised

this world of unrighteousness and have hated all its works
and ways in the Name of the Lord of Spirits:

"For in His Name they are saved, and according to His
good pleasure has it been in regard to their life."[6]

Enoch closed the scroll and said, "Our hope is not in vain."

"So shall it be," said the gatherers, and then they left the stone
altar to head back to Enoch and Edna's home. Another, but
simpler, meal was laid out for their breakfast, and over it, plans
were discussed for the day.

Markkah, ever the questioner, asked Enoch, "Who are the
'Gentiles'?"

Smiling, Enoch answered, "Why, that would be you and your
mother, and anyone who is not of the line of Seth, the brother
of Cain."

"So the Promise is really for us too?"

"From the beginning, dear one."

Both Kaliyah and Markkah treasured this one more assurance
in their hearts. Methuselah stated that he was taking the travelers
down to the refuge village on the next day. He turned to the
Kaliyah and Markkah and said, "This is our day of rest, and we
will do that today. Tomorrow's journey to your new home will be
one of just a half day."

Both women were overjoyed at the prospect of seeing soon
their long-missed cousin and sister, but they were also grateful
for a day of rest after their long journey. Hanan and Bahman were
thankful as well.

However, before the meal was over, the conversation changed
to the decree issued by Samjaza about not allowing all-human
babies to live. The Old Man had brought the subject up to inform
Enoch and Methuselah. It angered and saddened them all.

"This will change our operations somewhat, and the need for
our help will be all the more urgent," said Enoch. "We'll have a
little meeting before you leave, Methuselah."

The three men retreated to an area underneath a huge spreading tree. The meeting did not take long, and with resolute looks on their faces, they came back to join the others.

The rest of the day was spent listening to Enoch's teaching. They lounged on blankets on the comfortable, grassy ground in front of the cottage as he taught them about the revelations he received from the heavens. He explained that God is so beyond fallen mankind that to know who He is, He has to reveal Himself through priests and prophets. Knowledge of God and His plans for mankind can only come from Him, otherwise we would have no way of knowing at all.

To the four travelers, it was a wonderful thing to sit at the foot of a man of God and listen to the Word he learned in the heavens. Their hearts burned within them as he spoke.

During the evening repast, the Old Man addressed Kaliyah and Markkah, saying, "My children, there is something I want you to know before you leave from here."

"Of course," they both answered.

"Remember when I told you that I understood why you'd been taught that the serpent was God because you are descendents of Cain?"

"Yes," said Markkah, "and Ishmerai told me that Cain was your oldest son."

"Oh, and that's another thing. From now on, do not mention Ishmerai's name, even among your loved ones or each other. He is in a very dangerous position, and you never know that the wrong ears might hear. In fact, it is best not to talk about your escape at all."

That really put a damper on Markkah, for she was bursting to tell Lelah all about their adventurous journey.

"Now, back to what I wanted you to know," he continued. "There are people of the righteous congregation who will despise you because you are descendants of Cain, not to mention, dear Markkah, you being descended from a fallen Watcher."

"Watchers are not all fallen," Kaliyah added, reflecting on her vague memory of the one who'd come to her rescue from Abishag's assault.

"Indeed, and rest assured that not all the Watchers have lost their original estate. There are many, many more who remain faithful in their duty of watching and guarding mankind, especially the righteous and children.

"But this is what I want you to know and to hold in your hearts. When my Eve gave birth to our firstborn son, our Cain, we believed that the Lord of Spirits had given us the promised Seed. We treated Cain like he was the one who would redeem us. We favored him over and above all the rest of the many children we bore. To our shame and grief, we raised him to think he was better than all the rest. It was not until he murdered his brother, Abel, that we realized our terrible mistake.

"Cain followed the serpent and heeded him and not the Lord God. That did not stop my Eve and me from loving him, though, as we could not stop loving any of our children no matter what they did. This was especially so with my Eve. And she always grieved the ruination of our son and seeing such evil come to our Abel."

"You mean she never forgave herself?" asked Markkah.

"There is no such thing as forgiving yourself, dear Markkah. When we blame ourselves for our sins, the blame is well put. There is only one forgiveness that counts, and it comes from the Lord God. My Eve clung to that forgiveness, as do I."

The Old Man's eyes looked like they were swimming. He blinked, took a breath, and continued. "Markkah, you had asked about where she is now. She died some years ago, from a broken heart over her children and what has become of them. In no small part, it is for her that I have striven these days to help slaves to freedom. And it has not been just for physical freedom but more especially spiritual freedom as well. I want you to know this. It would have made my Eve so very happy to have known you two, descendants of our beloved Cain, who believe the Lord God and His promise."

He hugged them both. There wasn't a dry eye among any of them as they prepared for a night's rest before the final travel day.

PATIENCE

It was late in the afternoon by the time Nekoda arrived at Herathah's palace with Abishag moving stiffly in tow. They had checked in with the security office first and then were escorted to Herathah's official reception hall. Nekoda had been in the palace only twice before, and Abishag never. The massive entry corridor was lined with statues of Herathah and Samjaza's sons, clad in gold and standing nearly twenty cubits high, over twice their actual heights, as if their actual heights weren't already tall enough. As they passed by, Abishag unwillingly shuddered when he spotted Enkara's likeness.

Two of Chief Enkum's men stood rigidly at the enormous, ornately carved double doors to Herathah's reception hall. The escort directed the guards to open the doors. The doors opened to an enormous room paved in marble with a polished hematite inlaid pathway down the center. It culminated in a hematite dais upon which Herathah sat on one of two intricately carved stone chairs, made of red jasper with the motif of a serpent adorning the surrounds on the backs and on the arms. The men followed their escort between marble pillars that were the support for the arched roof far above their heads.

"Your Highness, I have brought the men you are expecting," said the man, bowing nearly in half at the foot of the dais.

Nekoda and Abishag also bowed. They remained in their bowed position until directed to rise by Herathah. She always took her time with that direction; she enjoyed the subservience and humiliation of others. Abishag's broken nose and face, as well as his bound broken ribs, pounded in pain in that lowered position, and he began to feel like he was going to pass out. Just as he started to wobble, the woman finally spoke.

"Rise," she ordered.

Abishag had seen Herathah many times but never up close and personal. He was astounded by her beauty. Her long, luxurious raven hair, some of which was tamed into a braid and the rest of which burst into masses of ringlets, nearly reached the floor as she sat. Her doe eyes were deep pools of brown and her lips deep red and full against golden bronze skin. She was clothed in a brilliant red gown that shimmered in undulating patterns as it curved around her curves. If he hadn't already have been petrified about how she would deal with him, he would have been petrified merely by her beauty. After he stole the glance at her, he immediately looked down to the floor. Herathah counted it the greatest of impudence to be looked in the eye by an inferior, and gratefully, his glance had gone unnoticed. Their escort bowed and excused himself to stand off to the left of the matriarch.

"Nekoda, how pleasant it is to see you again. Although, according to my son, you have unpleasant news to report to me. Please make your report."

"Your Highness," he began, taking care not to look her in the eye, "I have brought this man, Abishag, who is chief of the central and north sector city street cleaners. He was loaned a certain slave from Enkara's household to augment the street cleaner crews for the Great Gather, and he was the last one to have seen her before she went missing on the third day of the Gather. According to his testimony, he had taken her away from her assignment, intending to put her to work doing something else, locked her in a room in a building, and left her there. When he returned, she was gone. He inquired of people in the vicinity, and no one saw anything."

"That's according to him."

"Yes, Your Highness."

"And what has your investigation found?"

"I have found that he has told the truth, as far as I call tell. However, I also discovered that when he first borrowed the slave, he was unusually gentle with her, as opposed to his normal orientation routine."

Abishag was horrified to hear who he thought was a friend producing evidence that did not bode well for him.

Nekoda continued, "And furthermore, I learned that he has also been missing another slave, one who had been a partner of the one he borrowed. This one he had not reported."

Abishag could feel her eyes burning into his forehead, and he unwillingly began to tremble.

"And something that is also disturbing is the identity of the missing borrowed slave. Her name is Kaliyah, and she had formerly been a consort of your son and mother to one of your granddaughters. She was one of the survivors of Enkara's unfortunate incident at his compound last spring. Her daughter had been one who had perished."

A deadly silence ensued as Herathah digested the information. And before she responded, the entrance door opened and Chief Enkum approached. Attention was turned to the newcomer walking tall down the hematite course. He passed in front of the two men, bowed stiffly, and said, "My lady, may I have a word with you in private?"

"Does this pertain to the business at hand?"

"Yes, it does."

Turning to the escort guard on her left, she signaled for him to escort Nekoda and Abishag out of hearing distance. They were led to the far left side of the vast hall and made to wait. Nekoda could see Chief Enkum evidently giving Herathah some kind of information. He noticed that Herathah's complexion was getting redder and redder as the chief spoke. This made him nervous. He thought with a bit of panic, *What information is this that I haven't already found out about?*

At last, Chief Enkum turned and motioned to their escort to return the men back into Herathah's presence. The security men stood on either side of Abishag and Nekoda as they were once again in front of the matriarch. This time, both of them were afraid, as Herathah's countenance seemed to smolder.

"I have just been informed that not only are slaves missing but the supposed dead are actually alive!"

Nekoda especially was dumbfounded. He didn't know what she was talking about.

She continued in that evenly fierce tone, "My granddaughter Lelah and her mother, who had been reported to me by *you*, Nekoda, as being deceased last spring, have turned up alive and well living under the protection of Enoch and Methuselah!"

Nekoda still could find no words.

"And furthermore, this most recent missing slave, Kaliyah, was the one who 'identified' these dead ones, along with her own daughter. I speculate that it is highly probable her daughter is also still alive…and gone."

Her low-voiced, menacing tone changed. She abruptly stood and now screamed at Nekoda and Abishag, "You are both either supremely incompetent or traitors!" Her face was thoroughly red, her eyes bulging, and the veins in her neck pulsed violently against her skin. There was no beauty left.

To chief Enkum and the escort, she loudly ordered, "Take them both away from me! I want them interrogated until you get something useful from them. And I want my granddaughters back!"

The chief and the escort secured the shaking Abishag and thunderstruck Nekoda by the arms and pulled the men out of the royal hall. They could still hear the ranting and raving woman after the doors closed behind them.

Herathah fairly stomped from the reception hall and back into her private quarters, letting out angry, wordless yells along the way. She swept past her servants, who scurried to get out of her way as she passed. They knew to make themselves scarce when she was on a rampage. She swept past her lounge and headed for the incantation room. She entered the windowless room and slammed the door behind her. The room was lit by red glass sconces that lined the circumference of the five-sided, arched-ceilinged room, making her red gown shimmer a ghostly white.

Raging still, she opened the cabinet that housed her tools. She reached for the jar of dragon king's blood and the painting wand and then turned and stomped toward the middle of the room. She was certainly angry about the missing slaves and more so, her missing granddaughters, but she was the most furious about being bested by Enoch and Methuselah. Her hatred for them knew no bounds, and their slave-stealing insults stuck in her craw.

Herathah placed the jar on the floor and knelt to open it. Before she could do so, she was startled by a touch to her right ankle. She froze. The something was like a flickering lick that tasted her ankle and then ascended up her back. She closed her eyes and felt the tingling coursing up and down her spine and through her body as it flicked on her neck and under her ears.

A deep voice sounded—a hiss, almost purring—behind her, saying, "I love it when you're mad."

She opened her eyes and saw the end of great tail circle sensuously around her, just barely grazing her as she still knelt. The hair on the back of her neck stood up; she knew well the presence.

With a hissing in the voice, whispering closely to her ear, it continued, "You're not planning to conjure in your dear husband for help with this, are you?"

She found her voice, "Indeed I am."

"Maybe you should rethink that a bit," it hissed. The coils circling her came closer and assisted in her rising from her kneeling position, as if she'd had any choice about it.

She turned to face the serpent. His enormous head was well over two cubits in length and a cubit and a half wide in a triangular shape. His shimmery scales reflected the red lights of the room, except for the red scales, which appeared white, along with his normally red eyes and forked tongue, also showing white.

When she turned to face him, he flicked her neck again with his tongue and continued the same to her face.

"What is it then that I should rethink?" she questioned, trying to control the energy that still coursed through her, making her tremble.

"Do you really want your husband to know that you've lost control even of your children's households, not to mention the city? Do you really want to disturb him at whatever he's doing right now, only to find that you can't handle things?"

The suggestion about what Samjaza might be doing right now and what she might be interrupting cut her. When she'd decided that she'd borne enough giants, she had told him she wouldn't be doing so anymore. It was by no means completely an altruistic, in-the-interest-of-producing-a-supreme-race idealistic decree that Samjaza had declared the new law about banning all-human reproduction. His decree would legitimatize and even elevate his lust, as well as anyone else's with Watcher blood, to a "noble" purpose.

"I suppose I might not want to call him then," she softly said. "And what do you propose that I should do?"

"Dearest, you know that my advice is sound. You should have thought to ask me first," he chided. "Have I ever failed you?

Wasn't it I who delivered Samjaza as a lovesick puppy to you? Are not your children all dedicated to me?"

"Forgive me, my lord. I should have turned to you immediately."

"Indeed, my dearest, that you should have done," he hissed as he tasted her again with his flickering forked tongue.

"Lord, then how can I turn this around to put me in favorable light with my husband, and how can I exact revenge on Enoch and Methuselah?"

"Finally, you ask," he said with a feigned relieved hiss. He uncoiled the end of his tail from around Herathah and undulated his thick length of serpent body in mesmerizing patterns until he was a giant mass of tight coils mounded in front of her. He lowered his great head down to her again and flicked his tongue up her arm, neck, and right side of her face.

"You were going to send in the troops to storm the territory and take your granddaughters back, weren't you?"

"The thought had crossed my mind."

"That's what I've always admired about you, Herathah, your fire." He knew well how to manipulate her.

"I'm flattered, my lord."

"Now, I must admit, storming the territory does have its style, but let me suggest to you that you can do far greater harm by practicing a bit of patience and using your cleverness, my dear."

"How so?"

"Just the mere presence of your granddaughters in the territory of the 'righteous' will serve to drive a wedge between them, and I have confidence in your ingenuity to make the most of it," he said coolly.

"I can picture that."

"The possibilities are quite good that you will not only regain possession of your granddaughters eventually but also bring devastation to your enemies. Your husband will admire how very resourceful you are."

"I need a little more than resourcefulness to draw my husband back to me, I fear."

"Again, dear Herathah, must I school you in slyness once more?"

The great serpent began to shimmer and transform. Herathah watched in awe as the serpent shape morphed into the form of a white giant with great horns and ferocious face. He bent down to her, holding a clay jar in his hand.

"Take this, and you will bear children no more. You can still eagerly promote the super race, but no one can fault you if your body cannot produce children any longer. You've made your contributions already. It only takes one pinch mixed in tea to rid yourself of any child within."

"This substance would be very useful for our selective breeding program," she said in awe as she stared at the jar in his hand.

"Indeed, and I have already guided the hands of one of your herbalists to produce it as well."

"You truly think of everything," she remarked.

"Now still, do not begrudge your husband's other interests. The supreme race of the god-men must increase. It is as I promised long ago, you shall be as gods."

"Indeed, your promise is true. And, lord, thank you," she said softly as she took the jar from him. Then she added as an afterthought, "My lord, the two men I just interviewed, could you please tell me whether they are involved in the slave smuggling or not?"

"I probably could…but I won't. I'll leave that for you to figure out. I think I might drop by the interrogation room, though, for a little amusement," he said with a wicked smile on his grotesque face.

Before she could say anything more, he vanished, leaving the lingering smell of sulfur in the air.

IN DREAMS

*M*arkkah found herself sitting in a meadow filled with a profusion of brilliant daffodils. She was immersed in the wonder of it and drank in the brilliant color. As if it were the most natural thing in the world, she watched as a kindly old woman materialized in front of her.

Smiling, the old woman spoke, "Markkah, dear one, how wonderful to see you."

"Are you Eve?" Markkah asked.

"Why, uh yes, dear one."

"Are you still sad over what has become of your children?"

"No, I am not, my child. I am made most joyful to see you and others like you who have the blood of the gods in your veins."

"Gods?"

"Indeed. You possess the perfection of the gods."

"I am not a child of the gods," she said, confused about what "Eve" was saying.

"You are mistaken, child. You are descended from the heavens and are truly good."

"But my grandfather is not a god. He is a fallen one, and I'm descended from fallen man too. How then can I be 'good and perfect' when all the way around I've inherited nothing but imperfection and the curse?"

The kindly face of the old woman began to contort into something far from kindly, and she snarled, "Lies! All lies!"

Paralyzing fear seized Markkah as the vivid scene vanished, and she felt an overwhelming weight crushing down on her body. She tried to wake up, willed herself to move, and could not. In her mind she cried out over and over again to her mother for help, but her mother couldn't hear her. Finally, realizing the futility of it, she cried out in her mind to the only One whom she knew would be able to hear. "Lord of Spirits! Help me!" she called.

It felt like a giant hand reached down and pulled the crushing weight off her.

She woke up with a start, her heart pounding hard in her chest. In the dim moonlight filtering through the window, she was relieved to see her mother sleeping peacefully. Over and over she silently thanked the Lord of Spirits for heeding her call for help. But she was still too frightened to go back to sleep, lest the dream return. Instead, she went over in her head all the words both Enoch and the Old Man had spoken over the past several days. As she did so, the fear ebbed away and she was comforted, feeling almost like soft wings surrounded her in protection. And finally she drifted peacefully off into a dreamless sleep.

Herathah held onto the wall as she picked herself up off the floor. She was dazed. She'd been thrown from the middle of the room all the way to the wall to directly underneath one of the red glass lights. She knocked her head on the light as she stood upright. She burned with renewed anger, but at herself as well as her enemies. *I must be more clever and subtle still*, she vowed.

She let out a piercing scream that echoed throughout the room and even into the corridors beyond its closed doors.

TOGETHER

Methuselah, as usual, was mostly silent as he transported the travelers down from the top of Mount Moriah. He half-listened to the excited conversations of his charges but mostly mulled over plans for new and refocused smuggling operations. His heart was heavy as he considered the edict of the Watchers. There would be untold numbers of helpless babies who would be brutally murdered, families torn apart, and more desperate people, both slave and free, who would be in need of escape and refuge. The relatively small operations would necessarily need more willing smugglers and routes. The logistics of the task was daunting.

It felt as if the burden of the world's grief weighed down on his shoulders. He was driven by a passion to rescue lost souls. It would have been far easier to just write off the greater part of humanity and let them reap their deserved damnation. But whenever he considered that path, he was reminded of what the Old Man had said long ago and had repeated many times since:

Our Creator, the Lord God, loved my Eve and me so much that instead of destroying us, He forgave us, and He provided a way and a plan to bring us back to the state of being He intended. It was this statement, more than any other, that defined Methuselah. He knew that he couldn't dishonor this incomprehensible, undeserved love that the Lord God showed to the Old Man and all of his children by letting himself ignore and disregard the plight of lost mankind. After all, he couldn't credit himself with the deed of having been born to Enoch and of the priestly line. He, of all the righteous, if anyone could claim superiority, could claim it because he was in direct line from the Old Man through his son Seth and of all the anointed prophet-priest-kings who had ruled the righteous congregation from the beginning. But his circumstance of birth and family hadn't been his doing. He could just as easily have been born into one of the vast majority of families who did not know the Lord of Spirits at all and who worshiped the serpent. If he had, would there have been someone who would have shown him the truth? And if he'd been a slave, would there have been no one to set him free? And now even more urgently, if he were an unborn baby or an infant, would there have been no one to save his life?

Lost in his thoughts, he was a bit startled when the back of the transport erupted into squeals of delight. Kaliyah and Markkah spotted Melenah and Lelah in the distance, in the middle of the road. Lelah was hopping up and down, and Melenah was standing all by herself, leaning on her walking poles.

"Stop!" Markkah squealed! Before Metu could bring the transport to a full halt, Markkah leapt out the back and tore down the road toward her sister and cousin. As Metu resumed their approach, they all watched with smiles as both sisters ran to greet each other. There was no lack of tears, cheers, or embraces when they all came together. Hanan and Bahman were introduced and received as family. Cain, the wood craftsman, had watched from a few paces away and was called by Melenah to come over and be introduced too.

Metu stood back and took in the reunion. He felt not only responsible for but very protective of the two young Su-galam. He knew that it was not just the Old Man who chose individuals to receive the medallions. He knew that their embracing of these girls would be a problem for a number of the righteous, and now even more so in light of the brutal new decree of the Watchers. But he believed that the election of anyone to be saved was not based on that person's efforts, works, lineage, or bloodline "purity," for there was no person of whatever lineage in the entire world who merited rescue, even in the priestly line.

Metu turned to climb back up onto the front seat of the transport to travel farther down the road when Lelah ran up to him.

"Metu!" she exclaimed with more joy and animation than he could ever recall seeing in the normally reserved Lelah.

She took him by surprise, giving him a sudden hug around his neck and a kiss on his cheek. Just as quickly, she released him, and with tears of joy in her eyes, she said, "Thank you."

Normally in full control of himself, he felt momentarily flustered. Then they all roundly joined in thanking Metu for bringing them to freedom. It was several minutes more before he excused himself from the meal invitation as graciously as he could and turned back to the transport to journey farther down the road to the lower side of the refuge village. Lelah stole a glance as he pulled himself up into the vehicle, and she saw him as if for the first time. How broad and strong were his shoulders and great the unseen burden he carried. She thought to herself, *How could this be? I know giants and am the daughter of a giant, but this mountain man is larger than life itself. The meanness of my Digir-na father makes him seem puny in comparison with this mountain of a man.* And her heart did an unexpected little somersault in her chest. Blushing, she tore her thoughts away from Methuselah and turned her attention back to her beloved sister.

As Metu guided the transport down the road, he chided himself again for not spending the time with Melenah and Lelah that he'd originally intended. He knew they didn't fully understand the way of the righteous, even though they'd heard the Word from Enoch. He was, however, thankful for the tutelage that the Old Man had provided Markkah and Kaliyah, as well as Bahman and Hanan. He hoped that they would share what they'd learned with the two he'd neglected. He had tried to find the time, but always there were other demands on him, and it didn't look like it would get any less demanding anytime soon.

He steered his transport toward Ramuel and Corah's home and, arriving, jumped out of his transport and headed for their front door. As could be expected, their little Kam was out the door and in Metu's arms before either parent was halfway to their visitor.

"We figured you'd show up! I've got a meal all prepared," exclaimed Corah.

"I wish I could stay, but this is urgent," he replied. "Ramuel, we need to convene a meeting. I need you to get the word out." Ramuel responded with, "Yes, sir."

"Well, neither of you is leaving without food in your stomachs," Corah demanded. "If you can't stay to eat, you'll take it with you then."

She reclaimed the reluctant Kam from Metu's arms and quickly returned to the cottage.

"It must be pretty urgent, I presume," said Ramuel.

"Indeed it is. We have just become aware of a new edict issued by Samjaza. It outlaws all-human procreation, and they seek to expand this edict over all the lands. Only the race of god-men will be allowed to survive."

Ramuel was left speechless with his mouth agape at this revelation.

Terse in his order, Metu continued, "I want you to gather the men from the northern sector, as usual, and I'll summon the ones from the south. Use the regular transports. Meet at the cabin mid-morning two days after tomorrow."

Finding his voice, Ramuel answered with an emotion-filled and determined, "Yes, sir."

When Metu climbed back onto the transport and made to leave, Ramuel stopped him with, "You'd better wait until Corah brings you your provisions, or I'll never hear the end of it."

Metu breathed a sigh, not out of perturbation but just to allow himself a moment to relax just a bit from his driving urgency. When Corah returned with a leather pack stuffed full with more than one meal's worth, he sincerely thanked her for her kindness.

As he steered down the road, he realized just how hungry he was, and he thoroughly enjoyed Corah's generous edibles.

⋙   ⋘

Joy overflowed in Melenah and Lelah's cottage. The mother and daughter had spent most of the morning in preparations and were elated to host a feast for their loved ones and newfound friends. The conversation was lively, and Lelah and Markkah were especially absorbed with each other, as all sat down to the meal that included fresh bread baked by Lelah. She had been honing her culinary skills along with her clothes making. Fresh fruits and vegetables, several cheeses, and a savory stew graced the table.

"So you came by a different route here than we did," said Melenah.

"Evidently we did," answered Kaliyah. "I must say it was quite a trip."

"And you're not to talk about it either, I gather," added Lelah.

"And it's going to drive me absolutely crazy not talking about it too! Aahh!" Markkah chimed, to the knowing smiles and chuckles of her traveling partners.

"Well, with that reaction, I'll bet your trip was a bit more interesting than ours. But we need to keep secret and safe those who risked their lives to bring us to freedom. So the discussion of transit here is now forever ended," said Melenah with finality.

"So shall it be," they said in unison.

After a short silence, Cain spoke up with, "I have room at my place for you both, Hanan and Bahman. You are welcome to stay with me until we can get you a new place. We've had such an influx of new people in the past moon time that all the cottages are full."

"Thank you, Cain," said both at the same time.

"So, Bahman, you are a stone worker?"

"Well, that was my occupation as a slave."

"Excellent! You can join the construction team. We've been working on building more homes, and we could use a good stone mason!"

"We would love to have two new ones built here, next to ours!" exclaimed Melenah. "That is, if you'd like," she added, looking at Kaliyah, Hanan, and Bahman.

"If we'd like? We'd love it!" they answered.

"Then it's settled. We can begin building tomorrow!" said Cain.

"I'd enjoy having a hand in the design of it too," said Kaliyah.

"I've got a few ideas too," Melenah added. "I can think of a few improvements that would be really nice, like running water."

"I guess we're really in for it!" remarked Bahman, rolling his eyes.

"Indeed we are!" Cain laughed.

From that point on, the conversation was on planning and construction, not only of their physical homes but also their new lives.

That evening after Cain, Bahman, and Hanan left for Cain's home, Markkah and Lelah bedded down next to each other and whispered late into the night.

Markkah, who hadn't spoken a word to anyone about the horrible dream she'd had the night before, asked Lelah, "Have you had any weird dreams lately?"

"Weird? I don't know if I'd call it weird or not, but as a matter of fact, I did have a really vivid dream last night. It was quite amazing actually."

Markkah was a bit alarmed, but trying not to show it, she prodded Lelah with, "Tell me all about it."

"Well, I dreamed I was in a field of flowers. I think they were marigolds. I saw a road that rose from the field and wound up the side of a cliff that bordered the field."

"Did anyone talk to you?" Markkah asked, getting more concerned.

"No, there was no one with me. But I thought it would be interesting to walk up the road, so I did. I remember thinking how strange that I'd be climbing a mountain. When I reached the top, I saw a little cabin nestled in tall pine trees, just like the ones that surround us here."

"What did you do then?"

"I went to the cabin, opened the door, and walked in."

"What did you find?"

"There was a man standing inside."

"Did you recognize him? Who was he?"

"No, I didn't recognize him because I can't recall his face. But I got the most wonderful feeling."

"He wasn't a Watcher, was he?"

"No. I sensed that he was all-human and he was good. And then just when I wanted to always be with him, the dream ended."

"He didn't say anything at all to you?"

"I don't think so, but I got this feeling that he's the one I'm meant to be with."

"But you don't know who he is?"

"Can you keep a secret?"

"Of course, you know I can."

"I think it might be Metu," Lelah whispered, "but I don't know."

Markkah caught her breath and then said, "Do you like Metu?"

"Well, of course I like Metu. But I'm not like the other girls around here that throw themselves at him. And actually, I never thought about *really* liking him. It might just be him, though. I don't know."

"You're way too young to be thinking about that anyway," remarked Markkah. And then she thought to herself that she *really* liked Ishmerai, but she didn't know whether she'd ever see him again, and she couldn't even speak his name to her own sister. It saddened her, and her heart ached because she missed him. She was glad that Lelah's dream hadn't been as dreadful as hers, but she was still leery of it. She silently assured herself that it was a harmless dream, though, and really not like the one she had had. Finally, the sisters drifted off into peaceful, undisturbed sleep, with Lelah hoping she'd see the man of her dreams and Markkah praying she'd not see the old woman of hers.

THE ROOT

M etu arrived at the cabin in the dead of night, unhooking his oxen and releasing them into a pasture enclosure. Thankful the moonlight had illumined his journey, he trudged up the path to the cabin well before the mists of the morning set in. Opening the door he breathed in the slightly musty odor of cold stone and old wood. He would take no time to build a fire, but headed toward one of the soft beds to lie down. As exhausted as he was after the nearly constant travel, he had difficulty falling sleep. His mind wouldn't shut off. Again he mulled over and measured the words he would speak in the morning, but the final sensation before slumber overcame him was a warmth on his cheek where Lelah had kissed him.

Mid-morning arrived, and the smugglers he'd summoned over the past days began to arrive. It was not long afterward that Ramuel came, along with others in tow. The men were fourteen in number and included his great-great-great-grandfather, Enosh. All of them were relatives, both close and distant.

"Are the rest on their way?" Metu inquired of Ramuel after he took a quick head count of the group.

Ramuel pulled Metu aside and quietly said, "Jaireck, Achaz, Meshek, and Nevo are not coming. They're out."

"I'm sure I don't have to guess why either," said Metu darkly.

"Indeed, and they were especially adamant about it when they heard about the new decree."

"I expect so, considering the grumblings at the last Gather. And after I give my announcements to our group, we shouldn't be surprised if we don't have further defectors."

"I pray not."

"Same here."

Walking back to the cluster of men, Metu called, "Okay, men, let's get started."

He gestured for them to follow him into the cabin. They all filed in, with some claiming the several chairs, others sitting on the two beds, and four still standing, including Ramuel and Methuselah.

Metu began, "Thank you, men, for coming on such short notice. I'm sure you all are aware now of the latest decree by Samjaza for all Watcher-controlled lands and their intent to expand it to the free lands. I know we all share the same revulsion and condemnation of this heinous new law that will result in not only the murder of many thousands of innocent children, but I contend that it is the beginning of the systematic genocide of our entire race."

Heads somberly nodded in agreement.

He continued, "As you have perhaps surmised, this will mark a change in our focus and operations. Up until now, we have striven to reclaim those of our relatives and loved ones taken into slavery by the Watchers. But now, there will be others—not necessarily just slaves and not necessarily just our relatives—who will be trying to escape the rule of the Watchers in order to save their families and children."

One of the men cleared his throat and then nervously interrupted with, "I think I would like to hear, then, your explanation of and reasoning for the recent import into our community of the Su-galam child and her Cainite mother and how our welcoming of this sort countermands Samjaza's decree. In other words, why are we rescuing half-breeds when our new focus is saving the all-human race?"

Heads nodded again in agreement. They all wanted to hear Metu's answer. It was a question that Methuselah had anticipated. He'd gone over and over in his mind for the past two days how he would present their stand. And it was not just merely his opinion and determination but Enoch's, who was the ruling priest of the righteous congregation and the free lands.

He took a deep breath and began, "While we are in a battle now to save lives, it is not just physical lives at stake. This is a spiritual battle as well. Whereas the aim of this new decree is to eliminate the race of all-humans, we will strive to save lives and rescue those marked for slaughter. But what good is a saved life if one is spiritually dead? Up until very recently, those whom we've delivered from slavery have already been of the congregation of the righteous—that is, until the now two Su-galam and their Cainite mothers have come into our midst."

There was the look of surprise and some consternation among the hearers at Metu's revelation of the second Su-galam. But no one commented.

"I know there have been rumblings and questions about the nature of our mission, and because of this, I want to revisit the very root of our purpose here. I ask you a question. Who here deserves the mercy of the Lord of Spirits?"

No one dared raise his hand.

Metu continued, "What indeed is it that guarantees our acceptance by the Lord of Spirits? Is it because we behave better? Is it because of our bloodline? Is it our racial purity? Is it because we are good and the Watchers and their offspring and followers are evil? Do we take pride in our heritage, as if we by our own power were the ones who purposely orchestrated our own parentage and births? Or is it simply because we've earned it or that we are perfect in the sight of the Lord God?"

Metu paused as the men absorbed the rhetorical questions.

"I want to remind you all of a little history lesson. We have all heard and we all know what happened with Cain and Abel. Two brothers of identical heritage and parentage brought offerings to the Lord God. And the Lord had regard for Abel and his offering, but for Cain and his offering, He had no regard. It can be further said that because the Lord God had regard for Abel, He had regard also for his offering, and likewise, because the Lord God had no regard for Cain, He had no regard for his offering either.

"And what was the difference between these brothers? It was the difference between their hearts, which only the Lord of Spirits can see. Cain thought he should be accepted by the Lord of Spirits by virtue of who he was, on his own merits, and his bloodless offering reflected this pride and arrogance. He did this when knowing full well that his parents, after they had sinned, had only been able to stand before the Lord and be accepted by Him after God Himself had clothed them in the skins of animals whose blood had been shed for them. Do not be mistaken, our sin is so severe that death is the price that must be paid. It is far better to put our trust in the One who provides the sacrifice that makes us acceptable than to think we can win acceptance by ourselves. This is the sole reason the Priests of the Lord stand in the gap, making sacrifices to the Lord God, shedding the blood of animals in recognition that the earning of sin is death, and looking forward to the perfect sacrifice that the Lord God Himself will provide. It is *not* that the Lord God delights in the blood of sheep and bulls and goats. He delights in a contrite heart, in the one who looks to Him alone for the remedy of our fallen condition."

Metu paused to survey the men. He really wanted them to understand thoroughly, and he felt within his heart if there was ever anything any of them should understand, it was this.

He continued, "It is easy now to criticize Cain. It is easy for us to sit here and compare ourselves to him and say, 'We are not arrogant like him!' Isn't that in itself arrogance? We should not even take pride in our humility. The corruption we inherited from the Old Man is total. If we go back to what the Lord of Spirits said to the Old Man after he sinned, we remember that only the Curse was pronounced to him. The Lord did not say, 'You sinned this time, but I know you are just a man and if you try very hard to please me in the future, I'll forget this sin.' Nor did He say, 'You can redeem yourself if you make the right sacrifices and do everything I tell you to do from now on.'

"And it is well for us to note that the sin of the Old Man was not that he murdered anyone, or was filled with hatred or pride or consumed with evil thoughts and actions. The Old Man's sin was that he believed the Serpent's lie: *'Did God really say?'* The Old Man doubted the true Word of God. That sin was not just a simple misunderstanding, nor was it a minor 'sin.' It was and is the most major of sins that opens the door to every other sin, including disbelief, pride, the worship of creation over the Creator, idolatry, lust, envy, hatred, thievery, and even murder.

"Rather, we should believe exactly and only what the Lord said. The *only* hope that the Lord of Spirits gave the Old Man was the curse against the Serpent. He promised to send the Seed of the woman to crush the Serpent's head. That Promise is our hope and nothing else. If we dare to regard ourselves as 'the righteous,' it should only be because we follow the example of Abel. Abel, in humility, knew that he did not deserve the Lord's favor and neither could he earn that favor, but instead relied on God's mercy by faith in the Promise. Herein, Abel was counted as righteous by the Lord. If we hold to the Promise like Abel, it is the Lord God who counts us as righteous. Cain showed contempt of the Promise when he believed he could please the Lord all on his own."

He paused, and with piercing eyes surveyed each man in turn. With finality, he said, "Therefore, let us neither despise the Grace of God, nor His Promise."

Methuselah's voice reached a powerful crescendo in that statement, not so much with volume as with steeled conviction. One could have heard a pin drop in the cabin as the men absorbed the content. Those who had thought before to offer objections to the direction they thought the leadership was heading saw a new perspective. They all then waited expectantly for Metu to lay out their instructions.

"It is imperative from now on that all whom the Lord of Spirits calls into our hands to be delivered to freedom and safety be also instructed in the teaching of the Promise along the way. We can no longer assume that they know, understand, or have even heard of the Promise. Our aim is that they be free indeed. So you see, pedigree is of no consequence to any part of our operation at all.

"The word of this must be spread to all our smugglers, and I'm relying on you to spread the directive. If you all begin immediately to inform your contacts, we should have the word disseminated to the farthest lands within a year. If we lose smugglers because they disagree with the directive, then we shall strive to find other smugglers. And, Ramuel, I'm assigning you to the organization of instruction and further teaching of those who arrive at the refuge."

Methuselah scrutinized the men's faces and asked, "Does anyone have any objection to this directive?"

Together, they all said, "No objection!"

With raised hands, Metu solemnly said, "Praise to the Name above all names. May the Lord of Spirits have mercy upon us all."

As one, those sitting rose to their feet, and the boom of their voices seemed to vibrate the very foundation of the small building as they said in unison, "So shall it be."

GOD-MEN

As Abishag limped around on his rounds, he couldn't help but notice the new offices around the city. Samjaza's decree had spawned the Department of Family Protection and Development, the government agency formed to carry out Samjaza's directive, and certain storefronts throughout the city had been commandeered to house the new neighborhood DFPD offices. The enforcement was two-pronged: registration/marking and "implementation." Much like prior census takers before—and indeed with some of the same census workers themselves—the enforcement teams first systematically distributed notices to each household with orders to report on a specific day to their respective local office for registration. But this was far more than just a census.

With the initial phase, the outcome was the racial identification and certification of each person and the administration of the appropriate brand seared onto the back of his or her right hand, adults and children alike. And while this first phase was underway, the outer city that had been erected to house the temporary influx of pilgrims from all over Imin-sar for the past Great Gather was being converted to several other uses. One of these conversions was a massive compound intended to house breeding facilities. Upon Herathah's orders, the compound was called *Digir-na Garden*, or garden of the god-men.

Abishag rubbed his sore right hand, his ego chafing with each prickle of pain from his new brand, a mark that looked like two intersecting straight lines with a circle next to it. It was the mark of an all-human undesirable. His was just one level above the double circle of an all-human forbidden. The two higher levels, all-human desirables and the most-preferred Watchen, were marked with the single mark of two intersecting lines for the first and a tattooed five-pointed star for the latter. The only ones of whom the marks were not required were the Digir-na and their descendents.

In the determination of who fit into what category, several factors were considered. Evidence of lineage was primary, physical characteristics were second, and thirdly, demeanor or station. Digir-na were obvious: great size, larger eyes, somewhat elongated heads, and sometimes the double rows of teeth. They were the giants and their lineage unquestioned. The giants who married or consorted with other giants produced children like themselves whose lineage was also obvious.

The Su-galam, children of giants and all-humans, were a bit less obvious, their height noticeably greater than typical all-humans but nowhere nearly as tall as their Digir-na parents. These seemed to be a combination of the better traits of both lineages, with facial features being softer of brow and a more refined prominence of chin than all-humans and the more delicate-appearing features of the ethereal "god" grandfathers made more solid and vital by the strong bones and broadness of the all-human contribution. Their skin colors exhibited more variety than either of the pure strains, with variations of paler skin than the swarthy browns of the all-humans. Whereas all-humans exhibited only black, brown, or red hair, the "gods" had brilliant blond or chestnut hair. Hair color in the descendants was subsequently more variable also in the combination. But still, to the third generation, none of the descendents had the blue eyes of some of the "gods," or some of the children of both Digir-na parents, although many had the slight slanting of the eyes.

Of demeanor and station, those of the select Watchen class were deemed desirable even if their particular physical features were not necessarily the most select. Their devotion to and mystical education by the Nephilim rendered them suitable for breeding. Although in truth, the Nephilim selected only the most beautiful of them, and their female daughters were equally as shallow with any Watchen men they deemed worthy of attention.

Of the rest of humanity, their breeding quality was classified by height, facial features, strength, intelligence, and attitude. This applied to freemen and slaves alike. The shorter and coarser of brow, the less favorable was the classification. Any defect of form or feature and the determination that the person was intellectually inferior automatically classified the person as "all-human forbidden." Of course, much of the classification was subjective evaluation at best. A number of the wealthier who should have fit into the lower categories were able to bribe their evaluators into the higher ones, and those with no means to do so were sometimes relegated to a lower category merely by the irritation or whim of the evaluator.

Whatever the determination ultimately was, the mark made upon each person was a permanent one and the distinction between the marks were such that they could not be altered to become the mark of a higher rank.

Abishag's anger smoldered as he conducted his regular supervisory duties. It gnawed at his innards when he was not barking orders or lashing out at his underlings. More than ever before, the street-cleaning slaves walked on eggshells when they interacted with him. There was perhaps no one he didn't hate, but at the top of his list were Kaliyah and Hanan, seconded by Herathah and her henchmen. He even hated his former friend Nekoda, who had received the mark of an all-human desirable. They'd been branded at the same time, and Nekoda had ridiculed him when he'd received his marking. No doubt Nekoda's large frame and well-muscled physique had earned him the more respectable ranking. Blaming Abishag for his troubles, Nekoda delighted in the insult that was added to Abishag's injuries at the hands of the interrogators.

Abishag was absolutely bent on finding the person or persons who had helped the women escape. The connection had to be someone close; he could feel it in his bones. It was now his single-minded mission to unearth the rebels and traitors, and his delight was picturing in his mind what he would do with them; it would make even Herathah's torture-henchmen cringe. There was a common denominator, though, between the escape of his two wenches and the ones who escaped from Enkara's compound, and he was going to find it.

BOOK 2

YEAR 721 A.C.

RESIST!

A collective hush swept the crowd huddling close together in the cave that was rimmed and softly lit with amber lights. Movement was spotted at the westernmost wall, with the disturbance progressing to the dais slightly elevated at the northernmost point of the subterranean chamber. The air was heavy and dank with the odor of perspiration and anticipation.

As the movement neared the front, a few people said, "Resist! Resist!" The chant spread in volume and urgency as the man they'd awaited appeared. It changed from "Resist" to "Caleb, Caleb" again and again until he raised his hands, and they all fell silent.

"Fellow challengers, righteous of God, the trial has come to us, to our generation. If we shy from this battle, we will be the last of our generation, and humanity as we know it and as the Lord of Spirits created it, will vanish. This abomination of 'god-men' is the perversion of Creation. It is altogether evil, and we must act, oppose, fight, and resist!"

Again, those gathered began to chant louder and louder, "Resist! Resist!" adding to the chant a thundering collective stomp of their feet on the cold, dank cave floor.

The clamor subsided as Caleb began again, his voice resonating clearly off the ceiling and to the farthest reaches of the chamber. "We had formerly been willing to oppose this evil by merely living our righteousness, by helping and delivering those sold into slavery, by waiting and longing for the promised Seed, the Deliverer, to come to our aid. We have of late been able to minimize the advances of the enemy, but the evil has only grown stronger, and our meager defenses and our mere prayers and petitions have relegated us to the status of refugees and our being marked for extinction by these so-called 'god-men.' This is not the time to wait for a champion, a deliverer, to rescue us. This is the time for *us* to act. Deliverance is in our own hands, and by the strength of the Lord of Spirits, our Creator, in whose image we were made, we will prevail."

A diminutive figure slipped into the rear of the chamber as the crowd's attention was riveted on the speaker. Her stature prevented her from seeing Caleb as he spoke, even though he was positioned on the dais. This, however, did not prevent her from hearing.

"Our enemy would have us believe that they are improving the lot of humanity, that they are reforming humanity into a new and greater existence of unlimited potential and power, that humanity is upgraded by mingling with the blood of the 'gods.'"

The speech was punctuated by the hisses and boos of the audience. And Hulda thought to herself, *Such amazing ignorance this is!* She relished in her task of spy, and she delighted that these unenlightened souls were destined to fail so miserably. Not to mention, she was being compensated handsomely for her intelligence, more than making up for her losses in her fabric trade. She listened attentively for any details that would further improve her standing with her benefactress.

"From the Creation, has any benefit or progress ever been achieved by the human race by submission to organized and calculated violence?[7] Have we seen an improved humanity through the interference of the Watchers? Their way of life they claim is superior, their great cities and monuments, all have been built upon the backs of slaves, including many of you who had been stolen from your villages, lands, homes, and your families slain and your children seduced.

"We did not make this war. We did not seek it. We did all we could to avoid it. We did too much to avoid it. We went so far at times in trying to avoid it as to be almost destroyed by it.[8] Those of you delivered out of slavery would have been better served by being a part of a fierce resistance that would have prevented your enslavement in the first place. But we cannot look back, and that dangerous corner has been turned, and with every month and every year that passes we shall confront the evil-doers with weapons as plentiful, as sharp, and as destructive as those with which they have sought to establish their hateful domination."[9]

Hulda choked back a derisive exclamation and then joined in with the crowd as the mass cheered with even more exuberance and stomping of feet, "Resist! Resist!"

After many moments, holding his arms in the air to signal silence, Caleb then continued with, "Now for these past three years, an even greater evil than slavery and loss of freedom is upon us. Human babies are being murdered, families torn apart, the so-called weak and inferior are destroyed, and all of humanity as designed and created by the Lord of Spirits is marked for extermination. Many of you here had not been subjected to slavery but rather to a breeding program founded upon an abomination and the lasciviousness of so-called gods, who are no more than created beings who have left their assigned station, their own realm, and proscribed duties. The protectors became perverse predators."

After a pause, he then continued, "But not all have left their station. There are many more that are on our side, who watch over our affairs without taking our women and who remain loyal to the Lord of Spirits. They are our partners in this struggle…"

Again Hulda stifled a sneer, thinking, *Some protectors they are!* As Caleb continued speaking, her mind drifted off into images of the cities with their opulence and the great buildings and monuments built under the direction of the Watchers, who, according to these ignorant farmers, were the "fallen ones." *What have their Watchers done for them?*

Her thoughts returned to her surroundings as the mass shouted and stomped their final rounds of "Resist, resist," and "Caleb, Caleb!" She then began to wend her way through the crowd toward the wall to the west where the speaker was returning. Her nose was assaulted anew as she squeezed between the tightly packed gatherers, armpit-high to many of them. Her stature and physical appearance were a guarantee of her acceptance into this uncouth society as one who would be least suspected of collusion with the enemy. *Huh*, she thought, *if they only knew who my children are and who I count as friends! This ignorant lot should be exterminated!*

"Hulda! Good, you're here!" cried the familiar voice.

"Madam Kahjeera! At your service!" she replied as she neared her intended destination.

"And your service we need indeed! Come closer. We have need of the strongest fabrics you can acquire and, of course, at the best prices we can get."

"Of course! But I will need to get the specifications and what the fabrics will be used for." Hulda had already ingratiated herself with the ruling elite of the rebel humans by supplying the best prices for the highest-quality fabrics needed by the burgeoning army. She'd beaten all the other competitors primarily because she was aided and subsidized liberally by Herathah. Her great prices were mistaken for patriotism and loyalty.

"Astonishingly to us all, we've had word that Metu and the other pacifists are bringing new animals to us. They're making a token at supporting us, and this is at least a step forward for them."

"Here, here!" exclaimed those within Kahjeera's conversation.

Hulda's ears especially took in the news; another valuable tidbit of information to pass on.

"If that 'anointed' man and his fathers would get rid of the Cainites and abominations they've welcomed into their midst, they might see fewer of their followers leave," Kahjeera sneered.

Another chimed in, "And maybe we'd actually come back to their gathers!"

"Fat chance at that! Who needs to hear the prattling of an old man who spends most of his time in dreams and visions? Enoch isn't connected with what's going on in the world," said another.

"And who knows what son of man in our own midst might be that Deliverer who will lead us to victory and save us from our enemy," said Kahjeera softly.

Hulda could hear the name of Caleb whispered among those within hearing, and she noted that Kahjeera also heard and gave a hint of a smile and slight nod of her head.

"Indeed," Hulda said. Then she sidled up close to Kahjeera and said softly, "I have an idea that you might be interested in," and she added in a whisper, "In private."

"I'd love to hear it, Hulda," Kahjeera replied. She nodded to the others and then took Hulda by the arm and guided her away to a little alcove off the main room.

"Dear loyal friend, what is it you have on your mind?"

"It just dawned on me that Metu's peace offering might be put to good use."

"And how is that? We can't reconcile unless he and the sons of Seth renounced their acceptance of the half-breeds and Cainites in their midst."

"So true! But perhaps if we *appear* to reconcile we might gain access to the abominations and be able to 'return' them to their rightful place."

"The whole of our assembly won't go along with that, even if it were with the intent of purging the impurities from the human congregation."

"I thought of that too, but then perhaps if the overtures were from certain key leaders only, which of course includes you, the rest wouldn't even know."

"True, true." Kahjeera mulled the possibilities in her mind.

"And who better than you, who almost single-handedly created this whole movement, to also be the one to make the 'reconciliation'?"

Kahjeera flipped her long hair back over her shoulder, basking in the recognition she knew she deserved, and her mind began working the possible scenarios. "Dear Hulda, didn't you tell me you still have connections in Eriduch where you buy fabrics?"

"Yes, I do. Maybe it's not so unfortunate that I still get fabrics from them, even though they despise me," Hulda replied as she uncovered the hand that bore the brand of an undesirable." It had been small insult to her to submit to the mark, knowing she wasn't interested in having any more children anyhow. She knew who her children were and their exalted positions. Furthermore, it cemented her acceptance into the resistance.

"And we still get clothing made in Enoch's refuge village, much undoubtedly made by the abominations themselves," Kahjeera mused. "Meet me on the morrow at sunup."

"Yes, ma'am!" Hulda said. With a smile and an ingratiating bow, she turned to leave, spending her big payoff in her mind.

THE BREACH

L ife in the refuge village went on for the cousins and sisters, with Melenah and Kaliyah absorbed more into normalcy by their relationships with the men they had come to love. In the middle of their third year of residence there, the weddings were celebrated on the mountaintop, with Enoch presiding with a joyful sacrifice. Melenah and Cain, and Kaliyah and Bahman wed on the same day. And Kaliyah now asked to be called "Aliyah," or "ascender," because she felt she had truly been brought up and out of the depths. Her new name echoed the feelings of them all.

But as the joy of that day was unparalleled in the lives of those who'd once been slaves, there was in that afternoon an ill wind that arose. It came soughing through the trees at first unnoticed and then became harsh and urgent, twisting gnarled branches in woe-laden gusts. The sky seemed to darken prematurely that day; a thickness in the heavens brought shadows early to the mountain. The newlyweds wouldn't have noticed if it had gotten pitch black. They would have just assumed the arrival of midnight and counted it time of being together.

Enoch and Edna felt the foreboding and exchanged concerned but subtle looks between each other as the festivities and music continued. Two others experienced the chill not caused by a temperature change, Lelah and Markkah. Already they sensed a subtle change in newcomers to the refuge village, and not nearly as many people were staying to make it their permanent home as had happened before.

And noticeably absent from the celebration was Metu. At least Lelah felt his absence more acutely than perhaps anyone else, or maybe she just thought she missed him more than anyone there. As thunder rolled in the distance, ignored by most, her hair twisted across her face as the evening air grew chill. She and her sister gazed toward the west. He'd been gone for over three years now, and she did not know when he'd come back. Only bits and pieces of information about his whereabouts and activities floated back with the refugees who'd come through.

Markkah was more somber than usual. While both girls were happy for their mothers, they each felt something missing for themselves. Markkah had grown more introspective and contemplative and still had not shared with Lelah her feelings for her beloved Ishmerai—at least that is what she called him in her mind. It was as if her love was the more powerful for the secret that it remained. And equally, except for the earlier confession to Markkah about her feelings for Metu, Lelah also kept her private longings to herself and kept hidden the anger that smoldered just under the surface. But the ill wind was more than their longings and more than just the unmistakable feeling that there were increasingly more people who felt they didn't belong. The wind was a portent of an evil that was almost tangible. The two young girls moved closer to each other, shoulder to shoulder, and leaned their heads together. They had each other, and now with their mother's marriages, they each knew they would lean on each other now all the more.

Lelah and Markkah both stood on their front stoop, waving good-bye to Corah and her fast-growing little son. Their cart was full of newly made clothing. The girls' sewing business was flourishing, although regrettably to them, the items were more utilitarian than stylish. Their new stepfathers had built a separate cottage for the girls that stood between their parents' homes, and it was made with an added large room that they used for their sewing shop. The girls had requested it and were thrilled with their idyllic abode and newfound independence.

As they waved, Markkah spotted Bahman and Cain in the distance as they hauled more wood into the meadow where they were building a large, fenced enclosure. "I wonder what kind of animals are to be brought here."

"I wish Corah had known, because she surely would have told us more," replied Lelah.

Markkah noticed that Lelah had been more animated and much less solemn and taciturn ever since they'd heard that Metu would be arriving soon, and with a cargo that included more than refugees. Less and less they had looked forward to new faces. They both had received harsh looks from those who were escaping the breeding program of the god-men, but to see Metu after so long a time was indeed a thing to look forward to.

"I can't wait to see what these animals are," said Markkah as they continued to watch their new stepfathers building the final row of fencing. "They must be very special."

"I'm sure they must be. I can't wait to see them," Lelah said, even though she really wasn't interested at all in the animals, just the one who was to bring them. She added, "I must get Metu's gift out so I can give it to him right away. There's no telling how long he'll spend here, so I want to make sure he gets it first thing."

"You did such a beautiful job on it, Lelah. I'm envious of how you can sew skins so well now. I just don't have the strength in my hands like you," said Markkah as she followed Lelah back into their abode.

"Well, it took nearly a full year to complete it. And here I was worried that it wouldn't be done by the time Metu came back. I didn't think he would be gone this long." She thought, *And Metu has been gone so long that I'm no longer a girl. I'm a woman now*, as she glanced down to survey her curvier figure.

Lelah climbed up the wooden ladder to their storage loft and walked, ducking slightly, over to a carved chest. She knelt down and lifted the lid. Markkah joined her in front of the chest.

"Here, take these," Lelah said to Markkah, handing over the soft, brown, silk pullover top with long sleeves and the sturdier tightly woven silk leggings.

"This is going to take two trips," commented Markkah as Lelah reached back into the chest to pull out the much bulkier over-tunic.

"Not unless you can take this too. Just don't trip going down the ladder. I'll get the rest."

After Markkah eased herself, arms full, down to the lower level, Lelah balanced the unwieldy leather plates, along with the rest of the outfit, in her arms and followed.

"Let's get this on the form," said Lelah as she reached the bottom of the ladder, although Markkah was already in their workroom preparing the items she'd brought down.

Markkah had put her cargo down and was positioning the wooden form. They had several forms of different sizes that Cain had crafted for their clothes making. Constructed out of a lightweight wood, the forms were covered with a batting that allowed them to sink pins in as needed.

"I can't wait to see what Metu thinks of this!" said Markkah.

"For sure! I think he thought that we'd make the mahkur-tidnum skin into a rug or something."

"Not hardly! He surely didn't know about your leather skills."

"Well, I didn't have those skills then, you know."

"Very true, but now I don't think there is anyone better than you."

"I wouldn't go that far." Lelah blushed. "And if we didn't have such a wonderful tanner here, this skin would not have been nearly as easy to work with."

Markkah rubbed her hand over the leather leggings, marveling at the butter-soft feel, and added, "It is remarkable how soft and malleable this is. I think he said it was brain-tanned."

"Disgusting as it is, that's right."

The young women busied themselves with dressing the form. First were the silk underthings and then the leather leggings and shirt.

"Here, Markkah, help me get these plates inserted," said Lelah. These needed to be placed before they could get the outer tunic onto the form. They slipped the various leather plates into large pouches on the inner sections of the tunic. The plates had been meticulously constructed by the tanner. Multiple very thin layers of rawhide, with silk in between, had been pounded and sealed together with a special resin. Each thin plate was shaped to conform roughly to Metu's body contours. Together within the tunic, they made for armor far lighter than metal, but just as strong or even stronger. Although Metu hadn't been anywhere around, Bahman, who was nearly the same size as Metu, had volunteered to be the model.

At last assembled, they draped the tunic onto the dressed form. For the final touches, they fastened the belt, putting the armored dart holder just inside the left breast section and attaching to the belt the rolled-up pouch that carried the armor when it was not in the tunic. Since the dress form did not have a head, they attached the armored hat to another section of the leather belt.

After Lelah positioned the boots at the bottom of the form, they both stepped back to survey their handiwork. The outer tunic's leather had been tanned on the inside with the big cat's supple fur remaining on the outer. The longish fur had a yellow cream-colored base with a deep-brown pattern of wide stripes. Lelah had positioned the stripes to angle upward and outward from the middle of chest and upward to the shoulders. The same V shape of the stripes was repeated in the piecing of the back portion of the tunic top. It gave the illusion of wider shoulders, which in Metu's case, who already had very broad and muscled shoulders, would be positively massive. The boots likewise were fur covered, reaching up over the calves to the knees.

"Now that's impressive!" said Markkah.

"Not as impressive as when it's on Metu!" In her mind's eye, Lelah pictured her beloved in place of the dress form. She sucked in her breath at the thought.

They stood silently for several moments, absorbed in their own thoughts. Then whispering, Markkah broke it with, "Maybe Ishmerai will be with Metu."

Lelah was stunned. After another pause, she whispered too, "So Ishmerai is his name?"

Markkah had prayed so hard that Ishmerai would be with Metu that she truly believed he would be arriving too. She'd convinced herself that he was now out of harm's way. "Well, Ishmerai is his real name, but he is known in Eriduch as maggot."

Silence ensued for a few more moments until Lelah began to giggle. Through the giggles, she managed to say, "I can see why you're attracted to him."

Despite herself, Markkah giggled too. The giggles broke into outright laughter as the sisters then hugged each other. Their laughter was cathartic, releasing the tension that great anticipation can build. After laughing to the point of tears, the girls linked arms and retired to their living area. Sitting next to each other, Markkah told Lelah about Ishmerai. Her descriptions and feelings fairly gushed out of her, having been pent up and held secret for so long a time. Lelah listened, asked questions, and took in all that Markkah said, and she grew excited too, to meet this remarkable love of her sister's. They talked late into the night before finally crawling into their beds, exhausted.

Lelah found herself in the familiar field of flowers. Upon realization of where she was, she turned and fairly ran without touching the ground up the hillside road to the forest above. Since the first time she'd dreamed this dream, she'd returned to it several times over the past three years. She couldn't will herself into having the dream, even though if she could have, she would have. She knew who she'd meet with and talk. Within the dream, she knew she was dreaming, and even in the midst of it wondered whether Metu was also having the same dreams. She wondered when he came back if he would give any indication that he'd communicated with her this way over the years. It was a foolish hope, held both within and without of the dreams, but these things went through her mind as she approached the figure walking down a wooded path toward a cabin.

"Metu!"

Turning, the figure said, "Darling."

They walked hand in hand down the path, first without saying anything else. Then Lelah broke the silence. "I am so glad you're coming back soon."

"It will be good to come back."

"Will Ishmerai be coming back with you? Is he out of Eriduch now?"

"Ishmerai."

"Yes, Markkah's Ishmerai, you know, the maggot." She couldn't help but snicker gleefully at the thought of Markkah in love with a "maggot."

"Well, no, not yet. But I'm sure that Markkah will be seeing her maggot quite soon." The figure of Metu smiled. Lelah turned to look at her dream Metu, saw the smile, and then just before the dream faded away, she thought she caught something evil in that smile. It gave her a chill down her spine.

Lelah awoke with a start. It was the middle of the night, and she lay in a cold sweat on her bed with her heart pounding, trying to remember what it was that disturbed her. She knew she'd just had the dream but wasn't exactly sure what all had transpired. Usually, she would revel in the sweet recollection of every part of the dream, but this time it was foggy. She was shaken and couldn't piece together why.

"Aha!" breathed Herathah. The exclamation would have been a shout if she'd had the energy. It would take several minutes for her to gather her strength. Dream world was always physically taxing and she utilized it sparingly. She remained seated on the floor of her incantation room, cradling her head in her hands. It took all her willpower to take the time to recoup. *Unbelievable! Could it really be? Metu's little brother in the city all this time! And now I know what name he goes by! Thank you, Lelah! Listening to your silly prattle up until now has now been worth all the tedium.*

Finally recovered, Herathah put her hands on the floor and pushed herself up into a standing position. Once up, she fairly ran to the door and swung it open, the color of her flowing gown changing from an eerie white to red with the onslaught of the regular light from the hallway. She startled her personal aide, who had fallen asleep sitting outside the door. "Enkum! I need Enkum!" she shouted, even though her aide was right there. "I want my security chief now! Don't just sit there with your mouth open, fool! Run! Bring Enkum to my chambers now. I don't care where he is or what he's doing."

Berikah bolted to attention, nodded in assent, and then with a crisp, "Yes, ma'am," rushed off to obey Herathah's urgent order. Herathah turned in the other direction, and with purposeful steps and a wicked smile on her face, she headed down the hall to her personal chambers to await the meeting.

GIFTS

"They're here! They're here!"

The girls rushed to their front porch, and nearby, their mothers to theirs. It was Hanan who had sounded the call. She'd spotted the front part of the herd coming up the road as she had come out of the wool barn. She hastily dropped an armful of freshly shorn wool. The men ran for the newly finished gates of the large fenced enclosure and swung the double gates open for a funnel to herd the animals in.

Lelah and Markkah hurried down the path. Before they could see the beasts coming up the road, they heard them: a rhythmic sound of hoofs pounding the earth and snorts and whinnies filling the air. Closer to the wool barn and around the stand of trees, the girls caught sight of the herd. They climbed up and stood on a berm, well out of the way of the advancing animals, to watch the progression.

The animals were magnificent: fur-covered and hooved, similar to oxen but with the hoof in one piece instead of split.

These animals were taller, with more graceful features of form and movement and flowing manes and tails and of all sorts of colors and patterns.

"They're beautiful!" shouted Markkah over the din of the trotting beasts. "I think these are the animals we've heard about from the far north and east! Are not they called horses?"

"I believe they are." While certainly impressed by the beauty of the beasts, Lelah had her eyes peeled for Metu. Far back nearer the rear of the herd, she spotted several men astride the backs of some of the animals. She tried to distinguish their faces.

Likewise, Markkah turned her attention to the riders, believing with all her heart that she'd see Ishmerai among them. Neither young women were the overly chatty, excitable types; they were more inclined to retreat into silence, holding their emotions in check and relishing inwardly the fulfillment of long anticipation.

As the riders came closer, neither Markkah nor Lelah could make out any faces they recognized. They watched as the herd was funneled in through the gates. There must have been nearly two hundred horses in the drive, and it was not until the very tail of the herd that Lelah spotted Metu, along with another man she didn't recognize.

"Markkah, is that Ishmerai?"

"I can't tell just yet," she said, hoping beyond hope. After straining to see and holding her breath, she felt crushed. "No, I don't see him."

"Look there! I see Corah's husband, Ramuel. He's a rider!"

From their vantage point, they watched as the whole herd was finally ushered into the enclosure. With the last animal in, Bahman and Cain closed the gates. The riders, eight in all, began to dismount their horses, tying the reins to the fence posts. Up from the refuge village, the main street through which they'd just driven the animals, a number of people followed. A crowd began to grow, surrounding Metu and the riders.

Lelah and Markkah climbed down from their perch and headed for the wool barn. Looking behind them, Markkah turned to see her mother and aunt heading in the same direction. "Wait, Lelah."

The girls stopped to let their mothers catch up, and then they continued together down the path to the barn. Hanan appeared from among the crowd and ran up to meet the women. Everyone was all smiles, and the excitement was contagious.

All were talking at once. Lelah caught something about there being a feast in three days up on the mountain with Enoch. Surely a thanksgiving celebration it would be. The five women stood together, a bit off from the crowd around Metu and the riders. Lelah could see Metu, who was almost a head taller than anyone else in the crowd, except Bahman. As she watched him answering questions and responding to the eager entourage, he caught her looking at him. Their eyes held for longer than a moment until Lelah flushed and hurriedly looked away. She felt flustered and terribly self-conscious. She wasn't sure what she read in Metu's eyes, but she suddenly felt like running back to her cabin.

So she wouldn't put action to her impulse, she turned to the conversation occurring in the midst of her small family group. After several moments, she was startled to hear Metu's voice right behind her.

"How have you all been these past two years?" Metu noticed how Lelah jumped when he spoke.

Melenah retorted with, "Two years! It's been almost three full years since you were here!" Melenah walked to Metu, reached up, and gave him a warm welcome-home hug, almost knocking him in the head with a walking pole in the process.

"Indeed, I suppose that I have been gone that long." He returned her hug and patted her gently on the back.

Hanan spoke up, "Please, Metu, we have prepared a meal for you this evening, and lodging so you'll be refreshed for your journey to your father tomorrow. The other family groups will be hosting your riders also this evening."

"I would be honored," he sincerely accepted. "I shall take care of my horse, see that my men are settled, and then I will come."

Metu did not look at Lelah in the eyes again since that first meeting of their eyes. He was a bit taken aback by Lelah's looks. His memory of her had been the image of a tall, gangly youngster with a pretty face. He'd known she would be older but had not been prepared to see that she had become an outstandingly beautiful woman, dressed in a flowing deep-blue dress that revealed curves that had not existed that last time he'd seen her. It unsettled him somewhat, but not enough to decline the invitation from her family circle.

After some more small talk, he returned to assure that each of his riders had a place to eat and sleep that night. The townfolk had been prepared well for their arrival, and all were excited to host their guests and learn in better detail of the goings-on in the far reaches of the world.

The five women hurriedly headed to Hanan's little cabin, which stood to the far right of their little cabin compound. Hanan was hosting the meal and putting Metu up for the night in her spare room. All the women had helped to prepare the meal, including Corah, who arrived shortly after they got to Hanan's.

Markkah was especially quiet during the preparations. Only Lelah knew the reason for her lack of enthusiasm. She ached for her sister's pain and felt just a bit guilty about being able to see Metu in person again. The other women excitedly chatted while they worked, seeming not to notice the reticence exhibited by the two younger women.

Finally, the men arrived, and the joyous noise level in the home increased again. Around the meal table, mostly the women listened to the men discuss the world and latest events and heard about the newest monuments. Absent from the conversation was any discussion of events that could spoil the meal. That would wait for later. Suddenly, Bahman turned to Lelah, making her swallow her mouthful of food a bit prematurely. "Lelah, when are you going to show Metu that suit you made for him?"

Gulping as gracefully as she could and blushing a rich red, she replied, "Um, I could show him right after the meal, I suppose."

All at the table expressed agreement to the after-dinner activity, and Lelah felt even more unglamorous and awkward. She kept her attention riveted mostly on her food and her sister and steadfastly avoided looking at Metu.

After the meal and before the light of the day began to fade, the group made their way to Lelah and Markkah's cabin and shop. As they entered the sewing shop, Bahman gestured to the outfit that dressed the form standing in the center of room. Metu was stunned. He'd forgotten about the long-fanged tiger he'd killed and the pelt he'd given to the girls. He certainly hadn't expected what he saw before his eyes. Metu mostly hadn't given much thought to the clothes he wore. He just needed serviceable.

Lelah's heart was pounding. *What if he doesn't like it? What if he thinks it's too fancy or not good enough? Will he think I'm silly to have made this?* The self-doubt increased with every moment that Metu said nothing.

After standing still, staring for several moments, Metu then walked to the suit for a closer inspection. After several more moments of silence, Metu finally spoke as he felt the fur on the right sleeve. "This is amazing," he breathed, and then he repeated more loudly, "This is absolutely amazing."

Lelah, who had been biting her lower lip, breathed a sigh of relief.

Markkah pushed Lelah toward the dress form, saying, "Lelah, show Metu the armor and the dart holder.

At first Lelah was embarrassed about showing Metu the special features of the outfit she'd made, but then as she showed him, part by part, she forgot her embarrassment. She slipped out an armor plate from the tunic and described the process for making it and showed the dart holder and the tote bag for the armor when not in use. When she showed him the silk undergarments, she told that they would help to make the outfit "breathe." His close proximity animated her.

Likewise, Metu was affected by the close proximity of Lelah while she showed him the details of the clothes she made him. He smelled the sweet scent of her long, thick hair that was bound in a twist that flowed down her back. He was as amazed at her meticulous and beautiful handiwork as much as her incomparable beauty. This was not what he'd expected he'd find.

"Thank you, Lelah. I can't find the words to thank you enough. This is amazing."

"Try it on, Metu! Put it on!" sounded in the room.

"I will." It didn't take much coaxing for Metu to agree. The elder women herded the younger women out of the room, shutting the door behind them. The men remained while Metu exchanged his well-worn woolens for the new suit. Through the door they could hear the men commenting on the armored plates and various other aspects of the outfit.

After several minutes, the door opened and out stepped Metu. Lelah noted that he had a rare broad smile across his face. Lelah sucked in her breath, thinking that he looked far better than she'd imagined him to look. She thought that her heart might pound right out of her chest. She flushed bright pink, thinking that everyone else in the room might be able to hear it too.

He walked right to Lelah, pulled her to his chest, and swung her around in a circle. "This is the finest gift ever!"

Being set back down, now Lelah was flushed and dizzy. She could have stayed in his arms forever. The men clapped him on the back, and the women cooed about how great he looked. After Metu slipped the armor out of the tunic's pouches, he stored them in the bag made for them. "I can tie this to my saddle easily."

Lelah was glad that her idea of portable armor would work well, even with riding an animal she had known nothing about. They retired to the living area of the cabin and talked well into the night with the light of candles illuminating the room. The conversation turned to serious things as Metu related the more gruesome situations he'd found throughout the world. He told of the slaughters of all-humans who resisted the forced breeding program that had encompassed the entire world. All the various Watchers had embraced Samjaza's program and enforced it in their own territories.

Then, spitting in derision, he said darkly, "They have twisted the base murder of the innocents and made it into something they call holy and sacred. They slaughter babies on their altars to the 'Great Serpent' high on top of their ziggurats."

It was obvious why these revelations had not been made during the meal. At least they ended the evening's conversation on the topic of the new animals—their capabilities, usage, their beauty, and most importantly, how they would aid in the rescue and resistance efforts.

That night while Metu lay in bed, images of the grown-up Lelah flooded his mind. He was used to having other pressing matters on his mind instead, problems he could solve and people he could save. He tried to refocus, but to no avail. He thought to himself, *What would that look like or mean to the congregation of the righteous if I, the anointed successor in the priestly line, joined myself to a Su-galam? Wouldn't I be putting a stamp of approval upon the wicked practices of the Watchers?* Between that thought and this other, he struggled until he fell into a fitful sleep: *Is my preaching about the mercy of the Lord of Spirits all for naught? Does not the Lord's promise extend to all who believe, despite their lineage?*

As was Enoch's custom, his morning was spent alone in prayer. He was in one of his favorite spots, under a great spreading fir tree whose branches reached all the way to the ground. He could not be seen by anyone, save any from the heavens.

He saw a manlike being, tall, brilliant white with great wings, reaching down to take his hand. He looked back for a moment, seeing his prone body lying on the boughs underneath the fir tree and a thin silver cord attached shimmering and undulating between him and it. This state of being was neither the object of his efforts nor the result of any prayer that he prayed. It was simply the will of the Lord of Spirits to bring him here at various times. It was here that Enoch saw and understood far deeper and broader things than any knowledge he possessed in his body. The colors were incredibly vibrant, far richer than anything seen on the earth; his understanding was totally acute in that he knew exactly how far the measure was between himself and the far-away white throne in the distance; the number of worshipers bowing and singing before the throne and the Son of Man who stood at the right hand of the throne; and the name of the individual before him, who, as before, had brought tongs with a burning coal from the altar in front of the throne and laid it against his lips, saying, "Your sin is atoned for. Now you are not a man of unclean lips."

Raphael again spoke to Enoch, saying, "Enoch, whom the Lord of Spirits loves, behold the things that will come to pass. Take this tablet and write the visions that you see." Raphael, sweeping his arm wide, revealed images to Enoch, a progression of successive bulls that symbolized men, which he understood to have begun with himself, arose, reigned, and faded, one after the other. With the third one, which was all white, an event occurred that destroyed the whole world, and a new world began after the third. Many more bulls came and went. He saw slavery and deliverance, a great mountain and wanderings, and a great nation born, and a baby, the seed of the woman.

After Enoch wrote on the tablet the details of the vision he was shown, Raphael handed him another object, a small circular glass, and said, "The Lord of Spirits knows the end from the beginning. Trust always in Him."

Enoch turned the small glass over in his palm and then suddenly found himself on the ground under the fir tree again. His writing tablet was full, and he held a small piece of glass in his hand. From the vision, Enoch understood that the promised Seed would be many generations in coming and that many things would come to pass before the time was right for His advent among men. As for the piece of glass, he was not sure yet what that would be used for. He had no worries, though, because he wholly trusted the Lord of Spirits. It would be revealed to him when it was meant to be. Thanking his Creator, he pocketed the glass and returned to his abode to help Edna with the preparations for the feast on the morrow.

THE DRAGNET

Abishag was among the individuals whom Enkum had gathered together to search for the individual known as "Maggot." It would not be quite as easy as one might have thought. There were hundreds of thousands of people within and close by outside of Eriduch, both slave and free, who would have to be scrutinized. The nickname "Maggot," for all its appeal, would not necessarily be unique. It was a derisive term given to anyone particularly annoying. But it was something concrete to go on. And special persuasion was designed for the identification of the correct Maggot.

Although still chafing under the humiliation of being branded in the least-desirable category, Abishag was heartened at least that he'd been included in the final chase to capture the most wanted traitor in the city. He fairly salivated at the chance to catch the one he saw as the cause of his greatest miseries. And he felt it in his bones: he would be the one who would catch the right "Maggot."

He showed up at the main office of the Refuse Department in Eriduch. He'd already scoured all his own underlings for anyone called "Maggot," finding two men who were so called, both of whom were on street-cleaning duty under his own command. Both had been taken to Enkum's interrogation chamber. After numerous painful persuasions, it was finally determined that the men were not connected to the smuggling ring and neither was a brother of Metu. Still, they were released, only to be kept under close surveillance and monitoring.

With official papers in hand and authority vested in him by the Security Office, Abishag was admitted into the refuse-handling facility to continue the search for the traitor. He was ushered into the living quarters of the facility workers and began to question those present. It was not but just a few minutes until he was told that there was a worker there who was called "Maggot." Upon further inquiry, he learned that the man was then on a transport to the outer refuse-processing plant and would not be returning until the morning of the next day.

Abishag further learned that the man was so obnoxious that no one else wanted to be around him. He asked to be shown the man's quarters. Far from the standard worker quarters and through the expanse of the facility, weaving between piles of refuse of various sorted descriptions, he was led to what looked like just another pile of unwanted items and found that it had a door that led into a living space inside.

"Thank you for leading me here," Abishag said to the worker who guided him to the place. "Now please excuse me while I work."

The obviously curious worker reluctantly left Abishag alone in Ishmerai's room. Abishag caught a premonition that this was the man he was looking for. He tried to calm his excitement, though, to focus on being thorough in his search. He desperately wanted to get this right. He discovered something that piqued his curiosity: it looked like there might have been at one time a second sleeping area in the enclosure, separate from what was obviously this Maggot's usual bed. He searched through various but sparse personal items.

He found nothing of any consequence or of any telltale quality until he began looking for hiding spots. By poking and prodding refuse items that made up the walls of the space, he finally discovered a small wheel that was actually a door. When he pulled on the wheel, which was about a palm's width off the floor and behind a sitting chair, it pulled out a drawer with two items in it. The first item he grabbed was a medallion attached to a neck chain. He turned the object over and over in his hands feeling the embossed inscriptions and images on its surface. The lighting was dim in the confines of the Maggot's quarters, so he could not make out what it said. Thinking that perhaps the object was made of gold, he took his knife and tested the hardness of the dark, somewhat gold-colored metal disc. He let out a curse when the tip of his knife blade broke off as he attempted to scratch its surface. He had no idea what type of metal it was made of, but he was assured that it was not gold. Then he held it up to try to catch enough light on it to see it more clearly. He saw "the Name" written in the center on one side.

His heart began to race. He knew he had his man. He reached back into the little drawer for the second item and found that it was a child's toy, a puzzle. He knew the significance of the medallion. As for the toy, he held it up to the light, turning it around in his fingers, and then it dawned on him that one or both of the missing Su-galam children must have spent some time there and that the Maggot was especially attached to that child to have saved the toy as a treasure.

After he stuffed the incriminating puzzle into his pocket, he slipped the medallion over his head and tucked it safely under his shirt. Barely able to contain his excitement, he hurried out and away from the refuse facility straight to the Security Office. He had decided that it would be better to exercise discretion in bringing in the traitor. It was too much of a risk to try to bring the Maggot in all by himself, although he would have liked the recognition he would have gotten. He decided that it would be better to share in the glory and be guaranteed in the success of the capture. As he paced and waited for an audience with Enkum, his face contorted into a grotesque grimace as he salivated at the vision of anticipated revenge.

MIRACLES

Early on the morning of the third day was a bustle of excitement as the whole refuge village prepared to embark on their trek up the mountain. The gathering was set for midday, so most would be on their way shortly after daybreak. Metu and the riders had already gone up the mountain the day before.

As Lelah and Markkah were getting into their family's transport, they heard a commotion. It seemed to be coming from the center of the refuge village. Getting in, Cain steered the transport down their road and stopped at the junction where there was a clear line of sight to see what was going on.

"Well, someone of interest has come for the gathering, I would say," Bahman said, stating what everyone else thought.

"Should we go down and see who it is?" asked Aliyah.

"Let's not. We'll find out who soon enough," suggested Lelah, who was more anxious to get up the mountain and closer to Metu. She'd played over and over in her mind being twirled by the man and hoped that there would be a moment or two alone with him during the gather. "Plus, we'll be on the road in front of the crowd, and they won't hold us up."

Markkah was again hoping against hope that perhaps the commotion had to do with the arrival of Ishmerai, but she was not anxious to see her hope again dashed so soon. While the truth was still unknown about who the newcomer was, she could hold on to her hope. "Yes, let's just go up the mountain and get there before the big crowd," she said.

The liveliest conversation traveling up the mountain was between everyone except Lelah and Markkah. Lelah was picturing in her mind what she might be doing with Metu, and Markkah was picturing what she'd do if it were indeed Ishmerai who'd arrived. They were lost in their own thoughts so thoroughly that they barely noticed the hours of travel and were on Mount Moriah before they knew it.

Looking around quickly, Lelah did not catch sight of Metu, and both young women followed their mothers into Edna's kitchen to assist with the meal preparations. The large room was bustling with women, most of whom the ladies already knew. Everything was to be readied so that right after the sacrifice the meal would begin.

They heard commotion outside as the rest of the gatherers arrived. Someone stuck their head in the door and said, "We're about to begin. Come on out!"

That was the cue for the women to join the gatherers. Lelah had been waiting for the call and was the first out the door, with Markkah right on her heels. As they headed for a seat close to the front and left of the altar, Lelah was startled to see Kahjeera. A flood of emotions coursed through her at the sight of the woman who embodied all that Lelah hated. *What a blight on such a perfect day!* she thought . Never had she thought that that woman would dare show her face on the mountain again. Lelah and Markkah sat down next to each other, not far from where Kahjeera was. Just before Kahjeera bent down to settle into a sitting position, she turned and shot a smile to the two Su-galam. The gesture shocked and unsettled Lelah, and it further goaded her into stewing with her anger and resentment even more. Markkah, having never been stung so personally by the hatred and prejudice of the woman, was oblivious to the extent of her sister's inner turmoil.

A hush fell over the crowd as Enoch and Methuselah took their places on each side of the altar. Metu was wearing his new clothes, except not the furred tunic, just the leather shirt and leggings. The sight of Metu tempered Lelah's emotions, and she was pleased that he was wearing what she'd made.

"It is written," Enoch began, "that the sacrifices of the Lord are a contrite heart and a broken spirit."

"Amen," was heard variously through the crowd. Lelah noted that one of those *amens* came from the mouth of Kahjeera. She felt the blood flush hot on her neck at the sound of it. *The nerve of that woman!*

Enoch continued, "How is it that we please the Lord of Spirits? What is it that He demands from us? Is there anything we can do? Is there anything we can bring to Him that pleases? How well must we behave so that we've behaved well enough? Does He just tolerate imperfection? Overlook our failures? Does he turn away His head and not notice when we sin, when we harbor hatred in our hearts?"

When Lelah heard that last line, she felt a stab to her chest. She knew she harbored hatred in her heart. It wasn't evident most of the time, but it was always just under the surface. She resented and hated those who hated her because of who and what she was. She had cherished and nurtured her hatred, convincing herself that it was justified and right. This was the first time it had hit her that Enoch was saying that her hatred was deeply wrong.

Enoch continued to drive the dagger in with, "Hatred in the heart was the root of the first murder, when Cain slew Abel. It is the root of all murders to this day. Therefore, hatred and murder are twins. Just as surely as we harbor hatred against another in our hearts, we are guilty of murder. We may hate an evil, we may hate wrong actions, we may hate and despise evil deeds, as does the Lord of Spirits, but it is not our place to sit in the judgment seat to pronounce judgment upon those who persecute us or to hate those who hate us.

"There is only One who is the Judge, and it is to Him that we all must answer. Dare we pronounce judgment upon those who may hate us? Shall we dare hate any whom the Lord of Spirits has extended mercy and forgiveness?"

Instead of Lelah thinking that Enoch was speaking to Kahjeera or someone else, as she was wont to do, she felt that he was directing his talk straight to her, and she was cut to the quick. Lelah had become accustomed to hearing Enoch's teaching and sermons, and had even become used to thinking of herself as one of 'the righteous.' The realization struck her like a club to the heart that she had only been righteous in her own eyes; she was really one of the wicked, hate and murder-riddled to her core and deserving of eternal wrath and damnation. As Enoch preached, her thoughts whirled as she felt her soul was standing naked, filthy and guilty in the presence of Almighty God. She wrapped herself in her arms as if she were trying to cover her own nakedness. Her trembling seemed unnoticed by those around her as all attention was focused upon Enoch and his message. With her head bowed, silent tears of remorse and despair rolled down her cheeks.

Then through her misery, Lelah's broken heart began to swell with hope as she clung to the next words of Enoch, ". . . And if we harbor hatred in our hearts, is there a cure, a remedy? Yes. The Lord of Spirits, from the first sin of mankind, has given us this, His promise. The Lord of Spirits does not forgive our sins or count us as righteous because we can make ourselves behave better and can will ourselves to not have hatred in our hearts for one another. He counts us as righteous when we believe His promise. We believe that one day He will send the righteous Seed of a woman to restore us to His own image. Our redemption, our perfection, our restoration, and our forgiveness lie solely with Him and no other, including ourselves. Only He can heal what has been broken inside of us.

"If you have hatred in your heart, come lay it at the foot of this altar. If you have covetous thoughts, lay them at the foot of this altar. If you've wronged your neighbor, put it at the foot of this altar. Let the Lord of Spirits accept your broken and contrite spirit, look at your believing heart, and forgive you your sins, and count your belief in His promise as righteousness before Him."

One by one, people arose from the crowd and approached the altar. Passing a pile of sticks, each would pick up a branch, carry it to the altar, and lay the branch on the growing pile of sticks underneath the bound ram.

Tears were streaming down Lelah's face as she approached the altar, pleading silently, *Lord of Spirits, I cannot tear this hatred out of my heart by myself. You have to do it for me.* She laid her stick on the altar with these words, "Lord of Spirits, forgive my hatred and my sins, and take them away from me as the smoke rises from this sacrifice. I cling to Your promise." She spoke from her heart, as did each of the others who came to the altar, laying their transgressions at the foot of it, all except one.

She glanced at her mother behind her as she approached the altar with her branch in hand, and saw that she too had tears in her eyes. She had turned her back and begun to return to her seat when she heard the sound of rejoicing rise from the crowd. She stopped and looked back. The incredible sight of her mother rendered her dumbstruck and immovable. Her mother was standing in front of the altar, her arms raised in the air, taller. Her crippled legs were straight and beautiful again and her walking poles lay useless on the ground. Cain picked them up and laid them too on the altar.

At last finding words, Lelah said in awe, "Surely the Lord of Spirits is in this place!" And she joined in the praise.

In song, the remainder of the people laid their branches and sticks on the altar, and when Lelah noticed Kahjeera at the altar asking forgiveness, instead of seeing the woman as an enemy, she saw her with new eyes and forgave her outright for the pain she'd caused.

The joy was unparalled among all of the people, and especially with Melenah and Lelah; even the sun shone brighter that day on Zion. That familiar burden of lead in Lelah's chest had evaporated, and she felt as clean and new as a fresh bleached sheet billowing in a sweet smelling breeze.

Late in the afternoon, after the Gathering meal, the family groups visited with each other. Kahjeera, who had come up the mountain with two of her nephews, was greeted and welcomed by Enoch's clan. Lelah recognized one of the nephews as one of the boys who had been eager to talk with her at the very first Gather she'd attended, just before the rift. Of course, now he was a young man, and Lelah again caught him looking at her. The look in his eyes made her a bit uneasy, so she focused her attention on others as best she could.

As usual, Markkah, Lelah, their mothers, stepfathers, and Hanan were included in Enoch and Edna's family group, which, of course, also included Metu. Lelah could not have been more at peace. The fact that Metu was present and conversing with her and the others was just a bonus and not the be all and end all of her sense of wholeness. She felt like a new person.

Methuselah was not unaware of Lelah. He was struck with her presence, perhaps more so than ever previously. He kept stealing glances at her throughout the family conversation. He had the distinct impression that her face was radiating, and her beauty affected him profoundly. However, the greater his attraction to her seemed to grow, the fiercer his inner struggle became. *Should a priest of the Most High be joined with the daughter of a Nephilim?*

Does not the mercy of the Lord of Spirits extend to and include any who believe, despite one's bloodline? Isn't my attraction to this woman just a token to prove my point about the mercy of the Lord? Would that not ultimately be a stumbling block to the righteous? And why should I even be considering these things in the first place?

Interrupting Metu's warring thoughts, Kahjeera joined the family group. With a show of acceptance that bordered on gushing, she extended her hand and then pulled into an embrace at first Markkah and then Lelah.

"I am so very sorry that I have treated you girls so poorly. I was wrong. Will you please forgive me?"

The girls were taken aback at the suddenness of the overture, but both unreservedly accepted the apology. Turning to Enoch and Metu, Kahjeera bowed and offered her apologies for offending them also.

"Most honored Enoch and Methuselah, please accept my sincerest apology for misjudging your mercy and leadership. It is my hope that our congregations may again worship and work together. I personally extend thanks to you for the great gift of the horses brought to our resisters. They are greatly appreciated and will be put to good use in our struggle to defend our homes, families, and lands."

Both Enoch and Metu graciously accepted Kahjeera's apology. And then Edna began a song, to which the others all joined, in praise and thanksgiving:

"What shall I render to the LORD
For all His benefits toward me?
I will take up the cup of salvation,
And call upon the name of the LORD.
I will pay my vows to the LORD
Now in the presence of all His people.
Precious in the sight of the LORD
Is the death of His saints.
O LORD, truly I am Your servant;

I am Your servant, the son of Your maidservant;
You have loosed my bonds.
I will offer to You the sacrifice of thanksgiving,
And will call upon the name of the LORD.
I will pay my vows to the LORD
Now in the presence of all His people,
In the courts of the LORD's house,
In the midst of you, Mount Zion.
Praise the LORD!"[10]

The sun set on the gatherers to music and dance and the songs of praise. Melenah danced more than them all. All would sojourn on the mountain that night and leave to go home early the next morning. Lelah went to sleep feeling enveloped by angel's wings, and Markkah fell asleep with a heavy heart, praying silently for Ishmerai's protection. Metu at last fell asleep with the image of the beautiful Lelah and with the conflicting thoughts about her still battling in his mind.

Captured

As Ishmerai rolled his empty refuse transport into the main refuse terminal in the deep fog of the early morning, he was running over in his mind for the umpteenth time about when he would vacate his position in Eriduch. Of late, he had felt that the extent of his usefulness there was coming to an end. Almost everyone, if not all of those who were resisting Samjaza's super-race proclamation, had made their escape already or had died trying. There was little he could do in his position to help in the efforts to rescue the all-human babies marked for sacrifice. Smuggling babies out with the trash was not effective. Other means and smugglers were being more successful. But even those efforts were not sufficient enough to save all the babies.

Herathah and her loyal Watchen were fairly drunk with the blood of the innocents, with sacrifices conducted every full moon on top of the ziggurat. Samjaza was also present at most sacrifices, and the offering was dedicated to the Great Serpent.

Herathah always officiated the sacrifice, and Samjaza was always most interested in the cavorting that occurred in its wake.

"You, Maggot!"

Ishmerai turned to see one of the workers who especially liked to taunt him standing on the loading dock with his hands on his hips. He ignored him as he climbed down from the transport and began to unhitch the oxen.

"I said, you, Maggot!"

Annoyed, Ishmerai turned toward the speaker to give him a terse retort, but before he could speak, he caught something out of the corner of his eye. At the same time, he saw the movement, he felt sharp pain to the side of his head…and then everything went black.

"I think you've had enough fun, Abishag, at least for now."

Ishmerai heard the voice as his consciousness stirred. He slowly took stock of his condition without opening his eyes. He thought maybe his eyes were swollen shut, and his head throbbed relentlessly. His position hadn't been changed. He felt the heavy manacles on his wrists, his arms were still stretched out on either side, his ankles secured in irons, and he was seated on the same rough stool. He could also feel a warm sticky fluid on his face and in other places. The metallic taste of the blood in his mouth nauseated him and he willed himself not to vomit. Various parts of his body radiated pain, but instinctively, he knew that it would be better for him to remain as inert as possible. He listened through the pain.

A ragged voice answered, "I'm just not done with this pig yet."

"Oh yes you are, for now. You heard what Enkum said. He is to be kept in one piece and alive for the time being. He'll be of no use otherwise."

"Just one more round," Abishag begged.

"You sick dog, he's unconscious now. Don't you want to at least wait until he can appreciate your attentions?"

"Throw some water on him again. That'll wake him up."

"I told you, you are done. You'll get your chance again, but not now."

Ishmerai heard noise that sounded like Abishag was being physically ushered away. The sound of shoes on the stone floor indicated at least three, maybe four individuals were leaving his proximity. He heard the sound of heavy iron doors clanging shut. He remained motionless, listening through the cobwebs in his aching brain. He could hear the fading footsteps of those departing. After the clang of another door farther away, he strained to hear other sounds. He counted at least three, maybe four moans and the clinking of restraints from nearby cells. He had no doubts as to his whereabouts. Finally, he tried opening his eyes. He could only see dimly through red-tinted slits. Great relief washed over him like a flood at his torturers' departure, even though he was still shackled and in pain. *Thank you, Lord, for helping me through this,* he silently mouthed through split and bloody lips.

BETRAYED

O n the ride back to the village in the ox-pulled transport, conversation and spirits were lively. Kahjeera's transport and nephews followed directly behind the one that carried Lelah's family. Midday, the family group arrived at their cluster of homes. As they began to climb out of the cart, Kahjeera had her transport stop too, and she made a point to give her best wishes to the family and especially the two sisters in a farewell.

Knowing that Kahjeera and her nephews had much farther to travel, Hanan was the first to invite them in for a midday meal. The other women all joined in with the invitation.

"We'd be privileged to be your guests!" Kahjeera cooed with enthusiasm.

During the simple meal, Kahjeera told of the exploits of the resistance. She was sure to include that many of the clothes worn by their fighters had been ones that Lelah and Markkah had sewn themselves. *That surely explains the popularity of functional over fashionable in clothing demand*, thought Lelah.

"Would you two like to come visit and see the fruits of your handiwork?" asked Kahjeera.

"I'd love to!" said Lelah.

"That would be really nice," said Markkah. Both young women had been cooped up in one spot for so long, the mere idea of travel to somewhere besides just the mountaintop was very appealing. Added to that, the prospect that their presence was actually desired instead of abhorred was further incentive.

"Well, you could come with us right now! We've plenty of room, and just so you're not missed too terribly here, we'll make sure you get back before the next full moon."

Bahman, feeling protective, interjected with, "If you wait just a few days, both Cain and I can also escort you ladies."

"Ah, but our presence is expected on the day after the morrow. I wouldn't want our delay to alarm our people," said Kahjeera. Then she added, "But it would be good of you to come retrieve these young ladies in ten days' time."

The mothers were a bit reticent with the whole idea, but the sisters' excitement was hard to contain, and they were old enough now to make their own decisions.

"We'd be able to see what else we could design for clothing too," said Markkah.

Thinking of the special armored plates she had made for Metu, Lelah added, "And we've got some innovations that the resisters might really appreciate."

"Then it's settled! If you ladies get packed, we can be on our way in an hour!" Kahjeera was overflowing with joy. And it was contagious.

Kahjeera's transport was packed, and everyone loaded up before an hour was done. There was not much for Lelah and Markkah to take for such a short visit. Melenah and Aliyah had packed enough provisions for everyone for their three-day, two-night journey to the stronghold, and excitement was running high. As they set out, Kahjeera chattered about many things, although when questioned about the stronghold, she was evasive about its description and location.

"Oh, tell us about the stronghold. It must be quite a place," Lelah said with enthusiasm to Karbol, one of the nephews.

"Well, it's—"

Interrupting, Kahjeera said rapidly, "Oh, we want you to be surprised! It's an awesome thing, and much more impressive when you see it for the first time. We don't want to spoil the experience for you!"

With that exchange, both Markkah and Lelah felt a little uneasy twinge that went away as Kahjeera cheerily talked about other things and about what the girls might enjoy making. She stroked their egos by praising their sewing handiwork and telling them how much it meant to the resistance.

Their travel was uneventful, and the stop for the first night was at a cottage that Lelah recognized as the last stop before the refuge village when she and her mother had first come to the mountain. She whispered to Markkah, "I know this place. This is where my mother and I stayed the night before we got to the refuge village…and this is where I first met Metu." Her memories flooded back to her about that time and also the recollection of where they'd been the night previous to getting to that cottage. They had been at Kahjeera and Jaireck's home. The memory flooded back about the horrible things that Kahjeera had said back then and how devastated she had been. A surge of fear welled up inside Lelah. Her heart began to pound, and she asked herself, *Can a person really change?* Then she thought, *Well, I've changed. I know I have. It wasn't me who did it, though.* Assuring herself, she thanked the Lord of Spirits quietly in her heart for taking her anger away, and she asked Him to now take her fear away too. By the time they unloaded from the transport, her enthusiasm for the company she was with was genuine and unsullied by fear.

Markkah and Lelah shared a room in the cottage. They got to bed late and exhausted after a hearty meal and good conversation. It was good to be on an adventure, and they slept a dreamless sleep.

Well rested the next morning, the journey began with all in high spirits. The early morning mist surrounded the travelers when they loaded back into the transport. As they traveled farther down the mountain, the mists lifted to reveal a bright, crisp, clear spring day filled with the aroma of wildflowers and gentle breezes.

"It certainly is nice to travel in the open now!" Lelah couldn't get enough of taking in all the sights.

Markkah added, "I agree! This is wonderful. I love an adventure." Her mind went back to her unusual trip to the mountain and she thought, *although this adventure doesn't even come close, it still feels good.*

The road wound down into a meadowed valley beside a small lake. As they descended into it, a break in the trees revealed the panorama before them.

"Look!" Lelah pointed to a spot close to where they could see the road would take them. Several mahgid-gu with their great long necks and tree-trunk tails were feeding on the high branches of some trees near the shore.

To the girls' oohs and ahs, they descended ever closer, catching another glimpse or two through the breaks in the trees. When finally the road brought them closer to the animals, the great beasts paid them no mind as they continued to feed on their leaves.

"Look at how they hold their tails!" said Lelah.

"They don't look sad at all either," added Markkah.

"These beasts are free. I feel so sorry for the other ones," Lelah replied.

Breaking her morning's relative silence, Kahjeera interjected, "Well, they are just animals, and they don't have feelings."

Neither of the girls felt the need to beg differ with the woman, even though both of them believed that animals *did* have feelings. However, the comment did serve to change the topic of conversation. The women returned to the subject of sewing and fashions, function versus style, and combinations of both.

At the end of the valley the road turned to cut through another thick grove of trees, narrowing and turning a bit steeper than before. The oxen slowed, but the banter in the transport did not.

"I think I remember this part of the road," said Lelah, "although it's just by its steepness it seems familiar, because my mother and I couldn't see the surroundings when we came through here."

"Well, this would have been the way Jaireck would have brought you," said Kahjeera.

Just then, even over the rumbling of the transport's wheels, both young women heard rustling in the vegetation on left side of the road and their attention was turned to the noise. They expected to see an animal of some sort, and hopefully not one unusual to the area. Lelah had a momentary shot of fear race through her at the thought of the mahkur-tidnum attack years before. She gripped her sister's arm.

That momentary fear was immediately eclipsed by a far greater terror. Before either could speak, a thick darkness suddenly blanketed them. The transport came to a jolting stop, and confusion reigned. Through the unnatural inky blackness Lelah heard Markkah scream, "Get your hands off!"

And, just before she was seized by an iron grip that pulled her out of her seat in the transport and hauled her to the roadside, she heard an irritated whisper, "Not me, you idiots. She's behind me!"

Their frantic screams were silenced by rags roughly stuffed in their mouths. They were bound and stuffed into large bags. Fear, anger, and helplessness seized the young women as they were carried to another transport and tossed roughly into the back of it by the silent kidnappers. They could feel things piled on top of them and were close enough to each other to know they were together, but gagged—they could not speak. It was apparent to the girls that they were the only two taken captive. Of all the thoughts and emotions racing through Lelah's mind, the predominant one was rage. *What a fool I've been. That witch! I should have known. No one really changes.*

During the ride, being jostled around in the transport, bound in uncomfortable positions and unable to move, lying on hard boards and nearly smothered by being buried under unknown things, the only thing the young Su-galam women could do was listen and pray. At least Markkah prayed. Lelah was too occupied with her rage and images of what she would like to do to Kahjeera and her disgusting nephews. Lelah realized that their kidnapping had been a setup but didn't know whether Markkah had heard Kahjeera's words to the kidnappers or not.

Unable to talk through the gags, both women listened as best they could to their kidnappers, who were trying to keep their voices down. Neither Markkah nor Lelah could make out exactly what they were saying, except a few words. They did not recognize the voices.

"We could stop…wouldn't know…I'd like to…"

"She'd find…not good…"

"…be there…time."

Hearing what they thought they heard, both women prayed for protection from their kidnappers, although Lelah also envisioned thoughts of scratching eyes out, at the very least.

The ride seemed interminable and continued until it felt like the transport was now on stone pavement. There seemed to be the noise of jostling transports. They also thought they smelled a river. It was confusing to them. The year before, they had heard of the bridge Eriduch had constructed replacing the ferry crossing.

Ostensibly, it had been to promote better trading, but the people of the free lands thought it was really meant for better troop access to their lands instead.

Maybe they are taking us back to the city, thought Lelah. As unpleasant as being taken back to Eriduch by force was, it seemed there could be worse fates, like being taken and slain or worse by Kahjeera's ilk. The memory of her voice saying, *Not me, you idiots! She's behind me!* was seared into Lelah's consciousness. The tone of the woman's voice had that same quality of hatred and malice as it did when she'd first heard it three years before. *Just wait until Metu and Enoch find out! How could they have been so thoroughly fooled by that woman anyhow?* She was even angry at Methuselah. Rage and conflicting thoughts warred through her mind.

Lelah's rage prevailed until it was overcome by despair as the trip seemed to drag on forever. As hours, days, nights blended into each other, both women wept and were in pain to the bone by being bound so uncomfortably for so long. They were terribly hungry and thirsty and finally couldn't help but soil themselves. It was then that they knew what true and utter humiliation felt like. They cried through their gags and felt profoundly forsaken despite their prayers for mercy and deliverance.

Then when close to delirium and pain turned to numbness of body, both women heard dimly the sound of hoofs and wheels on stone sounding the streets of a city. Even though they were prisoners, they grasped to a hope of almost any kind of existence anywhere, if they could just get out of where they were. Eriduch would be a relief.

PRAY

Enoch surfaced out from under the fir tree and marched determinedly up to his cottage. "Methuselah!" he loudly called.

Usually soft spoken and not easily rattled, the urgency of Enoch's voice shot a charge of concern through Metu's body. He jumped out of his seat and joined his father before he was through the front door. "Yes, sir!" he responded. Instinctively, he knew there would be marching orders.

Edna followed Metu but stopped short at the door. Following a hand signal and shake of the head from her husband, she watched as he put his hand on their son's shoulder and steered him to walk with him away from their home. Her heart ached and cried silently. She knew loved ones were in danger, or else her husband would not be acting as he was. She watched the two and prayed with all her might that the Lord of Spirits would deliver her loved ones from harm. She turned away from the door and into the shadows, bowed her head, and smote her chest with an open hand. She had a feeling it involved Ishmerai and prayed, "Lord of Spirits, in Your mercy, remember Your servant, and remember the name You gave my son, Ishmerai, 'YHWH guards.' Please guard him and bring him home safe and whole."

After some moments, Metu burst into the house and turned into his room. Hurried movement was heard through the door. When he emerged, Metu was wearing the entire suit Lelah had made for him, including the armored plates and helmet. Edna held out Methuselah's medallion, which he took and slipped over his head. His mother put her hand over it as it rested on his chest and said, "May the Name of the Lord of Spirits be with you, and may He send His mighty ones to fight by your side. Remember the Promise!"

He covered his mother's hand with both of his and said, "So shall it be."

Releasing Metu, Edna quickly assembled a satchel of dried food and thrust it into his hands. She followed him to the door and then watched as her eldest saddled up his horse and swiftly departed down the mountain. Her husband returned in a brisk walk and said, "Mother, pack me some food, and don't stop praying."

She jumped to action while Enoch readied his ox transport for travel. Before she knew it, he was gone. And she did not stop praying.

He would have preferred to storm the city on his white charger with a hundred men behind him. But instead, Methuselah was concealed in a fresh vegetable transport headed for Eriduch. Old Enosh was the driver. They were on their way to the river and the new bridge. The false bottom of the transport was the hiding place, and they both prayed the inspectors at the gates of the city would easily pass them through.

Just before leaving, they had gotten word that Markkah and Lelah had been kidnapped and most likely taken to Eriduch too. Reportedly, Kahjeera and her nephews were beside themselves with grief, having put up a mighty fight against the abductors. As much as Metu wanted to believe Kahjeera's remorse, he had his doubts, although he kept them to himself.

Lord of Spirits, have mercy on us. Send Your mighty ones to fight by our side so that the captives may be set free.

THE PALACE

In the dimmest light of predawn, the transport was wheeled into a building with the gates shutting behind, and both Lelah and Markkah were near unconsciousness. It seemed to them a blur and just an impression of images whirling around them.

The action around them seemed frenetic, and they heard bits and pieces of conversation as they were being lifted out of the cart and carried somewhere.

"They are in terrible shape!"

"Well, orders were to get them here as soon as possible."

"No excuse! What were you thinking?"

"You could have…"

"Get them cleaned up… They need…water…"

"A doctor…now! Get attendants!"

"Right now!"

"Will be furious…"

And then blackness.

Lelah felt a hand at the back of her head supporting her and cool water gently brought to her lips and soothing her throat. The cobwebs in her brain began to clear, and when she opened her eyes, she tried to bring sense to the still-blurry images. *Where am I?* Disoriented and helpless, she closed her eyes again and received the ministrations of able hands massaging her limbs. She felt that she'd been washed and numbness and pain chased away.

As she lay there collecting her thoughts, an alarm of fear shot through her. *I'm not here because I asked to be! Who are these people, and what do they want? And where's Markkah!*

"Markkah!" Lelah thought she'd shouted, but it came out just a weak rasp as she opened her eyes again, jerked her arm away from the one massaging it, and managed to bolt herself into a sitting position.

"Lelah?" Markkah's soft voice sounded thick with confusion.

Lelah turned to see her sister lying on a bed with three women and a man surrounding her. She realized she'd been looking between two people right next to her, and turning her head to the left, she saw two more. Sitting so suddenly, the room started to spin.

"Easy, easy," said the woman who had given her water. "You are not in good enough shape to be getting up just yet."

"Where are we?" asked Markkah.

The man attending her said, "You're safe now. You're in your grandmother's palace. Here, drink some more water."

A kind voice said, "Food is being prepared for you two right now."

Being in no condition to flee, and reassured at least for now that these people meant them no harm, both Lelah and Markkah gave in to their attentions and accepted the relief they felt in being delivered from their hellish ride.

Herathah was in the great hall on her jasper throne, impatiently tapping the nails of her right hand on the polished arm of her seat. It made the man who was attempting to give the report concerning the successful retrieval of her two granddaughters very nervous. He was the one Watchen who'd accompanied the two other abductors into the free lands and was the one responsible for casting the darkness spell in the operation. The abductors stood silently behind the man, their heads bowed. They were handpicked all-human undesirables because it was thought that they would be the least suspected in the free lands of collusion with the god-men.

"It seemed safest to us to get to Eriduch as quickly as we could without stopping. If we had loosed the women, we would have had a much more difficult time not raising suspicion."

"Reger, you were the one in charge. You should have used better judgment. I am very disturbed that my granddaughters have been delivered in such appalling condition." Looking past the men, she then called, "Enkum!"

"Yes, ma'am." Enkum approached from the rear of the great hall.

"Please escort these three men to the dungeons. An overnight stay will clear their thinking. And check on our other guest down there while you're at it. Make sure that he is in the correct cell and that we're ready for any visitors he might have."

"Yes, ma'am." Enkum nodded, bowed crisply, and directed the men to turn and walk in front of him. Several security men at the back of the hall joined the escort on both sides of the men, who were not looking forward to their sojourn in the dungeons.

Out the great hall, past the massive statues of Samjaza's children, through an obscure door in the hallway on the left side just past the beginning of the statues and down many flights of stairs, they finally arrived in the dungeon.

Ishmerai, still chained and on the stool, lifted his head as the door at the far end of the hall opened up. The manacles cut into his wrists as his arms were still stretched out and up. He watched as the men approached, heading straight for his cell. He was glad to see that Abishag was not among them.

Enkum barked, "You two, take the maggot out and put him in the third cell on the right." Everyone continued to call Ishmerai maggot because his real name was too intimidating, or at the least one everyone wanted to avoid.

After taking keys from Enkum, two guards entered the cell, unlocked Ishmerai's wrist and ankle irons, and, hefting him under his arms, dragged him to the designated cell. In the rear wall of its three stone walls, there was a large carved-out indentation with a thin, dirty pad on it for a bed where they roughly laid him. There was a hole in the floor for a toilet and a horizontal slit at the bottom of the barred door to allow food and water to be passed through. It was a definite improvement in accommodations.

Ishmerai sat on the bed, collecting his thoughts, rubbing his wrists and ankles, and listening. His cuts and gashes had stopped bleeding, and crusted blood covered most of his body. He'd been stripped down to just a thin robe and short pants, both of which were blood soaked. In exhaustion, he lay on his side on the bed because his back was torn and raw. He strained to hear what was going on back in the cell from which he'd just been delivered.

He could tell by the rattle of chains, the cracks of whips, and the moans and cries that the three men were experiencing some of the attentions he'd recently experienced. One man was begging and threatening the torturers at the same time between strikes of the whip. "You would do well to be careful with me, fools. You don't know who you are dealing with," and, "It was the other two who hurt the girls! They tied them too tightly! They were the ones who wouldn't give them water! Please, no more!"

What girls? thought Ishmerai. He listened closer.

"You liar! Ah!" said one as he was lashed.

"You were afraid of the Su-galam! You thought they'd have something over on you! Aah!" said the other as he too was struck.

"None of you could carry out a simple kidnapping without messing things up, you imbeciles! I regret that I thought you could do it!" Enkum grabbed a whip from one of his men and proceeded to strike the three men with more force than before, evoking no more talk and far more screams and moans.

Could it be that Markkah and Lelah are back here? Ishmerai couldn't think of any two other Su-galam who would be kidnapped. They were the only two from Eriduch who had ever left the city or controlled territory under circumstances that would warrant them having to be kidnapped in order to return. And he knew that Herathah had wanted to get them back. Then he thought, *Are they all right? These men wouldn't be undergoing torture if everything had gone well.* He would be able to tell something by how long the men were tortured and if they were allowed to live or not. His heart pounded harder at the thought that Markkah might be injured or worse. Desperate thoughts and ideas of what he wanted to do raced through his mind. He closed his eyes and prayed for help and for protection for both girls.

When he opened his eyes, he was looking up at the ceiling. He noticed a curious stone in the center that was about the size of a man's palm. He thought he saw a light flash in it, or through it, just briefly. And he got a sensation that he was not alone.

ON OFFENSE

Caleb and his men waited. Patience was essential. Their forward scouts had identified a raiding party coming out of Eriduch that consisted of three Nephilim, numerous large animals and transports, and at least fifty men of either all-human or Digir-na lineage. It was not known yet where they were headed, but the initial direction indicated they could be heading to any one of several valleys of free land peoples. An increasing number of the free land peoples who had traded with the cities were being conquered outright. Only the young suitable-for-breeding or hard-labor prisoners would be spared. All others would be slaughtered.

When it could be determined where they were headed, the trap would be set. Caleb's scouts were riding the new animals. The gifts from Methuselah were rapidly being put to use in their resistance efforts. Experienced riders had been a part of the gift, at least for a time, for training. In the short time that they had these animals, communication on the front had already improved.

This upcoming operation would further reveal the value of the peace offering.

Two days before, the forward scouts had also seen a smaller party of travelers coming out of Eriduch, but it seemed of no significance to them. They were on the road to the river and the bridge newly built to replace the ferry crossing into the free lands, but they looked to be just merchants of some sort. After all, there still was commerce that occurred between Eriduch and some of the free lands.

The forward scouts pinpointed the destination of the raiding party. Sure of their judgment, they sped back to Caleb's forces. The new animals were improving the relay of information. Already, Caleb's troops had advanced nearer to the pass. They'd positioned themselves in an area that would be convenient for travel to any one of the three possible targets of the coming attack.

Thundering up to Caleb, the lead scout reined in his winded horse. "They're headed for the Karloah Pass."

Turning to Jaireck on his right, Caleb barked, "Ready the men. You take the north end of the pass. I'll take the south. Have Gerlag man both sides of the middle. Divide up the levers equally."

This was the first time they were attempting an assault on advancing raiders. They had previously resisted by fighting back with villagers as they came under assault or helping villagers escape from being captured in raids. Their ranks and the population in the stronghold had grown considerably. The massive systems of interconnecting caves had provided a secure refuge, and its inaccessibility made for a good defense. Thus far they had thwarted and slowed the slave trade but had not as yet been able to prevent the raiders of Eriduch from stealing villages and farmlands. With the increase in the number of Nephilim, there was a greater and greater need for food sources. The god-men had enormous appetites. The acquisition of more and more farmland and slaves to work it was a priority.

Caleb was intending to annihilate this raiding party, not just hamper or obstruct their goals. As quickly as they could, they headed to the targeted pass to set up their ambush before the raiders got there.

"Move out!" was heard just as darkness fell. The resisters would make their way to the pass and their positions and would be ready for action come the morning mists.

The morning mists lightened on the ridges of the pass while it still hung thickly and nearly opaque nearer the floor. Caleb and his men, manning the south end entrance, hunkered behind large boulders to remain undetected by the raiding party camped in the valley below, just at the mouth of the pass. He knew they wouldn't begin to move until the mists began to lift. They would wait until the entire party was in the pass before levering the boulders to fall and block the entrance. At the same time, Jaireck and his men would release boulders that would block the north end.

Caleb and his forces had spent many months readying areas for ambushes, targeting entrances to fertile farming free lands. They had been to Karloah Pass months before, digging around the selected boulders. It would not take much force to launch each boulder using a lever. They were set, and now it was just a matter of waiting.

As the morning sun climbed higher, the mist nearly cleared from around the resisters. They watched the top of the mists below. It was apparent where the raiders were by the torches they used, and it was apparent that they began to move. In the less dense upper part of the fog, Caleb could make out the tops of three heads, those belonging to the three Nephilim raiders. Nobody was looking up as they trekked along beside the river that channeled through the pass. The sun's position then hit the angle to cast bright rays into the pass. The mists thinned enough to reveal the leaders of the raiding party about a third of the way through.

When he was sure their prey was fully into the pass and too far in to run back, Caleb shouted, "Lord of Spirits, grant us victory!" He put the ram's horn to his lips, took a deep breath, and blew. Immediately, his men laid their weight to the levers, and the rumble and crash of great boulders deafened both raiders and ambushers. The great boulders took trees, other rocks, and debris with them as they crashed to the bottom. After several minutes, Caleb then blew the ram's horn again, and the middle resisters began their assault on the startled raiders. Already arrows had been whizzing up from below, striking no one. The shots had been fired in a panic and in the general direction of where they knew their attackers to be. Boulders, arrows, and debris rained down upon the trapped men, Su-galam, and Nephilim. Screams and roars were heard from the bottom of the river chasm.

Unseen by Caleb or any of his men, one man from the raiding party had been at the far rear of the group and close enough to the pass entrance to escape the first boulders. He wasted no time securing cover for himself out of harm's way. He had been sent back to retrieve a forgotten item at the camp, and the task he'd taken as annoying and demeaning became his salvation. Hidden, with his heart pounding and covering his ears to lessen the din, he felt the earth rumble. Fear seized him, and his first thought was to get out of there and back to Eriduch as soon as he could. Without stopping, he knew he could make it there in two days' time. Uncovering his ears, Kranagh looked at the five-pointed star tattoo on his hand. He was a Watchen and should be able to cast magic against the attackers, but even with that advantage, he had no idea how many he would be up against. The decision was made: discretion to him was the better part of valor. He fled.

After running for some time, Kranagh stopped to drink out of a stream and to sit and rest a few minutes. He was bent on getting to Eriduch as swiftly as possible, but the occasional rests were necessary. He slipped dried fruit out from his pouch and relished in its rejuvenating effect. Refreshed, he set off again. The only thing he was worried about was not being able to give a thorough account of the attacking force. He resolved to give them the best guess he could make and assure them that he'd verified it. There must have been hundreds if not thousands who had attacked them. It would have taken massive numbers just to move those boulders, so he felt confident in his guess. On the eve of the next day, he would reach Eriduch if he kept up his pace.

GRANDMOTHER

A deep hiss that almost sounded like a rumbling purr resonated throughout the room. Herathah stood with her eyes closed, her red gown shimmering white in her incantation room. She felt the giant coils caressing her and the electric charge coursing up and down her spine.

"I told you patience…ssss…would pay off."

"Mmmm…hmmm," she purred back.

"You've got your granddaughters back now. You've captured the maggot. And soon the biggest prize of all will be delivered into your hands."

"Life is good." She contentedly sighed.

The coils squeezed a bit sharply, and Herathah felt a momentary stab of alarm. "Don't rest on your victories just yet, my dear. There is still much to accomplisssssh."

She opened her eyes to see the giant head of the great serpent just inches from her face. The slick forked tongue lashed out to flicker around her neck, sending tremors anew down her body. It would be easy to swoon, but she fought to maintain her senses. *There is more to be done!*

Markkah and Lelah thoroughly savored the choice foods and drink their attendants served. Clean and dressed in exquisite and very comfortable robes, the aches and pains of the grueling ride were now just remnants. Neither engaged in conversation of any consequence, not with the strangers around. Their room was a spacious, high-ceilinged space with columns, carvings, and ornate paintings on the walls and ceiling. Their beds were sumptuously adorned and the bedding bright white and soft. The table where they sat was made of a shiny, translucent green stone with what looked like bubbles or domes embedded deep within it. The chairs were of a deep-red carved wood topped with embroidered cushions. These luxuries and accommodations surpassed any memories of the environment in which they'd ever lived, even before their father's rampage. This was the first time they'd been to their grandmother's palace, much less been guests.

"Mark the hour!" exclaimed a messenger who abruptly entered the room. "Ready our guests to be presented to their grandmother in one hour's time. Wait for the escort!" He turned crisply on his heel and then exited.

"Well, this is a meeting that's three years late," remarked Lelah quietly to Markkah. The sarcasm was thick in her voice.

"And thankfully, it is too late," Markkah replied cryptically.

Their attendants circled closer to the girls, taking plates and beginning the cleanup of the meal. It was an unspoken message to speed things up and begin to get ready for the upcoming event.

After a cold night on the thin pad of a bed chiseled into the stone wall, Ishmerai awoke with his empty stomach gnarling and tongue parched. Every bone ached and every move he made revealed another bruised or torn area of flesh. He heard footsteps in the hall, the wheels of a cart, the sliding of metal on stone, and sighs and moans of relief. He also heard the jailor releasing the three abductors who'd had their day and night of punishment. *One day and night in the dungeon and only one round of torture. The girls must not be injured badly!*

As the cart came closer to his cell, he sat up and stretched to make getting to the door a bit easier. Instinctively, he feigned more stiffness and weakness than was real, primarily because of the feeling that his every movement was being watched. He'd looked again at the unusual stone on the ceiling and felt that there were prying eyes on the other side. Even if he were imagining things, it would be advantageous to behave as if every move he made was being watched.

When the cart was pushed in front of his cell door, a young woman looking unkempt and overworked took a plate of meager rations and a bowl of water from the cart and slipped them through the slot in the lower part of the door. By the time she'd gotten to his cell, he was already squatted down by the provision slot.

Shooting a quick whisper to the woman while the abductors were making noise being released, Ishmerai said, "Tell me, what has become of the girls who the abductors brought in?"

That he spoke to her was startling in itself, but the woman then looked at Ishmerai's face for the first time, and gave another start. She recognized him from her days at Enkara's compound. After looking nervously to her side and determining that their conversation was unnoticed, she whispered, "You're the trashman. What are you doing here?"

"Yes I am, but never mind me, what has become of the girls those men brought in?"

Regaining her composure she whispered, "They have recovered."

"Who are they?"

"They're the ones who were taken to the free lands by their mothers three years ago." After another quick look to the departing jailor and abductors, she added, "The mother of one befriended me. But they questioned me brutally because they thought I might know how they got away."

Ishmerai could hear the bitterness in her voice. "What is your name?"

"It is Hazael, but they call me Merah." She straightened plates and bowls on her cart, making it look like she was spending a bit of time with that instead of communicating.

Ishmerai kept his head lowered over his plate of food and between bites said, "Would you like to escape from here?"

"More than anything."

"Get word to Markkah, one of the girls, that I'm here. My name is Ishmerai."

She nodded her head almost unperceptively and then rumbled her cart to the next cell. Ishmerai remained eating and drinking by the door. It didn't take long for him to finish.

The escort arrived to take Lelah and Markkah to Herathah. The women were dressed in long gowns, Lelah in a brilliant emerald green and Markkah in a deep sapphire blue. Being seamstresses, they admired both the design and the workmanship. Under any other circumstances, they would have been absolutely delighted.

Instead of receiving her granddaughters in the great hall, Herathah had them ushered to her private chambers. As the girls entered the room, they noticed the décor was similar to theirs, only it was twice as large with more living spaces. A number of attendants were seen either working at something or standing ready to take orders from their mistress.

Herathah was sitting on a lounge. She clapped her hands, and immediately two young men with effeminate mannerisms stood by her side. She gestured to them, and they hurried to escort her granddaughters closer.

"How lovely you ladies look," said Herathah. "Turn around… again. You are truly splendid, as well you should be."

Although thankful that their circumstances had improved considerably compared to the harsh manner by which they had been abducted, the fact remained that they were still in a place they had not intended to be, nor would they have chosen.

Perceiving their discontent, Herathah smoothly continued. "I am so sorry for your horrific travel here. The men responsible have been punished. I have dearly missed you these three years and have wanted you back where you belong. I had hoped that you would have come to see me of your own free will, and I am appalled at the manner you were brought here. I have learned that your friend Kahjeera received a handsome payment to hand you over. I'll have you know that I did not order, nor did I sanction, your kidnapping."

"Does that mean we are free to leave?" asked Markkah.

"Well, of course you are, but I would hope that now you are here you will at least spend a bit of time with your own grandmother."

Lelah stood there turning a bit red in the face as she reacted to the revelation that Kahjeera had even profited from their abduction. Her hatred boiled over, rehashing in her mind all the other offenses from all the others who had disparaged her because of her lineage. Markkah listened to her grandmother with a very skeptical ear.

"Please sit down, my dear girls. There is much I would like to speak with you about."

Both young women sat in the two chairs opposite her as Herathah continued. "First of all, I was devastated by your father's unfortunate outburst, and he is also very sorry for the hurt and destruction he caused. His remorse is complete. Secondly, I am sorry about your mothers. Lelah, if we had known how injured your mother was, we surely would have helped her right away. And, Markkah, your mother's position would have been restored right after the Great Gather. It was wrong that she had to work as a servant for as long as she did."

Again it was Markkah who spoke up. "If our father is so remorseful, why isn't he here apologizing to us?"

"He had no idea you two were going to be here. He is away from the city right now," she lied, "and when he returns, I guarantee that he will want to see you."

He was never interested in communicating with any of his daughters before. Why would we be so special now? thought Markkah, but she didn't speak her mind this time.

Lelah, under any circumstance, would opt to avoid her father altogether and forever. She said, "He doesn't have to apologize in person. It is enough that you say so. Thank you, Grandmother."

"My dear, sweet granddaughters, I am so proud of what beautiful and intelligent women you have become. I must say that I'm sure you have experienced unpleasant treatment from the all-humans who despise you because of who you are: daughters of the gods. They are jealous because you are so much more than they could ever hope to be."

Inwardly, Lelah agreed, but Markkah replied, "And all-humans would think that the Digirna are so much better than them because the birth of all-human babies is outlawed now?" Both strength and sarcasm were thick in her voice.

Herathah deftly handled Markkah's direct questioning with, "There have been many misunderstandings, my dear. All-humans have been apt to interpret reality quite differently. The truth is we know that it is inevitable that the blood of the gods will pervade all of humanity, in time. The race of Digirna is the future. It is the combination of the very best of all of us. It is our joining with the divine. Truly, the whole of mankind is being transformed into the image of the divine. Surely you see the great cities and monuments built, the modern conveniences made, and the improvement of mankind's condition with the advent of the gods joining with men. I'm sure also that just your presence among the all-humans has been a benefit to them, whether some will admit it or not."

Lelah, nodding, found herself being drawn into the words of her grandmother, thinking about the running water they had initiated for their humble abodes on the mountain. That was a thing new to the lifestyle of the human population there. And also, their innovations with simple sewing and clothes making could be attributed to their lineage, she thought.

Looking at Lelah in particular, Herathah continued, "I know how sometimes the ones we love have misunderstandings. There is no such thing as only black and white. There are just big areas of gray. Perhaps if all humanity could see that, we could all accept each other and live in peace."

If Metu were here to listen, maybe peace could be achieved! Lelah's mind drifted to pleasant thoughts of Methuselah, her Metu. *Wouldn't it be wonderful if there could be healing between our peoples? Clearing up the misunderstandings and practicing mutual respect would lead to a beautiful, exciting world for all!*

But Markkah bit her tongue, thinking a little discretion might be the wiser course at the moment. Instead of being provocative, she changed the subject with, "And where may our sisters be?"

Happy to speak on lighter things, Herathah replied, "Oh, some are married and have homes of their own now here in the city. Some have traveled to the far ends of the earth and begun families elsewhere. They have very rich lives. You are the only ones now here in my palace. Back at your father's compound are some younger sisters still under the care of their mothers. All are wonderful, just like you."

Markkah asked, "Are we free to move about your home or the city without restriction?"

"Why, of course, Markkah. I have let our servants know that you are not just guests here but are part of my family. They are instructed to obey your commands. There are just a few areas, though, that will not be accessible to you, unless I am with you. That is the rule for everyone here, not just you."

Herathah arose from her lounge and held her hands out to her granddaughters as they rose from their chairs too. "My dears, I expect you to eat at my table this evening, but in the meantime, enjoy yourselves by exploring. Balog, the escort who brought you here, is at your disposal to guide you wherever you wish." Then she leaned forward to kiss each girl on the cheek.

"'Til the evening, then."

"'Til then," the young women together replied.

TRUTH

"You have got to be out of your mind, Lelah!"

"Why? Because she makes sense?"

The two were back in their new quarters, having dismissed all the servants who were attending them. Lelah had asked the escort Balog to wait outside the door for them.

They were arguing in hushed tones, which, however, did not diminish the passion attached.

"It isn't that she doesn't make sense, it's that she is outright lying."

"There is a lot of truth to what she's saying!"

"What...like there's no black and white, no real right or wrong, just a bunch of gray areas? Just because we might not be able to tell the difference between the two, doesn't mean right and wrong don't exist."

"She still made some sense," Lelah replied. She felt the heat creeping up her neck as she obstinently refused to concede to her sister.

"And, like it's all just a misunderstanding, and we can all come together and make peace?"

"Yes, Markkah, there is truth in that."

"You just don't get it, Lelah. A lie can hold many truths, but the truth cannot hold a single lie."

"Hmmmph! You are just being stubborn. You can just stay here then. I'm going to have Balog show me the sights."

"Fine then."

"Fine."

Lelah turned on her heel and with her head held high, stomped to the door, opened it, walked out, and didn't look back.

Markkah was left in the room by herself. She knelt by chair, resting her arms on the seat of it. Looking up, she pleaded, "Lord of Spirits, by your holy Name, please deliver my sister from delusion and evil!"

She was interrupted by a soft knock on the door. Hastily, Markkah stood and walked to the door. Opening it, she found a weary-looking young woman who had a cleaning cart with her.

"Ma'am, I am here to clean your quarters," she said with a bow.

"Do come in," Markkah graciously responded, inviting the young woman into the room.

The young slave looked around the room. Nervously, she remarked, "Oh, ma'am, I thought there were two of you here."

"Oh yes, there are, but my sister, Lelah, has gone about touring just now."

"So you must be Markkah?"

A little alarm went off in Markkah's chest. *Why is this servant interested in me? And she knows my name?* Warily, Markkah responded, "Yes, I'm Markkah, and you are?"

She whispered. "My name is Hazael, but they call me Merah here. I knew your mother briefly. She was kind to me."

"Oh—"

"Before anyone else comes, I need to give you this message. Ishmerai is here, in the dungeon. And when you leave this city, I want to go too."

Markkah's heart nearly leapt out of her chest at the mention of Ishmerai. And he was here! "Quickly, how do I get to the dungeon?"

"As you enter the great hall of statues, just before the first statue on the right side, there is a plain door. It almost blends into the wall. It leads down a stairway to the dungeons. There is another entrance, but I do not know where it is. Just next to the dungeons is a kitchen. The other way out might be from there."

Just then, several servants re-entered the room.

"We're sorry ma'am. We thought you had gone."

Nodding a thank you to Hazael, Markkah said, "Oh, come on in. You may attend to your duties. I am going to do a little sightseeing now."

With a smile and a nod, Markkah exited her quarters. She tried to appear as if she were not on a mission.

Herathah received Enkum in her private quarters. "I would like a status report on the maggot, please."

"He is secured in the proper cell and being watched continually."

"Have you any indication about when Methuselah might arrive?"

"Not yet. We surmise he will most likely enter the city clandestinely instead of with force. I am anticipating that he could be here any day, and we are prepared."

"Remember, if you detect him before he gets to his maggot brother, just let him think we don't know. His capture will be more sure that way, and sweeter," she added with a wicked smile.

Mirroring the smile, Chief Enkum nodded agreement.

"By the way, you and my daughter are invited to my table this evening. It would be good for the girls to meet their aunt and uncle. I would also like you to pay attention to their demeanor and give me a report on your impressions afterward."

"Yes, ma'am. I am honored," he said with a bow.

After what seemed an eternity, Markkah found her way to the hall of statues. The palace was a bustling place, and true to her grandmother's word, everyone gave deference to her and servants obeyed. She exuded pleasance and curiosity as she asked questions and for directions. She'd made a mental note of how the palace was laid out, thinking it might be soon useful. In the hall of statues, she lingered, giving the appearance of admiring the images of each of her aunts and uncles, and her father too. It was at her father's statue at the beginning of the lineup that the door lay. It seemed to take another eternity before the hall cleared enough for her to slip through the door unseen.

Down flights of stairs she raced as fast as her gown would allow, circling down and down. At the bottom she stopped. There were two doors, one a regular heavy wooden door and the other an iron one. She had no doubt as to which led to the dungeon. She collected her wits and calmed her breathing, deciding on her course of action. She was torn between running into the dungeon to Ishmerai or going into the kitchen. She decided it was best to go into the kitchen to introduce herself and check the place out first.

"Hello!" Her cheery greeting startled the two servants working in the kitchen when she came through the door.

"Well, hello," said the elder one, obviously the man in charge.

Walking forward, Markkah held out her hand, "I'm Markkah, one of Herathah's granddaughters."

Shocked and hesitant, the man briefly took hold of Markkah's hand and then promptly let go. "Welcome to our kitchen," was all he said.

Trying to put the uneasy servants at ease as best she could, she said, "I'm sorry to bother you, but this is the first time I've been at the palace, and I'm having a wonderful time exploring everywhere. I found the passage down here and would love to explore your area too."

Having gotten the orders along with the rest of the servants of the palace to obey the orders of the two granddaughters, they were still surprised to see one of them interested in their area.

"And what are your names?" Markkah inquired.

Flattered that she would even be interested in their names, they introduced themselves with smiles. Aram and Gether showed her all parts of their kitchen, described their job of providing food to anyone housed in the dungeon, as well as the jailors when on duty. She listened with interest and asked many questions.

"When I want to leave, do I have to climb that whole flight of stairs back up to the top? Is there an easier way out?" This was the chief question she really wanted an answer to.

Aram gladly showed her the exit that was accessed through the pantry room. "This is the way we come and go and also the way we have our pantry goods delivered. There are no stairs, just a ramp that comes out and opens out into the loading docks."

"Are there any other exits from the dungeon?"

"There is one more exit, and that is through the jailor's office in the dungeon. It is used only by the jailors. The stairs you entered by are the route of entry and exit for all prisoners, and even the servants who work down here. We alone use the pantry route."

"How many prisoners are being housed right now?"

"We have only fifty-four at this time. Most of them are here for short terms," said Aram.

"This morning, they released the men who were punished for hurting you and your sister on your way here," added Gether. "They paid dearly for their error."

"I am very thankful for that." Markkah was sincere about it and then added, "I would like to see where they were, uh, punished."

"We don't go into the dungeon. Only our server delivers the rations to the prisoners. She will not be here until the morrow at just before dawn," said Aram.

"I think I might just be down here tomorrow morning then, just to see the dungeon with the server. Thank you so much for visiting with me during your busy day. I appreciate your kindness."

Aram and Gether bowed deeply to Markkah. It had been a special pleasure to be treated as an equal by a Su-galam. It took Markkah all her might and willpower to turn around and leave by the pantry exit without going into the dungeon to see Ishmerai. She needed a plan and the right timing, and this right now was not it, and she grudgingly knew it. *The morrow…before dawn… I've waited this long. I can wait until then.*

Markkah got back to her quarters just before Lelah returned from her explorations. She was treated coldly by her sister, and for the first time in their lives, they were at odds. Silently, they readied for the appointed meal with Herathah. Two servants assisted by bringing new clothing; however, both Lelah and Markkah discouraged them from assisting further. It was an uncomfortable thing to have servants waiting on them.

Soon Balog was at the door to escort them to Herathah's quarters. The sisters still did not speak to each other. Markkah was truly concerned about what was happening to Lelah but afraid to confide in her, and Lelah had so many conflicting thoughts running around in her mind that for the time being it was easier to just not think or talk. And both were still chafing from the words between them.

Balog announced them as they were ushered into the quarters and led to the far left of the room. The dining alcove was on an open terrace that overlooked the city. Great columns supported the perimeter of half the circular space. The setting sun showcased a profusion of bright oranges and azure blues, providing a dramatic backdrop for the lavishly prepared table. The young women recognized the oversized table and chairs from their days as children seeing their father's dining room, although they had never eaten at it. The chairs designed for the all-human sizes had steps up to a higher seat while the chairs designed for Nephilim were just oversized human chairs proportionately. The tabletop was shoulder high to the two Su-galam, making it about eye high to the average all-human.

As they approached the table, the backlight of the sunset obscured who was sitting at the table. They could only make out the silhouettes of three others, one of which included a Nephilim. Both young women felt a surge of alarm, thinking it might be their father. As they were led closer, the sun effect dimmed enough to reveal that the Nephilim was a woman. They were both struck by both her size and beauty. She was lithe and tall and had very similar facial features to Herathah, except her hair was long, brilliant, golden red twisted into a thick braid that draped over one shoulder and disappeared under the tabletop. Her skin was fair, and there was a smattering of darker little spots across her cheeks and nose. Her eyes were a deep hazel brown. The young Su-galam were awestruck.

"Lelah and Markkah," said Herathah, "may I introduce you to your aunt Isish and your uncle Enkum."

Both girls nodded and said, "Pleased to meet you." Nods were exchanged back.

"Be seated," Herathah directed.

The young women stepped up into their respective seats and beheld a variety of foodstuffs they had never before seen. A curious smell struck their noses, and they noted that there were several dishes that contained items that did not look like anything vegetable.

Herathah began the meal with, "Let us partake of the food of the gods."

It was a blessing that seemed confusing to both sisters. They both caught the gist that she was referring to them all as gods. And knowing their heritage, they were sure they had surmised correctly. Even Lelah, who had fallen for many things her grandmother told her, did not feel comfortable thinking of herself as a god.

Then, in a show of her magical powers, Herathah waved her hands, and the empty goblets in front of each person filled up with a bubbly red drink. Both Lelah and Markkah were not sure whether they really wanted to drink any of it. Instinctively, they acted like they were more interested in the food.

It was their aunt who immediately reached for platters of food to load her plate. And the others followed. Lelah and Markkah only put things on their plates that they recognized, being hesitant to sample the unfamiliar.

"Dear nieces," Isish said through a mouthful of food, "I understand that you are seamstresses?"

"Yes, we are," Lelah replied simply.

"What are your specialties?"

"We make many kinds of clothing," she said, neglecting to fill in that most of their creations of late had been for the resisters.

The small talk continued, with minimal information coming from the girls. Markkah was silently thankful that Lelah wasn't gushing in her approval of the whole affair.

Enkum picked up a plate of an unknown food that looked brown and crispy and garnished with baked apples and handed it toward Markkah. "Here, try this. I'm sure you'll find it pleasing."

"May I ask what this is?" braved Markkah.

"It is the flesh of a woolly amsi. Try it," he again urged.

The thought of eating the flesh of any animal was repugnant. The girls had never heard of such a thing. That was the job of carrion, worms, and wolves, not of any people. As far as they knew, all people had only eaten plants and the fruits of plants and trees from the beginning. Flesh was forbidden. They watched in horror as the others indulged in the forbidden food.

Just as the man was again urging the Su-galam to partake of the flesh, the far door of the chambers burst open. Herathah looked up at the scurrying newcomer with annoyance written on her face.

Bowing, the nervous messenger spoke, "Your Highness, please may I have a word with you? This is of an urgent matter."

Herathah descended from her chair with a scowl and said, "This had better be very urgent to disrupt us in this manner."

They could not hear what the messenger revealed, but it didn't take but a couple of sentences before Herathah turned to Enkum and said, "We need to talk. Now." Turning to her granddaughters, she said, "This meal is over. Please go back to your quarters."

Lelah caught a momentary look of rage and evil on her grandmother's face that distorted her beauty into something almost serpentlike. She even thought she might have heard a hiss. Lelah was horrified, and the sight sent a chill down her spine, making the hair on the back of her neck stand up. She remembered the words of Enoch, and she was grieved in her heart that she had let hatred back in and had believed Herathah's lies. Her soul silently pleaded, *Oh, Lord of Spirits, have mercy on me. Take my sin away from me, and cleanse me by the Word of Your Promise.*

The two sisters lost no time exiting the table, nodding to their elders, and hurrying to the door. Their escort awaited them outside the quarters and dutifully led them to theirs. Once inside, the young women finally broke their silence to each other. Together they dismissed their personal servants and told them not to return until they were summoned on the morrow.

"Forgive me, Markkah. You were right all along. I should not have been so blind."

"I'm sorry too, Lelah. I don't want anything to ever come between us again."

They held on to each other with teary eyes both until a noise could be heard coming from outside. Fear shot through the girls. What was it that had been so urgent? Something that so upset Herathah that they knew they would be for whatever it was and that it may be against whomever they might be for.

Running to the windows to look out over the streets below, they could see in the dim twilight and the lights of the city men being assembled and outfitted. They were fighting men, Su-galam, and at least twenty Nephilim. The girls continued to watch as carts of weapons and what looked like armor and shields were distributed, ranks ordered into lines, and orders being barked with authority and urgency. The mass swelled as more and more joined the ranks, and great animals were added to the bustle. When it looked like they couldn't see the end of the formations that spilled over from the gather area and down the streets, a horn blew and the command resounded, "Move out!" Slowly, division by division, the army marched down the streets headed for outside Eriduch.

"It must be something big for this to happen," whispered Lelah.

"Who are they moving against? I wonder if there's been an attack," wondered Markkah.

"They are going against the righteous."

"I'm afraid so."

"It was probably an attack, because if they had planned it, it wouldn't have been such a surprise to our dear grandmother." Then a thought struck Lelah. "What if Metu is involved? What if he has attacked? What if he is coming to rescue us?"

"He might not be coming just for us, Lelah."

"What do you mean?" Lelah turned to Markkah with a quizzical look on her face.

"Our dear grandmother has Ishmerai locked in the dungeons here."

"Your Ishmerai?"

"Indeed. My maggot."

Lelah inwardly kicked herself again for having been seduced by their grandmother. *Truly the best lies are the ones that hold many truths. Oh Lord of Spirits, forgive me!* She whispered, "Markkah, what shall we do?"

"Well, how thoroughly did you explore this palace?"

"I think I pretty much covered the whole of it, but I was not shown where the dungeons are."

"That I do know." Markkah then told her sister all about the servant girl's message, her explorations, and what she learned about the dungeon and its entries and exits.

"We need to plan," said Lelah.

"Indeed we do."

That night they forced themselves to get some rest, for the energy would be sorely needed very early the next day. Both young women went to bed with prayers on their hearts, with Lelah's mostly for Metu and Markkah's mostly for Ishmerai.

THE KITCHEN HELP

In the wee hours of the morning, well before dawn, two figures clad in dark clothing made their way down the long flight of stairs toward the dungeons and kitchen. The stairs were dimly lit by soft lamps at the turn of each level. The two Su-galam were thankful for the full wardrobe of clothing they found in their new quarters. The items they assembled were probably undergarments meant for insulating in cooler weather, but they were dark, soft, quiet fabrics perfectly suited for stealth.

At the bottom of the stairs, both put their ears to the kitchen's door. Hearing no sounds from inside, they carefully opened it and slipped inside. Markkah, leading the way in the dark, felt her way soundlessly by memory. Lelah followed close by, holding on to the tail of her blouse. They timed their entry into the kitchen to be before Aram and Gether would arrive. They laid in wait for them just inside the pantry exit route.

It seemed like forever to wait, but having not known exactly when the workers would arrive, they wanted to be sure to get there before they did come. Finally, they heard footsteps and jolly voices on the other side of the door. Markkah and Lelah crouched on either side of the doorway. After the door slid open with a rumble in its track, two figures stepped in. Just as one man turned the knob to switch on the room's lights, they were each struck in the head with a heavy pot.

The girls hastily took the men's outer clothing off and then dragged them, trussed and gagged, into a dark corner of the pantry. Just after the girls slipped into the men's clothing and tucked their hair up into their caps, the men came to consciousness.

"I am so sorry, Aram and Gether. It is much better this way so you can't be blamed for what we're about to do," Markkah whispered gently. "You won't be harmed."

Hurriedly, Markkah directed Lelah in preparing the food for the prisoners. She had paid close attention the afternoon before to all that Aram and Gether had shown and explained to her.

As they busied themselves at their task, another sound was heard coming from the pantry. Alarmed, both women hurried to the pantry door with pots at the ready. Ears to the door, they heard what sounded like a cart in the corridor.

"It sounds like we're getting a delivery," whispered Lelah.

"Do you think we can pull off receiving it without suspicion?"

"I don't know, but we can try." Thinking quickly, Lelah added, "Markkah, get behind that divider. If it looks like they won't accept us as the real thing, strike from there." Lelah rested her pot within quick reach and prepared to meet the delivery person or persons.

A quick rap at the sliding door resounded, and Lelah responded with, "Enter," with as deep a sounding voice as she could muster. The door slid open. Lelah could not see the man's face because he was holding a large crate of vegetables in his arms. "Put them down on the floor to the left," she added.

Instead of turning to the left, the man swiftly spun to the right, knocking Lelah to the floor senseless. Before he knew it, he was struck on the head, but the tough helmet he wore underneath the hood insulated him from the worst of the blow. Then Markkah launched onto his back with an arm around his throat. Another man rushed into the room, grabbing her from off the man's back.

Just before Enosh was to deliver a punch to Markkah's face, Lelah rang out with, "Metu! Stop!" She had come to and was stunned to see the boots the deliveryman was wearing. They were covered in mahkur tidnum fur.

Adrenaline rushing and hearts pounding, the struggling four instantly froze. *Could it be?* was asked in more than one head in that instant.

"Lelah, is that you? And Markkah?"

"I am glad I didn't hit you, young lady," said Enosh to Markkah, helping her to her feet.

"Lelah, are you hurt?" Metu asked as he leaned over to help her.

"I will be all right," she replied a bit dizzily.

Metu helped her to her feet and pulled her close to his chest. Lelah felt the world and its troubles melt away in those few seconds. She could have stayed in his arms forever. He held her tightly and whispered, "I am glad I found you."

"And I am glad I am still in one piece!" she added.

They all chuckled softly. The release of tension was cathartic, although brief.

"We are here for my brother," said Metu, finally releasing Lelah.

"Your brother?" asked Lelah.

"Yes, we came to free Ishmerai."

"I didn't know Ishmerai was your brother." Markkah was amazed at the revelation. She added, "We are down here to try to free him also." She quickly explained to the men what they had planned. Together they emptied the vegetable delivery cart and sent Enosh back up to the loading dock to prevent any suspicions regarding the delivery.

Food, plates, and cart prepared, they waited until just before dawn when the server Hazael would arrive. While they waited, Lelah asked Metu, "Now, did you come just to save Ishmerai, or did you come for me and Markkah too?"

The usually serious Methuselah couldn't help but say, "We did come only for Ishmerai, but since you both are so handy, I guess we can bring you home too." Then he smiled at her with a twinkle in his eyes.

"You are impossible!"

They all snickered. The levity seemed like the calm before the storm.

Soft steps were heard coming down the stairway. Standing out of direct sight of the door, all three watched to see if the newcomer was the expected one. It was.

"Oh!" Hazael jumped after she came through the door and was greeted by Markkah in the cook's uniform.

Before she could react negatively, Markkah introduced Metu and Lelah to the young slave.

Markkah added, "I have promised Hazael that we would take her out of here too."

Metu replied, "Your promise is my promise."

Smiling, Hazael was thoroughly willing to help out.

It didn't take but a few minutes to lay out the plan.

Despite Markkah and Lelah wanting to go into the dungeon, it was decided that the best action would be for just Metu going in with Hazael. He would be concealed on the lower shelf of the large cart.

Markkah was disappointed again because she was bent on going in too, but she finally conceded that the best way was the one chosen.

Readied, Hazael rapped on the iron door of the dungeon. Steps were heard inside and then a clank of keys in the lock. The door pulled open from the inside. The jailor held the door open for Hazael and the cart. As usual, she wheeled the cart down the hall toward the jailor's office. The jailor had just started his day's duty, having made the shift change minutes before. He walked faster than Hazael, past her and the cart. When he reached his office, he turned his back to her and unlocked his door. His usual routine was to enter his office, sit at his desk, and receive the breakfast that had been prepared for him. He would eat before the inmates. Instead, just as he entered his office he was knocked out from behind and his ring of keys was appropriated along with his outer clothes. Metu then quickly bound, gagged, and shoved him under his desk. Metu quickly searched for and found the exit door. He unlocked it with one of the keys on the ring.

Taking care not to look like routine was broken, Hazael again wheeled her cart around to start her rounds. She made her way from cell to cell down the easternmost row of cells. She did vary her sequence of cells from time to time, so choosing this row was not too unusual. There were hollers of protests from some of the prisoners who thought she was being capricious and hollers of approval from those who would now be first and not last.

At last she arrived at Ishmerai's cell and coughed loudly, looking back toward the approaching jailor. Metu decided that it would be good for him to get some food in his stomach before releasing him. Hazael leaned down and delivered the plate of food and bowl of water. "Eat quickly," she whispered.

Ishmerai did not have to be told twice to eat. He wolfed the food down and was pleased that it seemed much more substantial than anything he had gotten thus far.

Metu, in the jailor's clothing, walked down the corridor. The inmates were much more interested in the food being delivered than they were in the jailor. As Ishmerai was shoveling the last morsel into his mouth, Metu reached his cell door.

Metu whispered, "Move it out, brother," as he slipped the key into the lock and clanked it open. Ishmerai didn't have to be told twice with that command either. The ragged, bloodstained man fairly launched out of his cell, clapping his brother on the shoulder. "We need to move fast. This cell is being watched!" All three made for the door leading to the kitchen and stairs. Just as they reached it and opened the door, they heard the steps of guards running down the stairs. Metu slammed the door shut and locked it quickly. Turning, he told Hazael and Ishmerai to head out through the jailor's office. He was thankful that he had taken the precaution to unlock the exit. Hazael rammed the loaded food cart up against the dungeon door and then followed Ishmerai.

As Ishmerai and Hazael ran, prisoners shouted. By the time Herathah's guards were opening the dungeon door and trying to shove the cart out of the way, Metu had already unlocked several prisoners' cell doors. They immediately crowded into the corridor and got in the way of the rushing guards. The melee that ensued afforded Metu with just enough time to escape through the jailor's office and out through the exit door, locking it behind him just before the guards reached it.

Markkah and Lelah heard the commotion, and as soon as the guards went through the dungeon door, they stripped off the cooks' clothing and slipped out the pantry exit and up through the loading dock. Just before emerging at the dock entrance, they paused to catch their breath.

"Where do we go"—Markkah huffed—"from here?"

"Follow me. I explored all over around here yesterday."

The mist was so thick one could almost slice it with a knife. And in the dim pre-dawn, their dark clothing was concealing. They slipped out of the loading dock entrance onto the main dock. They could hear movement of some carts maneuvering into other dock entrances and the silhouettes of men directing and unloading. Lelah swiftly led them off the dock, through a gate, and around the corner to the left, hugging the stone wall. They were still on the palace grounds but on an inner street. Suddenly, bursting out of a door in front of them, four men appeared.

One was swearing. Lelah and Markkah immediately pressed themselves against an indent in the wall and held their breaths. The men heard the sound of someone running to the left of them and rushed in that direction.

After some minutes, Markkah whispered, "Well, I think they got away."

"I hope so."

"We can't run around the city looking like this. Do you think we should go back to our room for now?"

"That might be best, I think. Follow me. I know a back way to our room," whispered Lelah.

"Our separate explorations yesterday did us some good," Markkah whispered back.

"Indeed."

⊰ ⊱

The girls slipped up a servant stairway that led to their quarter's corridor. They only passed two servants along the way, who seemed to be preoccupied hurrying at their duties to give them any mind. Finally, they slipped back into their room. The first thing they did was begin to change clothing. When they were half dressed, a knock rapped on their door. A panic set in to shed the rest of their clothing and slip back into their nightclothes. The rap at the door repeated and was louder.

"Just a moment!" Lelah called.

Markkah jumped into her bed, pulling the covers up to her chin, and Lelah, wrapping a robe around her, stood in front of the door and said, "Enter."

Entering the room was Balog, accompanied by two large armed, obviously Su-galam, guards. "My ladies," he said with a bow, "we have a security issue in the palace this morning, and your grandmother has requested that you stay in your quarters until she summons you. These two guards will be posted outside your door to protect you from any harm. Your servants will attend you and bring you everything you need."

With another bow, he turned to leave. The huge guards, who were probably their cousins, preceded Balog out. Lelah could see them take up their stations as Balog exited and the door was shut again.

Lelah rushed over to Markkah as she was climbing back out of the bed. "We are in a fine mess now," she said.

Markkah replied, "But with this circumstance, we know that Metu and Ishmerai weren't caught."

"True. Locking us up wouldn't be a necessary precaution if they had been captured."

"So much for our being free here."

"Isn't that the truth."

"What do we do now?"

"I don't think there is much we can do right now, except wait for an opportunity," replied Lelah.

There was another rap at the door and then entered four servants, two who were bearing their breakfast. Apologizing for arriving without being summoned like the women had directed them the evening before, they proceeded with their duties. Both Markkah and Lelah treated them with respect and deference, knowing that kindness could produce better results than not. Also, both women felt deep in their hearts that all people of whatever station or lineage deserved respect—that is, until proven otherwise.

Both young women waited. Both were confident in the men they loved and even more confident in the God they believed. While the servants were there, they prayed silently. It was just a matter of time.

SEEING RED

The wait seemed interminable. All day long they waited. Servants came and went, and at no time were the girls left alone, either by them or, of course, by the guards outside the door. Finally they went to bed, disappointed that something, anything, hadn't happened as yet.

They were abruptly awoken in the wee hours of the pre-dawn. After a hasty morning meal was served, two servants arrived bearing brilliant red gowns and an announcement that their company was desired by their grandmother. Before the hour was done, they were to be escorted to her.

Markkah and Lelah both allowed the servants to dress and ready them for their meeting. Great care was taken, even with preparation of their faces and hair. For the first time, powders and colors were added to their faces and eyes. Looking at each other, the girls thought the effect was gaudy. Although not pleased with it, they did not resist. Instinctively, they felt their acquiescence was the wisest course for the time being.

They were ready when Balog arrived to escort them. This time, though, instead of escorting by himself, two more guards accompanied them. Through corridors, down stairs, and into an area that neither had been before they were taken. Finally, they arrived at curious-looking, gnarly, red-lacquered double doors. The young women noticed the carvings framing them; twining serpents and unknown symbols adorned the wide stone molding. At the very top outcropped a large stone viper's head with eyes that looked like they were blazing. At closer inspection, they could tell the eyes were made of translucent, blood-red agate, and the light from corridor lamps was showing through. It gave the sisters a distinct foreboding feeling. Balog rapped a pattern of knock on one door. The doors swung open.

Balog stepped aside and gestured for the women to walk in. For the women, it took all the nerve they had to obey. Standing tall, they entered. In the center of the large, high-ceilinged room, they saw their grandmother , dressed in a red form-fitted gown similar to the ones they wore. Red lights rimmed the walls of the circular room, and even though light poured in from the corridor, it was still a dimly lit room, and they couldn't make out the details of most of it.

Behind them the doors clanged shut, and with it, the lighting changed. An oppressive heaviness accompanied the change, and it was unnerving for them to see how their red gowns all seemed to glow a sickly white.

"Welcome, my granddaughters," spoke Herathah darkly. "Come over here."

The girls obeyed, although dread enveloped them both like a heavy shroud. It was not until they stood beside their grandmother that they noticed they were standing in the middle of a pattern drawn on the floor. The lines, palm-width wide, were glowing the same sickly white of their gowns and formed a five-pointed star made with one continuous line, and a separate circle was drawn on the outside of it.

"My dears, here you shall meet your grandfather and any others he wishes you to enjoy."

Both Markkah and Lelah, standing on both sides of Herathah, looked at each other in great alarm. Markkah gestured with eye movement to Lelah. She looked at Lelah and then looked up. Lelah caught the message and nodded. They began to pray.

Herathah began an incantation, the words of which the girls paid absolutely no attention to. Their silent cries of help to the Lord of Spirits were not eloquent, nor were they even complete sentences. It was as if their hearts were crying out. It did come to both their minds, however, to plead that Herathah's efforts be thwarted. Heads bowed and closed eyes in the intensity of the struggle, both saw flashes of light sparking in the blackness of their clenched eyelids. Their grandmother's voice chanted louder and louder, as if with more volume and passion she could produce the outcome she desired.

The desperation and anger that entered their grandmother's voice encouraged the sisters to continue their pleas. As the struggle continued, Lelah suddenly felt hateful hands from behind gripping around her neck and squeezing. Instinctively, she opened her eyes and reached up to try to pull the strangling hands away, but they were not physical. She looked over to Markkah and saw her choking also. *Lord, take these away from us!* she screamed in her mind. And then it felt as if something forcefully dragged those strangling hands away from her neck. She immediately broke into thanks and praise in her mind.

Herathah's raging words were interrupted then with a song that came out of both sisters' mouths. The silent praise erupted into sound.

The girls sang a song of praise they had learned on Zion:

> Give unto the LORD, O you mighty ones,
> Give unto the LORD glory and strength.
> Give unto the LORD the glory due to His name;
> Worship the LORD in the beauty of holiness.

The voice of the LORD is over the waters;
The God of glory thunders;
The LORD is over many waters.
The voice of the LORD is powerful;
The voice of the LORD is full of majesty![11]

Herathah nearly choked on her rage as she screamed. The sisters stepped away from their frenzied grandmother just as she tried to gouge them with her talons.

Karloah Pass

U nseen by the mortals below, save the few surviving Watchen, were ethereal contenders in hand-to-hand combat above the pass. The Watchens' magic spells and curses were thwarted as they gnashed their teeth in great fear and frustration.

Caleb and his men were still fighting the remnants of the raiding party. It looked as though there were just a handful of men who were still putting up a fight. It was apparent that the three Nephilim were still alive, and whether they were injured or not was unknown. Most of the raiding party had been killed during the initial assault. The ambushers had run out of boulders to send down into the pass and were now using just arrows. Instead of shooting randomly, they waited for targets to present themselves. The survivors had hunkered down under shelters of boulders and fallen trees. A few had attempted to climb the walls of the pass to reach their ambushers but had either been killed or driven back to shelter. The river that ran through the pass began to rise because of the damming effect of the boulders at the south end. There were boulders at the higher elevation of the north end, but they and the debris had not been dense enough to cut off the flow of the river into the canyon. Caleb and his men would wait it out. It was too risky to send men down into the pass to finish off the raiders. Time, circumstance, and the rising waters were on their side, and they would not leave until every one of the enemy was dead.

Throughout the night, Caleb's men took turns on watch, occasionally sending torches down into the chasm to reveal if any of the remaining raiders were trying to climb to the top. Only twice did they reveal a climber and swiftly sent arrows down on each climber's head. It appeared that the remaining raiders were moving or changing their shields upward as the river waters rose. And occasionally they heard the roar of a Nephilim. It was curious to the resisters that the roar that usually sent great fear into all-humans now seemed like cries of desperation instead. Although they needed to be prepared for when the Nephilim did emerge; it looked like that was only a matter of time too.

As the water rose in the dammed-off chasm, an unknown number of surviving raiders managed to creep up the side of it, keeping just above the waters. It seemed evident to Caleb's men that the three Nephilim were pushing logs up with them, using the logs as shields from arrows and rocks. It was a feat of strength almost unfathomable, and one that gave Caleb's men concern. While the resisters stood watch, Caleb, Jaireck, and Gerlag took council to discuss courses of action. It was a luxury to have the time to plan rather than just make snap battlefield decisions. They considered well the price of victory.

After crossing the new bridge at the mighty Alagan-ida River, the great army of Eriduch made its way swiftly, in spite of its size, through the terrain leading to Karloah Pass. They followed the road but spilled over the sides of it into the fields surrounding. The carts pulled by animals of all sorts were kept on the road, while the foot soldiers massed on both sides. Su-galam, Nephilim, and all-human warriors were armor clad and loaded with weapons of all sorts—bows and arrows, blow darts, maces, clubs, and spears. There were so many that the ground rumbled as they moved through the early morning mists, and the sound of the multitude was deafening, with grunts, roars, the clanging of metal and the rhythmic pounding of thousands of boots. A great fear rose in all the people who saw the advancing army. Never before in the free lands had they seen such a sight and all fled from its path. What didn't get out of the way in front of them got trampled into the ground. They had marched all through the night and wouldn't arrive at their destination until the next day. Rest and refreshment would be minimal. Samjaza's army would pulverize the ones who would dare assault their own.

With the taste of victory in its mouth, the great army grew closer to its destination as the morning sun burned off the last of the mists. It was noted by some who knew the terrain that the normally mighty Karloah River was dry. But they marched on with the leaders, bent on reaching their target in better time than was even planned.

The forward troops reached Karloah Pass. They found it completely blocked off with boulders and debris reaching nearly to the top of the steep banks on either side. There was no other way to reach the trapped raiders or to reach the army they were to slaughter.

"Climb!" shouted the large Nephilim general.

The rugged debris was easier to surmount than the bordering cliffs, so the whole of the army bunched in direct line to the blocked southern entrance of the pass.

The Mighty Ones

The great doors of the incantation chamber flew open with a resounding crash, and in burst two men. The largest one charged directly at Herathah, knocking her sprawling and senseless across the floor.

Even before the light flooded the room from the corridor, Markkah and Lelah knew that it was Methuselah and Ishmerai. Lelah ran to the man covered in mahkur-tidnum fur and Markkah to the one she hadn't seen in three years but whose form and face she still remembered, even through the cuts and bruises that marred it.

There was no time to linger, and the men swiftly led their women out by the hands and into the corridor, stepping over bodies of the fallen. They ran full tilt down the corridor and toward a flight of stairs. Arriving at the foot of the stairs, they heard a rush of footsteps descending. Quickly they turned and ran down another corridor. Far behind them they heard Herathah's screaming orders. They ran upstairs and down and around in what seemed like a maze, turning at points to avoid approaching pursuers. Instead of finding a way out and away, they seemed to be herded closer to the central part of the palace.

After what seemed an eternity of running, they found themselves in the hall of statues with pursuers coming from both sides. There was but only one choice: enter the great hall, the throne room.

Gasping for breath, the winded four burst through the great doors and into Eriduch's seat of power. They halted midway to the center of the chamber. To their chagrin, they saw Herathah, hair disheveled and gown torn, sitting with her hands clenched white and nails dug into the arms of her throne.

"You have nowhere to go now, you filthy swine!" she roared in a voice that was much deeper and masculine than anything they had heard out of her mouth before. She laughed a maniacal laugh and said, "Now I have you just where I have wanted you, Methuselah!"

The great hall filled with guards and warriors coming from several entries. They encircled the four.

Immediately, Methuselah and Ishmerai pushed the girls behind their backs and faced outward at the ready. They slowly circled with backs to each other and Markkah and Lelah in between. Both men had dart shooters in hand and swords at their sides.

"In the name of the Lord of Spirits!" boomed Methuselah.

"Remember the Promise!" yelled Ishmerai.

The girls bowed their heads, crossed their arms over their chests, and prayed. From all sides they were rushed. A great light flashed above them, and the onrushing attackers fell back. Metu and Ishmerai shot their darts, and screams and thuds followed. The attackers drove forward again.

Markkah and Lelah lifted their heads and arms and began to sing praises:

Oh come, let us sing to the LORD!
 Let us shout joyfully to the Rock of our salvation.
 Let us come before His presence with thanksgiving;
 Let us shout joyfully to Him with psalms.
 For the LORD is the great God,
 And the great King above all gods.[12]

The sisters saw above them great beings with wings fighting in hand-to-hand combat. The brightest ones were beautiful, perfect in form, and struggling with others who looked much the same, but there was an evil exuding from them; perfection was not there. They heard these words: "These are my children! You have no right to them!" and, "This is our territory! These are our claim!" and from the perfect ones, "Samjaza! The Lord rebuke you!" and, "The righteous belong to the Lord of Spirits!"

And the sisters still sang:

 In His hand are the deep places of the earth;
 The heights of the hills are His also.
 The sea is His, for He made it;
 And His hands formed the dry land.[13]

The door to the great hall broke open again, bashing with such force that they broke off the hinges as they slammed against the stone walls. In stormed Enkara, Markkah and Lelah's Nephilim father, followed closely by Nekoda. The giant's eyes were blood red with rage. Lelah saw the look in his eyes, having seen the rage before. Instead of cringing in utter fear and crumpling down in a heap, she turned to face him directly, still singing:

 Oh come, let us worship and bow down;
 Let us kneel before the LORD our Maker.
 For He is our God,
 And we are the people of His pasture,
 And the sheep of His hand![14]

Enkara swept his mighty hands, knocking, breaking, or dismembering all within his reach. The attackers fell against each other, fighting and slaying each other in utter confusion. Enkara roared a deafening roar and turned to the four. The floor shook with each stomp he took toward them. Methuselah drew a dart from the pouch in his tunic, put it in place, took aim, and said, "In the Name above all names." He shot the dart. It found its home deep in Enkara's right eye.

The great Nephilim's roar stopped in midstream. His hand went to his face, but before it could get there, he twitched violently and fell to the right. He landed on several attackers, including Nekoda, who screamed as they were crushed. At first the nerve toxin paralyzed him, and then he died.

Lelah and Markkah, still singing, saw their father's spirit rise out of his lifeless body. At first it looked much like his physical body, but then it morphed into a gnarled, misshapen, lizard-like form that they understood to be profoundly evil. They heard a bitter cry behind them, turned, and saw Herathah standing before her throne, screaming. Out of her mouth came an enormous snake, with fire-red eyes. It raised its head high to the ceiling, opened its mouth, large enough to swallow the four whole, and positioned to strike downward.

Looking up, they sang still:

Oh, sing to the LORD a new song!
Sing to the LORD, all the earth.
Sing to the LORD, bless His name;
Proclaim the good news of His salvation from day to day.
Declare His glory among the nations,
His wonders among all peoples![15]

As they sang, a great mighty one with a flaming sword in his hand and more than twice the size of Enkara blazingly appeared between the four and the serpent, stopping the strike.

Lelah and Markkah still sang:

> For the LORD is great and greatly to be praised;
> He is to be feared above all gods.
> For all the gods of the peoples are idols,
> But the LORD made the heavens.
> Honor and majesty are before Him;
> Strength and beauty are in His sanctuary.[16]

"Out of my way, Michael!" hissed the great serpent. "I am the god of this world, and these sinners belong to me!"

Michael boomed, "Thus says the Lord: 'I will put enmity between you and the woman, and between your seed and her Seed; He shall bruise your head!'"

"That hasn't happened yet! I claim the half-breeds! They are blood of the Fallen Ones!"

"They believe the Promise. It is counted to them as righteousness. You cannot claim them. The Lord rebuke you!" roared Michael, holding the sword to the serpent's face.

Then Methuselah began a new song, and the other three joined in:

> The LORD looks from heaven;
> He sees all the sons of men.
> From the place of His dwelling He looks;
> He fashions their hearts individually;
> He considers all their works.
> No king is saved by the multitude of an army
> A mighty man is not delivered by great strength.
> A horse is a vain hope for safety;
> Neither shall it deliver any by its great strength.
> Behold, the eye of the LORD is on those who fear Him,
> On those who hope in His mercy,
> To deliver their soul from death,
> And to keep them alive in *distress*.
> Our soul waits for the LORD;
> He is our help and our shield.
> For our heart shall rejoice in Him

Because we have trusted in His holy Name.
Let Your mercy, O LORD, be upon us,
Just as we hope in You.[17]

When they finished their song, the only sound in their ears was their own breathing. Herathah lay unconscious at the foot of her throne, and the great hall was littered with bodies. For some moments, the four surveyed the carnage all around them, marveling in awe of their deliverance. Ishmerai caught the sight of his own medallion, blood-stained on the floor next to Abishag's head doing a final spin, and he stooped to reclaim it. Lelah spotted the slain Isish and her husband, Enkum, as they stepped over and around bodies. The other-dimensional visions were gone, but all four felt the brush of wings by their sides as they left the palace unhindered.

SACRIFICE

Both the rising waters and the great trees pushed up by the Nephilim were coming closer to the pass ridge. The three leaders knew that it would not be much longer before massive arms would launch those trees onto their men. They positioned themselves strategically, ready to pounce. What they were about to do, they felt they could not ask of any others.

Up high on the ridge, Caleb, Jaireck, and Gerlag kept their eyes peeled on the ever rising tree trunks. Just as Caleb detected that the Nephilim were winding up to heave the great trunks, raising them higher and then lower for the launch, he yelled, "In the name of the Lord of Spirits!" and jumped. Jaireck and Gerlag flung themselves off a half second later. They each landed on a trunk, with just enough force and angle to teeter the throwers, their logs, and the raiders under them into the water that was not far below.

Just as the largest Nephilim reached the topmost boulder blocking Karloah Pass, water started spurting out between the boulders, rubble, trees, and debris. There was a great rumble, shaking the dam and those scaling it. And as the army below, in terror and confusion, came to a halt, the dam burst upon them, rushing a great wall of water along with boulders and mud, trees, rocks, and the bodies of men and giants. Those who survived the torrent fell to arms against each other in confusion, until there were none left alive.

The resisters gathered on the ridge above the valley at the entrance to Karloah Pass. Below them were strewn countless bodies of men and giants. The entire army was decimated. The forty men carefully climbed down the cliffs to search for their leaders to bring them home.

EXODUS

There were not many people in the streets, but the ones there fled and hid from Methuselah, Ishmerai, Lelah, and Markkah as they walked out of Eriduch. Terrified faces looked out of windows and peeked around corners as the four made their way up the wide street leading to the northern gate of the city. The great ziggurat stood forlorn on the east side of them. Unseen by the four but seen by all who gawked was an escort of four beings as tall as the tallest buildings, with blazing blue eyes and flowing white-blond hair dressed in battle gear, tunics, and leggings, all a brilliant white. They flanked their charges so closely that the fluttering feathers of their great wings brushed against them.

As the four, or rather eight, approached the north gate of the city, they heard a mass of people moving and the reverberating stomp of something very large. The two sisters jumped when a more than very loud roar pierced the air. Through the gate they could see on the road heading east people walking, riding in carts, and many little ones being carried. And when the source of the roar arrived just on the outside of the gate, a squeal of delight issued from Markkah.

"Lugal!" Markkah broke from the group and ran headlong toward the beast.

"Markkah!" Horrified, Lelah made an attempt to run after her to drag her back. Metu grabbed her hand, stopping her.

"She will be all right," he assured her.

"But…" she sputtered.

"Watch."

As they hurried closer, they watched Markkah run to the gate. She climbed the steps near the left gate that led to the top of the wall next to it. Then Lelah noticed a basket-weaved harness on the beast with a man riding on the top of it near the giant gisgal-usumlugal's neck. She watched in awe as the man coaxed the beast closer to the gate wall and to her sister. He held out his hand and helped her over to the beast's back to sit behind him.

"It's the Old Man!" Lelah gasped.

Laughing, both the brothers said together, "Indeed!"

Lelah turned to Metu and asked, "Is that how she and the others got out of Eriduch before?"

"Well, part of the way," he answered.

"And all we got was a stinking rotten trash transport!"

"Would you like to have the honor this time out?" asked Ishmerai. He smiled an impish smile as he bowed and motioned toward the massive beast that snorted and stomped with impatience.

"Yes, I would!" The excitement was written all over her face.

The Old Man kept his Lugal at the gate waiting for them. Lelah's heart was pounding as she climbed onto the mighty dragon king after Ishmerai. Metu climbed on last and sat behind Lelah.

To Markkah, Lelah said, "I am amazed that you kept this a secret for all this time!"

"Believe me, it was not easy!"

They all laughed as the Old Man coaxed his beast away from the gate. They ambled easily a little distance from the road filled with the travelers.

"Who are these people?" asked Lelah, "And there are so many children!"

The Old Man said, "While you were busy in Herathah's palace, we were outside on the west emptying out the breeding facilities and the places they were keeping the all-human children until they would be used for sacrifices." His voice had a bitter edge to it. The others knew that he would have preferred to have gotten the children out of there before any of them had died. He added, "We gave those in the breeding program a choice of whether to stay or leave. Most of them chose to leave and come with us."

The sisters recognized three of the men riding horses: Ramuel, Bahman, and Cain. Old Enosh had his transport loaded with laughing children and one adult. It was Hazael, no longer called Merah, laughing with the children. And they even saw Enoch with his cart loaded with women holding tiny babies.

Ishmerai held Markkah close.

Markkah, with tears in her eyes, said to him as they swayed back and forth to the rhythm of Lugal's gait, "I am so glad you are coming with me this time."

Ishmerai gave her a squeeze and said softly, "I am very, very glad too."

She then shifted in her seat and turned to drink in Ishmerai's face. With a twinkle shining through her moistened eyes, she ran her hand over his broken lip and said, "I always knew you'd clean up really well."

They all broke out in a hearty laugh.

Lelah and Metu relished their closeness also, although not in words. Metu rode with one arm wrapped around Lelah's waist, his other hand holding on to Lugal's saddle. Lelah nestled her back into the chest covered in mahkur tidnum fur. The Old Man chuckled when he looked behind him.

He remarked, "You know, there has already been one match made on the back of old Lugal here. I think I might nickname him 'the matchmaker!'"

Lugal let out one of his ear-shattering roars that startled everyone about. More than one person jumped, and more than a few babies cried, even though they were a good ways away from the traveling crowd.

"Shh, shh, Lugal," the Old Man said as he patted the beast's neck, "I didn't mean it."

They all moved steadily toward the free lands and the bridge built to transport hostile armies. It now was the bridge to freedom.

THE NAMES

Lelah awoke to a cool morning breeze wafting through the open window, and the smell of fresh baked bread filtering through the cracks in the door. She rubbed the sleep out of her eyes and remembered what day it was. They shared a bed in a small room, Metu's room. Metu and Ishmerai had slept in tents outside Enoch and Edna's home, along with all the other tents. Her heart swelled with anticipation and boundless joy. This was her wedding day! And, Markkah's, too! The day had finally come and she felt she had to pinch herself just to make sure she wasn't dreaming it all.

She shook Markkah awake, "Markkah! It's the day!"

Just as Markkah stirred and sat up, there came a knock at the door.

"Come in," said Lelah.

Both their mothers came into the room.

"All right, sleepyheads," Melenah said with a broad smile, "It's time to get up and get ready."

Neither bride needed further encouragement to get out of bed. Lelah looked at the wedding garments hanging on the wall. Both Markkah and Lelah had put as much or more care and skill into those dresses as Lelah had put into Metu's mahkur tidnum suit. The garments were made of brilliant white silk, as soft as butter, and adorned with lines of sparkling jewels in the folds. They ate a small breakfast first, and then the women set to preparations with much laughter and cheer.

The celebration on Mount Moriah was the largest ever attended. There were so many present that the whole mountaintop clearing was littered with tents and camps packed with people. The resisters were present, and there were also a number of people there who were a bit lighter skinned and lighter haired who were a bit taller than the average all-human. Kahjeera was not among them, although the rest of her family was present, except the husband who sacrificed himself along with the two others in the battle of Karloah Pass.

Excitement and spirits were running high, and many children were running and playing. But just before it was time to gather in front of the altar, there was another smaller gathering inside Enoch and Edna's home. Methuselah, Lelah, Ishmerai, and Markkah were there, among the grandfathers and most of the grandmothers.

"Let us gather in here. I think we can all squeeze into this room if no one sits down," Enoch beckoned.

Everyone did fit in around a large table in the middle of the room.

"The medallion," he said.

All those present either fingered the medallion hanging around his or her neck or pulled it out of a pocket.

"We all know the story on the one side. We know the Name of our Creator, the story the medallion tells, and the map it holds for the salvation of our souls. Turn your medallion over. We can see the promised Seed is at the center of it. We also know these medallions were forged in the heavens, not made by human hands."

They all turned their medallions over and waited for Enoch to go on. He held his own medallion out in front of him and then pulled a small glass out of the breast pocket of his tunic. Holding the glass in close to the medallion, he said, "These tiny letters are names all run together, and this is how they read beginning at the outer: Adam, Eve, Seth, Hanna, Enosh, Elloe, Cainan, Hilliel, Mahalalel, Moriah, Jared, Eunice, Enoch, Edna, Methuselah, Lelah, Ishmerai, Markkah."

There was a hush in the room. The Old Man put out his hand to take the glass and look at his medallion himself. After a long look, he said, "True. But I cannot read the many names after Markkah." He passed the glass on to Seth, who stood beside him.

Seth concurred. "The glass does not reveal the names that come after Markkah."

One after another all solemnly looked at their medallions through the glass, including Lelah, who held hers with a trembling hand. And finally the glass was passed back to Enoch. They waited expectantly for Enoch's next words.

"Praise to the Lord of Spirits, King of the Universe. He knows the end from the beginning."

They all held their medallions and said together, "And our trust is in Him."

Enoch opened his arms wide and said, "Now, people are waiting. It is time to go out. We have two weddings to conduct!"

"So shall it be!" They all cheered.

The eldest filed out first, leading the way to the altar. And lastly, Methuselah, Lelah, Ishmerai, and Markkah followed.

The doubts that Metu had previously were long since evaporated, but seeing the names on the medallion made his heart sing. He turned to his beautiful bride and cherished her as his gift from heaven.

AFTERWORD

Before these things, Enoch was hidden, and no one of the children of men knew where he was hidden and where he abode and what had become of him. And his activities had to do with the Watchers, and his days were with the holy ones.

And I, Enoch, was blessing the Lord of majesty and the King of the ages, and lo! the Watchers called me Enoch the scribe and said to me: "Enoch, thou scribe of righteousness, go, declare to the Watchers of the heaven who have left the high heaven, the holy eternal place, and have defiled themselves with women and have done as the children of earth do and have taken unto themselves wives: 'Ye have wrought great destruction on the earth: And ye shall have no peace nor forgiveness of sin: and inasmuch as they delight themselves in their children, the murder of their beloved ones shall they see, and over the destruction of their children shall they lament and shall make supplication unto eternity, but mercy and peace shall ye not attain.'"

Enoch, Book 1, Chapter 12:1-6

And the two hundred Fallen Ones asked Enoch to make supplication for them before the Lord of Spirits. They were asked why they should be asking a man to make supplication for them when instead they should have been the ones making supplications for man. The judgment remained the same. They would see their offspring, the Nephilim, murder each other, and then the two hundred would be locked in chains for all eternity.

LIST OF CHARACTERS

Melenah: slave consort of Enkara. A descendent of Cain, the firstborn of Adam
Lelah: A Su-galam (Stretcher). Melenah's daughter by Enkara
Kaliyah: Slave consort of Enkara. Melenah's cousin
Markkah: A Su-galam. Kaliyah's daughter by Enkara
Metu: A priest.
Enosh: An old priest, in the family of Enoch
Elloe: Enosh's wife
Enoch: "dedicated," High priest, father of Metu
The Old Man
Ishmerai: 'YHWH guards,' a slave in Eriduch, known as "Kisim" in Eriduch (means "maggot")
Jaireck: a worker in the underground
Kahjeera: Jaireck's wife
Corah: resident of the refuge village, a teacher
Ramuel: Corah's husband
Hazael: "God sees," called Merah (bitter) in Eriduch, a slave

Hanan: "gracious," a slave woman in Eriduch

Bahman: "good mind," Hanan's son

Samjaza: chief of the fallen Watchers, of the guardian class of the sons of God; worshipped as a god.

Herathah: Wife of Samjaza, sorceress and sovereign of Eriduch

Enkara: "weapon," oldest son of Samjaza and Herathah; a giant or Nephilim, and as with all giants prefers to be known as a Digir-na, or god-man

Abishag: "my father strays"; slave master of street workers in Eriduch

Nekoda: "marked"; slave master of the household of Enkara

Enkum: "guardian"; security chief of Eriduch

Glossary of Terms

Places:

Imin-sar: The whole world, all lands, Pangaea, the world before the continents were divided.
Eriduch: the capitol city of Imin-sar, seat of power for Samjaza
Idim-kur: The Wild-lands
Mul-Eriduch: the Star of Eriduch, the ziggurat, or stepped pyramid bordering Eriduch on the east
The Mountain: Mount Moriah, Enoch's seat of rule

Terms:

Digir-na: god-man, preferred name of the giants, the children of the fallen Watchers
Su-galam: A child of a giant. Means Stretcher, or stretched tall; grandchildren of the fallen Watchers.
The Watchen: Followers of the Watchers; the 'upper class' of all-humans, sorcerers, determined to join themselves or their

children with Watchers, the giants or the Su-galam as spouses
or consorts; the elite of the believers in the race of 'god-men'
Lugu-la: despot
Lugal: King

Animals:

Sutum: lizard.
Usum: dragon
Gisgal-Usumlugal: Mighty dragon king
Umbin-sutum: Talon lizard
Mahgu-usum: Great bird-dragon
Mahgid-gu: Great long-neck
Essimudusu: Three horned beast of burden
Woolly amsi: Woolly elephant
Mahkur-tidnum: Great fanged tiger
Uzka-Sutum: Duck-billed lizard

ENDNOTES

1   Adolph Hitler (1889–1945), German dictator. Speech, Nov. 6, 1933. Quoted in William L. Shirer, "Education in the Third Reich," ch. 8, The Rise and Fall of the Third Reich (1959).

2   Norman Cameron and R.H. Stevens, trans., (Oxford, 1953), Hitler's Table-Talk, p. 51. This quote is altered in the story. Full quote: "The law of selection justifies this incessant struggle, by allowing the survival of the fittest. Christianity is a rebellion against natural law, a protest against nature. Taken to its logical extreme, Christianity would mean the systematic cultivation of the human failure."

3   Ethiopian Enoch, translated by R.H. Charles, 1917, 1:3b-4; and Jude 14-15.

4   Genesis 1:1-2:2

5   Ethiopian Enoch 46:1-4

6   Ethiopian Enoch 48:1-7

7 Winston S. Churchill, British PM. The Defence of Freedom and Peace (The Lights are Going Out) speech. Broadcast to the United States and to London on October 16, 1938. From Churchill, Into Battle (London: Cassell, 1941), pages 83-91. Renewal copyright Winston S. Churchill © 2001.

8 From Winston S. Churchill, Unrelenting Struggle, p. 365, December 30, 1941. Speech in House of Commons of Canada, address to the Parliament of the senior Dominion of the Crown.

9 Ibid.

10 Psalm 116:12-19

11 Psalm 29:1-4

12 Psalm 95:1-3

13 Psalm 95: 4-5

14 Psalm 95:6-7a

15 Psalm 96:1-3

16 Psalm 96:4-6

17 Psalm 33:13-22